Heartsong Sonata

Heartsong Sonata

SHEILAH R. CRAFT

STARLIGHT BOOKS

STARLIGHT BOOKS

Cover photograph drawn by Sheilah R Craft. It represents Angelica's drawing of her birth father. Back cover photograph of Angelica taken by Sheilah R. Craft.

First Starlight Books edition April 2016

ISBN-13: 978-0692481301

ISBN-10: 0692481303

DEDICATED TO L. J.

HAVING A PLACE TO GO—

IS A HOME.

HAVING SOMEONE TO LOVE---

IS A FAMILY.

HAVING BOTH—IS A BLESSING.

--DONNA HEDGES

PRELUDE

In *Heartsong Sonata*, I have endeavored to explore what defines family. Traditional definitions hinge on common ancestry—blood ties—that connects people. Parents create and give birth to their child, and they are a traditional family: father, mother, child. What about couples who cannot have their own birth children? What about children whose parents are dead, who have no biological families?

These two questions form the foundation of *Heartsong Sonata*. Our story opens on March 11, 1964 in Paris, France. Our three principal characters—Julien Lacoeur, his wife Aurélie, and young teenager Angelica—meet that day. Their lives change forever. What unfolds in the course of the year ending on March 11, 1965 shows what defines a family.

What else happens demonstrates the price of love. With love comes joy—and heartbreak. I know that well. These characters are part of my soul. Writing their story has been a privilege. I love them. I rejoiced in their happiness. I cried at their sorrow. They filled my heart with happiness and pain. I gave birth to them. They are my children, my family. I truly understand the emotional heights and depths they experience.

Ultimately, this is a story about the power of love and the bonds and connections it fuses between people. The Lacoeur family proves that love is the strongest component of a family. Love is eternal. Love comes with a price, yes, but the alternative is unthinkable.

S.R.C.

MOUVEMENT UNE

Tourists, diners, window shoppers, and pretty much everyone else watched as he walked down the Paris, France sidewalk. In a city bursting with beautiful people, he commanded interest simply by walking. He nodded and smiled at people as he walked, never seeming to notice the frenzy he created. He stepped into a fine jewelry shop, and left several minutes later with a very special piece safely encased in a velvet box and tucked in his jacket pocket. He walked to a floral shop, and exited with fifty long-stemmed red roses. How romantic, many women thought. For whom had he bought the jewelry and roses? they wondered. As they stared, they noticed that he headed toward a nearby café, and suddenly several other people decided they needed refreshments at that café, as well. They trailed him as if he were the Pied Piper himself.

He strode to a table at the sidewalk café, and all attention suddenly turned toward him. He was alone, although many of those staring at him would have more than happily kept him company. "He's luscious," one woman whispered to her friend. As he approached a vacant table, people noted his tall, lean, genteel physique. Too bad it was covered by a grey suit—Hitman by Nino Cerruti, the fashion conscious noted—crisp white shirt, black tie, and black Oxford shoes. His brunet hair was well groomed, with just one tendril escaping to curl on his forehead. His face was perfect, too perfect to be real. Adonis-like features exuded assurance and compassion beneath the beauty. His brown eyes reflected the smile he gave the waiter when he ordered a coffee—"With crème, no sugar"—in his cultured French accent. The waiter smiled as he heard several women audibly gasp and sigh.

"Merci," the gentleman said to the waiter when the coffee cup was placed before him on the table. More enraptured sighs followed, and once again the waiter smiled. He noticed that many people had their cameras out, video recording or taking pictures of the gentleman. Really? He was merely sitting there, sipping his coffee and reading a newspaper. There was nothing extraordinary about either. The waiter had served celebrities and film stars over the years, and he expected them to receive this kind of attention. But this man? Why?

The waiter took a moment to study the gentleman. It wasn't just the suit, the face, the figure. It was the combination, some magical concoction that defied explanation. This gentleman, unlike many attractive people, didn't seem to realize just how beautiful he was. He honestly didn't notice the way people reacted to him. Why not? Most men relished such attention, especially from women, but this man remained unfazed. He paid them no mind.

Suddenly, the gentleman waved his left hand, and for the first time his audience saw the gold ring. A wedding band. Many women groaned or gasped, disappointed to see the ring. No wonder he had ignored them. People watched the scene play out as if they were watching a film. The gentleman stood as a woman approached him, and the couple embraced and kissed. "Ah, ma chère, how I have missed you," he said as he held her chair as she sat.

The woman laughed, looked at her watch, and replied, "It has been just two hours, mon amour."

"Oui, but I love you, ma beau jeune femme," he smiled, lifted her hand, and kissed it. "Happy twenty-fifth anniversary to the only woman I will ever love."

"Happy anniversary, Julien," she said with adoration evident in her eyes. "I love you."

Even those who had not overheard presumed the woman was the gorgeous man's wife. "She's pretty," someone whispered.

"And lucky," another woman added. "She's got him. I mean, look at him. And it's not just that he's drop dead handsome. He's so in love with her."

"I know. What I wouldn't give for a man like him," someone else sighed.

"That's Julien Lacoeur," a man leaned close to inform the captivated women.

"The hotelier? I had no idea he looked like that," a woman replied.

"Oh, yeah, he inherited the Hotel du Raphael from his father. "

"And a fortune."

"Sure, but he's no playboy, you know. He's a serious artist, and his works exhibit in some of the finest galleries," yet another admirer informed everyone.

"And he runs a charity for terminally ill people. A lot of that money he inherited goes into helping with their medical expenses and care," one woman said in a defensive tone.

"Really? I had no idea. Just look at how he's looking at her. He really is dreamy," a young woman smiled.

"That's his wife, Aurélie Grosvenor. They've been married twenty-five years."

"Well, she's one lucky lady to have him, that's for sure."

People watched the romantic exchange in silence once more as Julien pulled the jewel box from his pocket and offered it to his wife. "For you, my Aurélie."

She wept when she opened the box, and said, "This is exquisite. I will treasure it always. I will wear it every day. Do you have any idea what this truly means to me?"

"I do, my dear. The first gift I gave you was a dime-store version of this, a token from my ten-year-old self to the first and only girl I have loved," Julien proclaimed in his gentle French accent. Those who heard wept, too, as they watched a real life love story play out before them, one more romantic than Hollywood could ever script.

Aurélie smiled through her tears. "Yes, and I have worn that one every day since you fastened it around my neck," she said, and pulled a chain from under her dress. Suspended from the chain was a clear plastic heart. "Our love has endured for 35 years, and it will endure for eternity, mon amour. Will you?" She held the jewel box out to him, and he removed the necklace, stood, and fastened it around her neck. When he finished, he bent and kissed her cheek. Many of those watching sighed and cried when they saw the heart pendant made from 25 flawless diamonds.

Aurélie looked down and gently fingered both hearts. "I love them both, Julien, and I love you with all of my soul. You remain my very best friend since we were ten years old. You are the only man I love. Oh, I always saw how very beautiful you are. Who doesn't? But I love you and I married you for your mind and your soul, not for your beauty. You, my love, are an enigma, the antithesis of the French playboy. You are a man of integrity, intellect, seriousness, compassion, poetry, music, family, and loyalty. What more could I ever desire in my life partner? You, dear Julien, are my dream man come true."

Julien held her hand aloft and tenderly kissed it. "I was created to be your eternal husband, ma chère. God destined us to meet, to become friends, and to marry. Together, we will continue to blaze our path of love across the universe. Long after we depart this earth, the trail left behind will glow in the sky like a transcendent vapor," Julien said and handed Aurélie the red roses.

"Our flower," she said through her tears. "They are perfectly beautiful," Aurélie said as she breathed in their fragrant perfume. "This is a gorgeous bouquet, but why so many?"

"That is simple. Fifty red roses symbolize unconditional love," Julien smiled as he clasped her hand.

Aurélie buried her face in the roses, her body trembling as she cried. Julien moved to the chair beside her and held her close, her head resting against his shoulder. "I do love you so," she sniffled, kissed him, and smiled up at him with her green eyes shining.

"And I you," he replied, kissed her, and dried her cheeks with his handkerchief. "I thought we would spend the rest of the day exploring the little hidden gems and nooks of Paris together, things we do not normally get to see. Just you and me, celebrating our forever love. What do you think of that?"

"I think it sounds delightful," Aurélie smiled, held the roses in one arm, and put her other arm around Julien. They began their leisurely stroll through Paris as people continued to watch them. For a few hours, the couple browsed tiny shops and galleries as they made their way to out-of-the-way areas of Paris. Suddenly, they smiled at one another when they saw a small church. They entered, walked toward the altar, and knelt to pray.

When they finished, both made the sign of the cross and stood staring up at the crucifix. "My life really is perfect, Julien. I have my best friend and his love. I would never have survived everything if you hadn't been beside me. I would not. You are my tower of strength."

Julien sighed, bowed his head, and fought his tears. "You are the one who kept me strong, Aurélie. You and God. I should have crumbled and withered without you both."

She nodded. "We are a trinity— you, me, and God. It is just the three of us. We are meant to exist alone. I will never know why, but that's the way God planned it to be."

"I know," Julien whispered. "I do not understand it. I never will. It took me a long time to realize that I do not have to. It took me a long time to release the pain, to see the truth that I am not the one who is in control. There is something else in store for us, Aurélie, something we never dreamed of or planned for, but something beyond the confines of our minds and control." He walked to a stained glass window and stared through it at something only he could see. "We talked for years about growing up, getting married, having children, and being happy. A happy family. That is all we ever wanted."

"I know," Aurélie said through her tears. "I know. That is what we wanted. Desperately wanted. But it is not what he wants for us. There must be something much bigger, much grander, in his plans for us. There must be. Why else would he deny us children, children we will love and who will love us? This life is all about love. So there must be something more for us, Julien, or none of this makes any sense."

"Yes, I know, my dear. Perhaps we should try once more to have our own child. Perhaps that is our test of faith."

"Oh, Julien, we have been through this. Isn't four miscarriages and one stillbirth enough? How much more pain can our souls endure? There is a limit. Is not the message clear to us both? We are not meant to give birth to a child. That is the one thing we cannot experience and have."

Julien turned, looked at his wife with tears streaming down his face, and nodded. "I know. God help me, I know. Oh, Aurélie, I am so sorry, my love. I am so very sorry. I have failed you."

Aurélie rushed to him, embraced him, and held him tightly as he cried. "Never. You could never fail me, Julien. Maybe this love of ours, that is larger than the heavens, is meant for something or someone more. Maybe our love is meant for someone like us who is alone and in need of a family."

Julien held his wife for several moments while her meaning became clear. "You mean adoption? Adopt a child?"

"Well, there are so many children who are all alone, who need parents. I know we both dreamed of our child, but if we adopt, then the child becomes ours, truly ours. Birth does not create a family, Julien. Love does. We find the child we love, and we become a family." He shook his head as he tried to reconcile himself to the idea. "We do not have to decide anything today, darling. But you are the one who always says that everything happens for a reason. There is a reason we do not have children, and there is a reason we came into this church today and are talking about this. God brought us here, to this place and to this discussion. Maybe, just maybe, this is God's plan for us, Julien."

After several minutes of reflective silence, Julien smiled and nodded. "Maybe it is, my beautiful bride. Maybe it is. If it is meant to happen, we will find our child. Our child will find us. God is directing this play, and he will bring us together when the time is right." He kissed Aurélie, bowed his head to pray, and then made the sign of the cross.

Aurélie pulled three roses from the bouquet and placed them on the altar. "Red roses also represent Christ's suffering as well as strong desire. We, too, have suffered horribly, the deaths of five babies. We desire a child. A child will complete our human trinity and make our lives whole. That is what I pray for to God on this very special day, my love."

Julien smiled, kissed her, and softly said, "So do I, Aurélie. So do I."

§§§§

"We have weathered so much in our twenty-five years. Your father's illness and death, the deaths of my parents, the deaths of our babies. So much pain and loss. I think we have grown closer and tighter because of it all," Aurélie said as they slowly walked down a wide cobblestone street.

Julien squeezed her shoulder and nodded. "I know we have. Lesser things have torn apart other couples. Like Darren and Shirley. The setbacks and rough patches turned them into enemies, not close friends and lovers. They grew apart. We grew even closer, deeper friends. We had only each other even before our parents died, because we could not burden them, and we held tight to one another. We shared these experiences, truly shared them. We opened our souls to each other during our grief. We trust each other as we have never trusted anyone. We understand each other. We are best friends, and we are lovers. We are a unit, a solid unit, that nothing can destroy," he said and kissed the top of her head.

Aurélie sighed and snuggled closer to him. "Yes, we are, darling. For that I am grateful."

Julien suddenly gestured toward a café on the opposite corner, suggested they relax over coffee, and smiled when she nodded. Still snuggling, they entered, surprised to find no other patrons on such a lovely afternoon. There was just one person, a young lady, sitting at a piano and playing a beautiful melody. Julien and Aurélie stood and listened. Aurélie sighed in response, and the young pianist stood quickly, realizing that she had customers.

"I'm so sorry. Forgive me," she said as she rushed to show them to a table.

"No, no, no. Do not apologize. That was absolutely breathtaking, especially today," Julien told her as he smiled at Aurélie and held her chair for her.

"Happy anniversary."

"How did you know?" Julien asked the girl.

"The way you look at each other. Yours looks like lifelong love, not new love. That and the roses. So many red roses must mean true, deep love. Is it your twenty-fifth?"

"Yes, it is," Julien smiled at her. "You are very perceptive." Julien sat across from Aurélie. "Two coffees please. Crème, no sugar in mine. Crème and sugar in Aurélie's."

The girl curtsied and said, "Of course. I have to make some fresh coffee. There hasn't been anyone here for hours. It will take a few moments. I hope that's all right."

"Of course," Aurélie smiled up at the girl. "We are not in a hurry. We came in here to relax."

As she made the coffee, the young lady stared at Julien. Something about him was so familiar, and yet she had never met him before. He looked up and caught her staring, and she looked away. Not before he saw the sadness on her face, however. He watched her, his brow furrowed, and Aurélie noticed. She looked over her shoulder, saw the girl preparing their coffee, and wondered what was wrong. She quietly asked her husband.

"I am not sure. She was staring at me so intensely."

Aurélie smiled and patted his hand. "Every woman stares at you, Julien." He looked at her in amazement. "They do. You are gorgeous." He literally brushed away her comment with his hand, and she giggled. "Fine, my dear, but you are. You really have no idea the effect and power you have." Julien made a face. "All right. I will stop. I know this makes you uncomfortable. But I am not surprised that she is smitten," Aurélie said with a wink.

"Hush. She is coming," Julien whispered.

The waitress carried a tray to their table, placed Aurélie's coffee before her, then Julien's in front of him, and finally a small white-and-red frosted cake in the middle of the table. "Happy anniversary," she said as she placed dessert plates, forks, and a cake knife on the table.

"Thank you. This is very sweet," Aurélie said. "Please join us."

"Oh, thank you, but that isn't allowed."

"But there is not anyone else here, is there?" Julien asked.

"No, but. . . ."

"Then sit with us. Help us to celebrate our anniversary. Get yourself a cup of coffee, a cake plate, and join us," Julien insisted. When she hesitated, he said, "Go."

The young lady poured herself a cup of coffee—her first all day—picked up another plate and fork, and sat between the couple. Aurélie cut and served the cake, and looked at Julien when the waitress bowed her head and seemed to pray.

"May God bless you and fulfill your dearest dreams," she softly said to them when she raised her head.

"Thank you," Julien said. "Aurélie and I prayed for that ourselves this afternoon in a small church not too far from here."

"I pray for that every day," the young lady very softly said. "I wonder if my dream is meant to come true." Aurélie and Julien barely heard her. They looked at one another, stunned by her overwhelming sadness. She seemed too young for such heartache.

"This is the best-tasting coffee I have ever had," Julien said, hoping to shift the mood.

"Thank you. I suppose it's easy to do something well that you do very often."

"Perhaps, but not necessarily," Julien countered. "I have met plenty of people who are mediocre at best at things they do very frequently. I believe the key is to, at some level, enjoy what you are doing. If you enjoy it, you want to do your best. You strive to do your best. Like your piano playing. You are remarkably gifted. You learned well from your teachers."

"Thank you, but I've never taken lessons. We never had extra money for such luxuries. Still, I was blessed to have someone who cared for me and who taught me. I really can't and shouldn't complain about my life despite everything."

Aurélie flashed her husband a concerned yet puzzled look, and he nodded once. "Your life was not easy?" he asked the girl.

"Oh, it's not that life was difficult. It's just that Renée, the woman who raised me, didn't have very much money. She cleaned others' homes for money, and we never went hungry. We lived in a small two-room house in a lovely village where we had what we needed. The neighbors were kind and friendly. The pastor at the church allowed me to play the piano there during the week. That's where I practiced."

"The woman who raised you? What about your parents?" Aurélie asked, maternal concern evident in her voice and on her face.

"My mother died minutes after I was born. I never had the chance to even see her. I've been told that she was very beautiful, with dark brown hair and blue eyes. Renée told me that everyone adored my mother," the girl smiled.

"And your father?"

"He was. . . . He died when I was a baby. That's when Renée took me to raise. She homeschooled me once I was old enough. I especially like history and art. Monet and Renoir are my favorites," she replied with a small smile.

"You are lucky that Renée adopted you," Aurélie said.

"Oh, she never adopted me. She simply took me when my father died, and she let me live with her in her simple house. That's where I lived until late last year when Renée died and I came here to find a job."

"She never adopted you? But what about the authorities? No one asked questions?" Aurélie asked.

The girl shook her head. "No. We lived in a very small village, and Renée told people that I was her niece. I believed her until just before she died, when she told me the truth. I'm not related to her, but I should use her family name as mine to avoid any problems. So I do. Angelica Sabine."

Aurélie inhaled sharply, but Julien squeezed her hand as a signal not to say anything. "Where are your relatives?" he asked.

"I don't know if I even have any. Renée never mentioned any, no aunts, uncles, grandparents, or cousins. I don't know what name I'd search for anyway."

"How old are you, Angelica?" She was unusually, surprisingly honest with them, which stunned Julien. He had to know.

"Fourteen. I'll be fifteen in eleven months. Please don't tell the café owner. I know it was wrong, sinful actually, but I lied about my age and said I was sixteen when I asked him about this job. This job allows me to have a room over the café and a small salary to live on. I need to keep this job until I really am sixteen and can find a better-paying job. Please." Angelica looked at them with fear and anguish in her eyes, and Aurélie covered her mouth with her hands to stifle her own tears.

Julien held Angelica's hands gently and promised, "We will never tell a living soul, Angelica. But you are still too young to live alone. You are not safe."

"Oh, no one pays me any attention. I spend most of my time here except to attend church every Sunday morning. It's the little church around the corner, St. Mary the Virgin. That's the church you prayed at, isn't it?" Julien nodded. "I don't own much, so the small room upstairs is all I need. I have a job, a bed to sleep in, and enough money for clothes, food, and once in a while a book to read. I can play the piano when no one else is here, so that is the best of all. Every moment, I do wish my parents were alive, especially my father, but no one can change that. So, considering everything, I really don't have any excuse to complain about my life, even in silence to myself." Angelica looked alarmed. "Forgive me. I didn't mean to be such a downer and take so much of your time, especially on such a very special day."

"You have not, believe me. Will you play Aurélie and me another piece before we leave?" Angelica looked both surprised and embarrassed by the request. "Please, for me," Julien requested tenderly and smiled at her. She suddenly appeared—what? Sad? Unsure? Julien didn't know, but her expression touched his heart deeply for some unknown reason. Aurélie noticed, as well, and she was more baffled than Julien.

Angelica nodded, slowly walked to the piano, sat, and played from her heart a composition she made up at that moment. She stared at Julien as she played, and he felt compelled to study her. What was it about her that made him feel as if he had known her before? Had he met her through his foundation or his charity work? If so, he didn't remember the meeting. He forced his mind back into the present as she finished, and he applauded with his wife.

"Thank you, Angelica. That was beautiful," Aurélie smiled.

"Yes, extremely beautiful, Angelica. Thank you for making our anniversary even more special," Julien said and kissed her hand. "I pray for you that all of your dreams and desires come true, my dear child," he said, pulled 10F from his wallet, and left it on the table.

Aurélie picked up the bouquet, kissed Angelica's cheek, and handed her one of the roses. "So do I, darling. Thank you for a lovely afternoon."

"Thank you. I'll never forget either of you," Angelica said with a sad smile as they slowly walked outside. She watched Julien until they were gone.

Angelica sighed, got the tray, and began clearing the table. Suddenly, she spotted Julien's wallet, and she ran after them yelling his name. He and Aurélie turned just as she caught up to them.

"Your wallet. You left it on the table," she breathlessly said and gave it to him.

"I was not aware I did something so careless. Merci, Angelica," Julien smiled.

"My pleasure. Enjoy the rest of your anniversary."

"Thank you. We are going to the theatre soon," Aurélie smiled up at Julien as they turned and began walking. "She is such a sweet, sad girl, all alone. Why not ask her to go with us, Julien?"

"Yes?"

"Yes. You were thinking the same thing, too, do not tell me you were not."

"I admit it. I was. I will go get her," Julien kissed his wife and turned back toward the café. He felt his heart skip a beat. Angelica was slumped against the café building, her back toward him. Had she fallen and hurt herself? he wondered in alarm. He walked to her quickly, and knelt facing her. "Angelica? What happened? Are you all right?"

She lifted her head and looked at him just as he saw the red stain on her white shirt. He watched it grow larger by the second. "You are bleeding," he said, panic in his voice, as he quickly took off his suit jacket and pressed it to her chest. By that time, Aurélie neared to find out what was wrong. "Call an ambulance. Hurry!"

"No. I'm already dead," Angelica murmured as Aurélie ran into the café to make the call.

"Do not talk, darling. You will be fine," Julien reassured her, although he was terrified. She was barely breathing, and she was losing so much blood. His brain whirred as he tried to understand what had happened in just a matter of seconds. He glanced around. Pedestrians talked, laughed, and walked as if nothing untoward had happened. No one had seemed to see what did happen. Julien had neither seen nor heard anything out of the ordinary.

"The ambulance is on its way. There is a doctor on board to start treatment right away," Aurélie said as she ran to them and knelt beside Angelica. She looked in horror at the red stains on her husband's shirt cuffs as he tried to staunch the bleeding.

"Angelica, look at me," Julien commanded. "Angelica." Her eyes flickered open, and she looked at him with that same longing he had noticed as she'd made the coffee and stared at him. "The doctor will take care of you. You will be all right."

"It's okay. I'll be with my father again," she barely said just as the ambulance sped to them.

Before Julien could say anything in response, the doctor rushed to Angelica and told him to move. The doctor quickly wrapped thick cotton bandages tightly around her chest and ordered a medic to insert an IV and start a blood transfusion. In moments, she was placed on the gurney and lifted into the ambulance. The doctor turned to Julien and Aurélie. "There is room for one of you to accompany your daughter to the hospital."

Aurélie pushed Julien forward, told him to go, and asked to which hospital they were taking Angelica. "You go. I will get a taxi and be there soon. Go."

Julien quickly climbed into the ambulance. Soon it was speeding as a medic relayed vital information to the surgical team awaiting them at the hospital. Angelica looked into Julien's eyes and pulled the oxygen mask away from her mouth. The medic reached to replace it, but she shook her head and said, "I am so sorry I ruined your anniversary."

Julien fought his tears, replaced the oxygen mask, and held her hand tenderly. "You did not ruin anything, Angelica. You just let the doctors make you well. That is the most important thing. All right? The three of us will go to the theatre when you are well, and we will have a glorious evening. I promise."

She nodded while tears filled her eyes, and she feebly curled her fingers around Julien's. At that moment, the ambulance arrived at the hospital, and the medics quickly removed Angelica from the ambulance and wheeled her inside. Julien ran to follow them toward the operating room. Just outside the operating room doors, the doctor turned and told him they had to get her to surgery. "We will take the best care of her, we promise you that. Someone will update you halfway through the surgery. We must take her in now."

Julien nodded and bent to kiss Angelica's forehead. "God is with you, dear child. Aurélie and I will be here when you wake up." She touched his hand as they wheeled her into the operating room. Once the doors closed, Julien leaned against the wall and cried.

§§§§§

"We have been sitting here for almost three hours. How much longer? When are they going to tell us anything?" Aurélie asked as she twisted a handkerchief in her hands. She and Julien sat alone in the hallway, the long wait only increasing their fear.

"I do not know," Julien said, forcing his voice to remain clam while he tightly clenched his hands together. "I do not know. The surgeon said someone would update us halfway through her surgery. I do not know how long this surgery is supposed to take, so how can I know when it is halfway over? Someone needs to tell us something," he exclaimed, the fear tinging his voice.

Julien stood and paced the hallway for several moments, but stopped when he saw someone in surgical scrubs approaching them. Aurélie noticed, too, stood, and tightly held Julien's arm. What would they hear? Was Angelica all right? Was she alive?

"Mr. and Mrs. Lacoeur?" Julien gripped Aurélie's hand, and they both nodded. "I'm Dr. Sutfield's medical assistant, Dr. Forbes. He asked me to give you an update on your daughter."

Aurélie and Julien looked at one another. That was the second time someone had presumed Angelica was their daughter. Aurélie saw the look in her husband's eyes and quickly answered the doctor. "How is she? We have been so worried just sitting here and waiting."

"I understand, Mrs. Lacoeur. Dr. Sutfield had intended to update you sooner, but. . . ." The doctor paused, and Aurélie put her arm around Julien when she felt him tense.

"But what?" Julien whispered, barely able to speak.

"Sit down, please."

Aurélie stifled her scream with her hand, and Julien put his arms around her. "Tell us. Please, just tell us," he pleaded.

"Angelica had a .44 caliber bullet lodged just next to her main pulmonary artery. By the time we began surgery, she had lost nearly half of her blood, but since the transfusion had been started at the scene, that was in her favor."

Aurélie began crying, and she uttered a strained, "Dear God, no." Julien held her closer as he fought to control his own terror.

"The surgery itself is very delicate, as I'm sure you can understand. Every move that Dr. Sutfield makes is very deliberate, precise, and very cautious. He has performed a sternotomy to gain access to Angelica's heart. The first third of the surgery went well."

Julien breathed deeply, and asked, "What happened?"

"Angelica is stable now. Dr. Sutfield and our team resolved the issues, I assure you."

"What happened?" Julien repeated, standing ramrod straight and clenching his fists.

"Angelica's heart stopped beating just before Dr. Sutfield was ready to remove the bullet."

"Her heart stopped? What does that mean?" Aurélie asked, her eyes wide and tear-filled.

"Angelica died," Julien stated—not asked. Aurélie shook her head in denial.

Dr. Forbes took Aurélie's hand in his, and his eyes looked at her in concern. "For just a few minutes, yes. Dr. Sutfield restored cardiac rhythmia relatively quickly."

Aurélie began crying, while Julien stood rigidly straight and still, as if afraid to move. Dr. Forbes was unaccustomed to such discussions; Dr. Sutfield usually dealt with his patients' families. He cleared his throat and patted Aurélie's hand. "Your daughter has the best cardiac surgeon in Paris, and she will, in time, recover from her ordeal. She will. I must return to the operating room now, but Dr. Sutfield will speak with you when the surgery is over and Angelica is in recovery."

Aurélie blew her nose on her handkerchief and gave Dr. Forbes a small smile. "Thank you."

When the doctor had left, she turned to her husband, who still stood unmoving. "Julien?" Aurélie gently touched his cheek. "Julien. She will be fine. She will. They are taking care of her. She will be fine, mon cher."

"She has to. We cannot lose another child."

"Oh, darling, no. Do not do this to yourself. I know the doctors presume she is our daughter, but she is not. Do not torment yourself, Julien."

Julien looked at her with an expression that Aurélie had never before seen. She gave a small jump in her astonishment. "She is, in all but name, Aurélie. Angelica is the child meant for us, the child God brought to us. She is our daughter."

Aurélie froze, stunned—not by the incredulity of Julien's words, but by the truth in them. A few hours earlier, they had stood in a church, discussing God's plan for them. They had left the church in agreement that God would bring their designated child into their lives. Then they had met Angelica, sweet, sad, gentle Angelica. This young girl, so thoughtful, so musical, so alone, had looked at them with such longing. She needed them as much as they needed her.

"Oh, Julien, dare we believe that our dream has come true?"

"It has come true," Julien replied as he clasped his wife's arms. "Angelica is our daughter. She is. The way she stared at me in the café, as if she knew me, recognized me, it shook me, Aurélie. It astonished me. And I felt as if I had met her before, too. I cannot explain it. But I feel it, and I know that this is real and true. I know that she is our daughter."

"I know," Aurélie whispered. "I think I knew all along. That is why I wanted her to come to the theatre with us to celebrate our anniversary. Oh, Julien, she will be all right. God would not bring a sixth child into our lives, only to take her away. He will not. He cannot."

"He will not," Julien stated, his voice firm and confident. "When she recovers, we will take Angelica home with us, and our human trinity will be complete."

§§§§§

Julien and Aurélie sat silently, heads bowed in constant prayer and holding hands, for the next two hours and forty minutes. Their quiet was suddenly disturbed by Dr. Sutfield's voice. Julien quickly stood, his heart pounding, and looked at the surgeon, questions and anxiety evident in his eyes.

Aurélie slowly stood, holding tightly onto her husband's hand, all the while not daring to breathe. She could not help but stare at the blood stains on his surgical scrubs, the same blood that still stained Julien's shirt cuffs.

"Angelica is in recovery. Her vital signs are stable, but we are, of course, closely monitoring her. The first twenty-four hours are crucial, but there is every reason to hope that she will make a full recovery."

Dr. Sutfield explained some of the more technical elements of the surgery and projected recovery. Noticing that Mrs. Lacoeur looked pale and that Mr. Lacoeur appeared anxious, the doctor realized that his explanations meant little to them at that moment. "She is still unconscious, but you can see her now."

Aurélie and Julien looked at one another, and then nodded to Dr. Sutfield.

Aurélie whimpered when Dr. Sutfield escorted them into Angelica's recovery room. The girl who had talked, smiled, and so vibrantly played the piano just a few hours earlier now lay still, pale, and connected to multiple monitors. Julien gently hugged her as they neared Angelica's bed. The room was silent except for the beeps and ticking of the machines. Aurélie bent, kissed the girl's cheek, and said yet another silent prayer.

Julien smiled reassuringly at his wife, and then gently kissed Angelica's forehead. She opened her eyes oh so briefly and very softly murmured "Daddy" as she looked at him in the instant before her eyes closed.

Aurélie sharply inhaled. Julien tenderly held Angelica's hand and said, "I am here, darling."

§§§§§

While Julien and Aurélie kept vigil in Angelica's private hospital room, around-the-clock guards maintained alert protection at the door to her room. Only Dr. Sutfield, Dr. Forbes, and Nurses

Ramsey and Schwitzer were cleared for entry. Police had begun investigating the shooting as soon as Angelica's injury had been reported. However, no one had seemed to have seen or heard anything out of the ordinary at the time of the shooting. Since no one had heard a gunshot, police presumed the shooter had used a silencer. Until they could question Angelica, and hopefully get a description of the shooter, they had no leads.

Twelve hours after surgery, Dr. Sutfield examined Angelica and, with Nurse Ramsey's assistance, changed her wound dressings. While they waited, Julien and Aurélie went into the hospital gift shop, where Aurélie bought a pretty nightgown and robe and Julien a teddy bear. "She needs someone she can hold onto and feel safe with," Julien said, as if justifying the purchase.

"She has you, Julien, son père," Aurélie smiled and snuggled close to him as the cashier handed him the bag.

"How can I tell you what I felt when she looked at me and said that? She called me Daddy. This girl who is meant to be our daughter called me Daddy. My heart felt such joy and happiness at that moment, Aurélie. I cannot describe how I truly felt."

"You do not have to, darling. I felt it with you. This is meant to be. It must be."

"Oui, mon amour, oui. You, me, and Angelica are a family," Julien smiled as they entered her hospital room.

"She's resting comfortably," Nurse Ramsey quietly told them before she left.

Aurélie kissed Angelica's cheek, quietly placed the gown and robe in the dresser drawer, and then walked to the window. "I am feeling it all now, Julien. I am exhausted."

He stood behind her, placed his hands on her shoulders, and kissed her neck. "Go home, darling. Eat, sleep, shower, and come back later. You can bring me a change of clothes when you do."

"I cannot leave you here alone," Aurélie said as she turned to face him.

"I will be fine. I will order some food, and I will take a shower when you return. Go on. I will call you if anything happens."

Aurélie nodded. "You are right. We need to take care of ourselves so that we can take care of her. I will be back in a few hours. Je t'aime," she said, kissed him and Angelica, and left.

Julien tenderly placed the teddy bear next to Angelica and wrapped her arm around it. She moaned, opened her eyes, and looked at him. Tears filled her eyes and sliced through him. "Oh, Chouchou, I will call the nurse to bring you something for the pain," he said and reached for the call button.

Angelica shook her head and said a weak, "No. That's not it."

"Then what? Why are you crying?"

"Memories," Angelica whispered and pulled the teddy bear closer. "I had a teddy bear when I was a baby. It was in my crib with me when I took naps and at night. I remember it had a red felt tongue. I don't know what happened to it. I never saw it again after my father was. . .after my father died and Renée took me."

The utter sadness in her eyes and voice filled Julien's eyes with tears, and he had to force himself to swallow them so he could speak. "You will always have this one, Angelica. Always."

She smiled at him through her tears and reached for his hand. She feebly curled her fingers around two of his fingers, and Julien wrapped her weak hand in his strong hand. He stroked her hair with his other hand, kissed her forehead, and said, "Sleep, little angel, and I will be here when you wake up. I will always be here."

When she was asleep, Julien bowed his head and cried. He couldn't explain it, even to himself, but this girl whom he had just met felt like his daughter as surely as if he had made her.

§§§§§

Aurélie entered Angelica's hospital room with two suitcases containing her and Julien's clothes. Julien stood and kissed her while Nurse Ramsey finished checking the teenager's vital signs.

"She has remained stable. It's going to take time for her heart to recover from the wound and the surgery, though.

I know how hard this is on you," Nurse Ramsey said in her habitual near whisper.

"It is," Aurélie replied. "It is."

"I wasn't aware you had any children," Nurse Ramsey said, and then apologized. "I'm sorry. I don't mean to pry into your personal lives, but, well, Monsieur Lacoeur, you are in the newspapers frequently."

"It is all right," Julien assured the nurse. "Actually, my wife and I are adopting Angelica, so she is our daughter."

"Adopting?" Nurse Ramsey sounded perplexed, but quickly explained. "Forgive me. Adoption is wonderful, it really is. My nephew was adopted when he was an infant. I wholeheartedly support it. It's just that Angelica resembles you, Monsieur Lacoeur, and I just assumed. . . . Forgive me."

"No need, Nurse Ramsey. None at all. Merci," Julien smiled as the nurse quietly left. "She resembles me?" Julien asked no one in particular as he stared straight ahead.

Aurélie stood behind him, put her arms around him, and rested her chin on his shoulder. "Yes, she does. You did not see that at the café? I thought that is why you watched her."

Julien shook his head. "No. I was too stunned by how she stared at me. It was like she knew me. No. I did not see myself in her. Do you really think she looks like I?"

"Yes, I do. Look at her, Julien. She has the same cheekbones, the same chin, the same face shape, the same complexion, the same coloring, and the exact same eyes. Those brown eyes that have that perpetual sad look, no matter how you feel. She has them, Julien."

"Mon Dieu. She really is meant to be our daughter, chéri," Julien whispered. "She loves music and literature and art. She loves all of the things I love. Of course she is our daughter."

"Julien, darling, I know. That must be destiny. You will call your lawyer soon and start the process, oui?"

"Yes. Yes, of course. I will call Rogier now," Julien said and moved toward the door.

"Julien, wait," Aurélie grabbed his arm. "We should talk with Angelica first. She is fourteen, not a baby, and she has thoughts and feelings about this. We cannot just decide her life for her."

"You are right. We can wait. Well, then, I think I will take a shower now, change clothes, and appear fresh and proper when she wakes up. I love you." Julien kissed Aurélie, picked up his suitcase, and went into the bathroom of Angelica's of hospital suite.

Aurélie sat in the chair next to Angelica's bed and watched her. She placed her hand over Angelica's left hand atop the teddy bear. "Oh petite fille, you were brought into our lives, and we into yours on a special day. We three are meant to be a family. I believe that. I know that in my heart. I pray to God this come to be."

"Mrs. Lacoeur?" Angelica weakly asked.

Aurélie smiled at her and said, "Oui, Angelica darling, I am here. Julien and I are both here."

"You were here before," Angelica said.

"We were. We have been here since they brought you here."

"Mr. Lacoeur came in the ambulance with me," Angelica said with a look of bewilderment. "You barely know me. Why?"

"We care about you, ma petite. We want to be here with you," Aurélie responded and tenderly stroked the girl's hair.

Tears filled Angelica's eyes. "Did you mean what you said?" Aurélie's expression asked what the girl referenced, and Angelica explained, "Just before I opened my eyes."

"You heard that?" Angelica nodded. "Yes, I did mean it, Angelica."

"What did you mean, ma chère?" Julien asked as he entered the room looking dashing in a navy blue suit. He and Aurélie heard Angelica inhale sharply when she looked at him.

"She overheard my prayer, Julien," Aurélie said while she gave him a knowing look. Julien nodded, understanding his wife's meaning.

"Our prayer," Julien clarified and looked into Angelica's eyes. "Yes, we do mean it. We both want this, Angelica, we do, more than my words can say."

Angelica looked at Julien and Aurélie for a few moments. "Why me? You just met two days ago."

"Yes, we did, but that does not mean that I, that both of us, are not drawn to you, connected to you. You opened yourself up to us, and I in particular share so many similarities with you. And I will tell you that, from the beginning, I felt that I knew you. I cannot explain that, but it is true, Angelica. You are familiar to me even though we just met." Julien placed his hand over hers. "You felt that, too."

Angelica nodded as tears filled her eyes. "I did," she whispered through the tears that choked her. "There is so much about you that is very familiar." Tears slid from her eyes as distant memories flooded through her mind. "I feel safe and comfortable with you. I can't explain why, either, but I do."

Aurélie put her hand on her husband's back when Julien cleared his throat to keep from crying. "You do?

That makes me glad. You heard Aurélie's prayer?" Angelica nodded. "You know what we long for more than anything?" She once again nodded. Julien looked deep into her eyes again. He saw love, trust, and hope in them. His heart leapt. "How do you feel about our prayer, Angelica?" He wanted her to answer honestly, so he did not want his questions to lead her in any way.

Angelica looked at Aurélie and then at Julien, straight through his eyes into his soul. "I'm not sure what to think. It would be more than I ever thought possible, more than I deserve."

"Oh, Angelica, whatever makes you think you do not deserve a family?" Aurélie asked with pain in her voice.

"Because I had only my father so briefly. After the first months of my life, I never had a family. That was more than I ever dared pray for," Angelica admitted. "I believed that God meant my life to be this way, alone. I mean, I know I had Renée, and she gave me the necessities, but she, well, she was never a mother to me. I am grateful to her, but that's true. She wasn't any semblance of a mother.

So I accepted that I would never have a family—parents—of my own."

Julien clasped her hand in both of his. He had to ask her the most direct and important question he had asked in twenty-five years. "What do you think about Aurélie and me becoming your parents?"

"I think it would be the most fabulous gift," Angelica softly answered as tears spilled from her eyes.

"So do we," Julien agreed with a tender smile as Aurélie leaned against him and cried tears of joy. Their prayer had come true.

§§§§§

The next morning Angelica ate a few strawberries, her first food since the anniversary cake three days earlier. The fruit made her nauseated, so Aurélie sat on the bed beside her, holding her and gently stroking her hair. "Close your eyes, ma petite, and take deep, slow breaths. Let your body adjust to food again."

Julien smiled as he watched his beloved wife doing the one thing she had long dreamed of doing—being a mother.

Aurélie's maternal instinct had been noticed in her occasional visits with patients that Julien's foundation served. She had held sick children, comforting and soothing them. He always knew she would be an affectionate, loving mother to their children. Now, after years of hope and heartbreak, Aurélie was a mother. Oh, it was not legally official yet, but Julien would speak with his lawyer very soon. He had made an appointment while the doctor had examined Angelica before breakfast. He, Aurélie, and Angelica would be a family soon.

Aurélie kissed the girl's head, and smiled at her husband. "She is sleeping," she whispered.

Julien nodded, kissed his wife, and left to get them both coffee. They had practically lived at the hospital since Angelica had been rushed there. He stopped walking, suddenly overwhelmed, stunned, and euphoric by how quickly and unexpectedly everything that happened. One moment he and Aurélie had prayed in the church for God to give them a child. Moments later, they had met her at a café, only to nearly lose her to an assassin's bullet. Julien shook his head to clear the discombobulation from his mind.

Nurse Ramsey watched Julien, understanding the stress and fear he had experienced since Angelica's shooting. "Monsieur Lacoeur?" she said as she approached him. "Is everything all right?"

Julien forced his attention back to the present, and he gave the nurse a tired smile. "Oui. Yes, everything is all right. Angelica is sleeping right now, and Aurélie is holding her. I was on my way to get us some coffee."

"No need for that, my man," a gentleman in a suit said as he walked toward Julien. "I bought coffee for the three of us: you, me, and that charming wife of yours. So this is where you have been the past two days. I wondered where you two had gotten off to this time." The man looked at Julien from head to toe. "Just what is going on Julien? You make an appointment to talk about adoption, yet you tell me you are staying here, at the hospital. Who is sick?"

"The girl we want to adopt. Oh, Rogier, we finally found the child meant for us, only to have her nearly murdered,"

Julien explained and then began sobbing, unable to hold his tears inside any longer.

Rogier put one arm around Julien as he held the coffee in his other hand. He turned and asked Nurse Ramsey, "Is there somewhere we can talk in private?"

She nodded and led them to a small waiting room nearby. Rogier asked her to take one of the coffees to Mrs. Lacoeur and to explain that he and Julien were meeting. Once she left, Rogier revealed his shock. "Murdered? What happened?"

Julien told his lawyer and friend about his and Aurélie's twenty-fifth anniversary, going into detail about their visit to the church followed by the café where they met Angelica. "Rogier, I saw the bloodstain grow larger and larger, and I was so very scared. I thought she would die, and I was so scared." Julien's eyes were filled with tears—and love—as he looked at Rogier.

The intensity in Julien's eyes stunned Rogier. He had seen that depth of emotion related to only one other person—Aurélie. Aurélie was the true love of Julien's life, his soul mate and best friend. Rogier knew that Julien loved this girl; he saw the feelings when he looked into his friend's eyes. The whole story was improbable and incredible, but Rogier, the logical-minded lawyer, never questioned or doubted his friend. "I know, Julien. But she did not die. She's going to be all right, isn't she?"

Julien nodded and sipped his coffee. "Oui. She will, it will just take time. But yes, she will. She has to stay here for a couple of weeks. There is so much to do before she comes home, Rogier. I want everything ready for her. I want her to leave the hospital for the only real home and family she has had since she was a baby. I want her to leave here and go to love, warmth, and security," Julien smiled for the first time since Rogier's arrival.

"Well, the adoption itself takes time. But," Rogier quickly said to offset Julien's concerns, "I will file a petition with the court naming you and Aurélie as Angelica's legal guardians. I will do that after I leave here today," he assured Julien. "After I do that, I need to assign one of my aides to investigate Angelica's family. We need to know if she has any living relatives." Rogier recognized the fear in Julien's eyes. "There's a huge chance that, if she does have relatives, they don't know about her. They most likely won't oppose or contest the adoption. But I have to check, Julien. The last thing we want is an unknown relative to suddenly appear and make a claim. This is a preventative measure."

Julien nodded and took a deep breath. "When can we begin the adoption?"

"In a couple of months, maybe more. A lot of this takes time if we want to do this with the caution and prudence this process deserves. Julien, once you are her legal guardian, she will live with you and be your daughter in every other way."

"She is my daughter. Nothing and no one will ever change that. Mon Dieu, Rogier, when she awoke from surgery, she looked at me and said, 'Daddy'. Angelica called me Daddy. At that moment, I finally understood what men talk about when their children say daddy for the first time. Aurélie and I have prayed for this so very long. You know that, Rogier."

"I do know that, and that is why we are erring on the side of caution. The more thorough we are now, the smoother and quicker the adoption process. Believe me. Trust me."

"I do trust you. We have waited this long. We can stand a few more months." Julien grinned. "After all, the typical pregnancy is nine months."

Rogier smiled, too, and asked what Julien knew about Angelica and her family. Julien repeated everything Angelica had told them in the café and in the hospital. "Well, that's not much, but having Renée's full name is a help and a start. Since she worked for Angelica's father, maybe, just maybe I can find out something about him from any records about her. We need Angelica's birth name."

"What if you do not find out?"

"Then she is presumed to have no known family, and we proceed with the adoption. In normal circumstances, a minor who has no family to care for her or him becomes a ward of the state. Such a child is able to be adopted. That means you and Aurélie would be able to adopt Angelica without any contestation."

"She will legally be ours?   We could not bear it if something prevented this," Julien said through clenched teeth.

"Nothing will, Julien. That's why I insist on going to these extremes to find out all I can about her, to find her family, and to assure that they will not contest the adoption. Julien, I will do all in my power to ensure that your adoption of Angelica is uncontested and legal," Rogier said as he placed a hand on Julien's arm.

"I know, Rogier. I know you will. Spare no expense in your search for her family. It does not matter how much the research, travel, and documents cost Rogier. Angelica is priceless."

"I will begin the research as soon as I return to my office.   I will do whatever it takes, Julien, I promise you that. You really do love Angelica. When can I meet this girl who has changed your life?" Rogier asked with a smile.

"Now, if she is awake. Come on," Julien said and led Rogier to Angelica's private room.   The two police officers guarding the door nodded as Julien introduced Rogier and quietly entered the room.

Julien carefully leaned down to kiss Aurélie and then Angelica. The girl opened her eyes and, just as she did after her surgery, said, "Daddy. I love you, Daddy." She smiled up at Aurélie and added, "I love you, too, Mom."

While Aurélie fought her tears, Julien smiled and said, "We love you, Angelica." He smiled up at Rogier, an expression of pure elation clearly evident. "Angelica, I would like you to meet Rogier Sandorf, my trusted friend and lawyer. He is going to help us with the adoption."

Rogier stepped around the bed to meet Angelica, only to stop, dumbstruck at his first sight of the teenager. A moment later, he regained his composure and said, "I'm honored to meet you, Angelica. So you're going to become Julien's and Aurélie's daughter."

"I am their daughter," she said. "I feel like their daughter already. I feel loved and protected with them. They are the first family I have had since I was a baby," she said and looked at Aurélie and Julien.

"Then I will return to my office now and begin the necessary work. I promise you that this will become legal as well as sanctified. Get healthy and strong, Angelica," Rogier said as he placed his hand on her cheek.

"Thank you, Mr. Sandorf," Angelica smiled. "Thank you for everything."

Rogier nodded and then looked at Julien. "Walk to the elevator with me?"

"All right. I will be back in a few moments, my darlings," Julien said to Aurélie and Angelica.

In the hallway, Rogier stopped walking and put his hand on Julien's arm. "It's incredible, Julien, just incredible. That girl looks like you. She could be your birth daughter she looks so much like you."

"That is what Nurse Ramsey and Aurélie both said, Rogier. We have known her for three days, and you are the third person to tell me that. To me this means that Angelica is meant, destined, to be our daughter. Make it happen, Rogier. Do whatever you need to do, but make this happen for us. Please make it happen."

"I will, Julien, I promise you, Aurélie, and Angelica that. I will," Rogier said and set off to begin the process.

$$\S\S\S\S\S$$

That afternoon Julien and Aurélie ate lunch with Angelica. While they ate, Julien told Angelica about the day he and Aurélie met. His eyes sparkled, and Angelica felt his love for Aurélie as if it were palpable. She had never seen true love; she had only read about it.

"It was a nice summer day, June 19, 1928, my tenth birthday. My parents held a party in the hotel ballroom and invited all of the children who were guests at the hotel. There were dozens, children of all ages from toddlers to teenagers. My mother went all out on the decorations, and my father had the hotel chef and his staff prepare the most expansive and luscious buffet of food and sweets.

"The party was not about gifts for me. I knew how fortunate I was, and, quite frankly, there was nothing I needed or wanted. Except one thing. I am an only child, with no brothers or sisters or companionship. The children in our neighborhood were friendly and nice, and I did play with them at times. When I was at father's hotel, I talked and played with the children whose families stayed there. But they eventually left. I never had a true friend during my first ten years.

"I longed for a friend, a true and lasting friend. I longed for someone with whom I could share my thoughts, ideas, and dreams, someone who would likewise share hers"—Julien smiled at Aurélie— "with me. Someone who would share everything with me. I wanted one true friend more than I wanted anything else. In fact, when it was time for me to blow out the candles on the cake, several people reminded me to make a wish first. I closed my eyes, but I did not make a wish. I prayed. I asked God to send me such a friend.

"He did. That friend was already in my presence, and our friendship would begin momentarily. The cake and ice cream were served, and the children gathered in small groups as they ate. They talked and laughed. Except one girl, who stood alone looking out of the huge window, watching the outside world. She seemed so introspective and thoughtful. I picked up two plates of cake and ice cream and walked to her. I offered her a plate, and she smiled at me when she took it. She said, 'Thank you. It is your birthday, but you are treating everyone else. Happy birthday, Julien'.

"That was the first time Aurélie said my name, and even then, at the age of ten, I felt my heart soar. She introduced herself, and we spent much of the day talking. Her family was staying in the hotel for the summer, and so we had three months to get to know one another. Aurélie became my very best friend. She is the answer to the prayer I made that day."

Julien smiled at Aurélie and kissed her. "My father ended up getting a job near the hotel, and he bought a house nearby, too. So we became neighbors, and we were able to see each other every day. We even attended the same schools. We really were and are best friends. I married my best friend, Angelica, and I am so very happy," Aurélie gushed.

"I am, as well," Julien agreed. "The prayer I made on my tenth birthday came true that very day when I met Aurélie. The prayer made on my twenty-fifth anniversary came true that day when I met you, Angelica. God brought me my best friend, who became my wife, and he brought me my daughter." Julien held Aurélie's and Angelica's hands. "I am so blessed and so happy. I love you, my beautiful girls," Julien said and kissed their hands.

"I knew when you came into the café that you shared a very special and strong bond and love. The way you looked at one another, the looks you gave each other, I knew how much you love each other. I felt it. When you left the café, I felt sad, because, well, because it felt so special with you there. It felt lonely again when you left." Angelica's brown eyes filled with tears as she looked at Julien and Aurélie. "I don't feel lonely anymore. I feel warm and complete. That you chose me to be your child over all of the thousands of orphans is unbelievable. Thank you."

"We did not choose you, Angelica. God brought us together in answer to our prayer," Julien said and squeezed her hand. "Our union is destined. We are meant to be a family. I really do believe that everything in my life is how God intends it to be and that it all happened for a reason."

"But why me?" Angelica asked. "Why did God choose me?"

"Only he knows for certain, darling, but he obviously knows how special and generous you are," Aurélie said with firm conviction. "Yes, there are many children who need families, and Julien and I had decided to pursue adoption the other day in the church. But we both also had faith that God would bring us and the child meant for us together. He brought you and us together that day. I knew it. That is why I wanted you to go to the theatre with us. God knew that we needed each other, and he brought us together. We three have been blessed, Angelica, and we need to accept that with faith. We need to believe that he has a purpose for us, for making us a family. We may not know his purpose yet, but we must trust him."

Angelica remained quiet and thoughtful for several moments while she subsumed all that Aurélie had said. "I do. My father was. . . . My father died when I was nine months old. Everything in my life after that—the years with Renée and then my coming here to Paris—brought me to the time and place for us to meet. I do believe that we were meant to meet.

This all happened so quickly that it must be fate. If it is not, I can't explain any of this. But I don't have to, because what I feel is real. All I can say with one hundred percent certainty is that I love you both. I do love you," Angelica said and reached for Julien and Aurélie.

They gingerly hugged her, and while Aurélie cried tears of joy, Julien said, "We love you, Angelica. Aurélie and I love you."

§§§§§

The following morning, Dr. Sutfield greeted Angelica, Julien, and Aurélie. "How are you feeling, Angelica? How is your pain?"

"I can deal with it, Dr. Sutfield."

"You shouldn't have to deal with it. That's what pain medication is for. I'll give you some after I examine you." Dr. Sutfield looked at Julien and Aurélie, and told them, "You two go for a walk while I examine my little patient."

Julien and Aurélie nodded and kissed Angelica just as Nurse Ramsey entered the room. They went to the chapel to pray, arm in arm as they walked.

They drew the attention of others in the hallway, although they were oblivious to the stares and whispers. They were too focused on Angelica and her healing to care about attention.

Nurse Ramsey removed Angelica's wound dressings, and Dr. Sutfield listened to her heart and lungs. Her heartbeat was irregular, and he made a mental note to monitor that very closely. After he examined the surgical incision, he asked Nurse Ramsey to redress the wound. While she did, he made notes in Angelica's medical chart.

When he finished, Angelica asked him, "When can I go home?"

"Patience, my dear little patient," Dr. Sutfield said as he sat in the chair beside her bed. "You will be here at least two weeks. Your body, your heart, need time to fully recover, Angelica." He noticed her disappointment. "I know how anxious you are to leave and resume your life, but you need to recover before you do. The last thing you want is to suffer a setback. Right?"

Angelica nodded, disappointed but realizing that he was right. "Yes. Thank you, Dr. Sutfield."

Dr. Sutfield patted her cheek, smiled, and said, "It's my pleasure, my dear. You just do everything we say so you keep getting stronger and healthier." Angelica promised she would. "And I promised you something for the pain. Nurse Ramsey, give her eight milligrams of morphine." Nurse Ramsey nodded, prepared, and administered the medicine. "In a few days, you should be able to get out of that bed and began walking again. You will become stronger and healthier, but only if you approach your recovery in stages."

"I understand, Dr. Sutfield," Angelica assured him. He and Nurse Ramsey left, and for the first time she was alone in the hospital room. Angelica looked across the room, at the cloudless sky through the window. "You kept me alive for a reason. I don't know why yet, but I will let you guide me to it. You've already brought me to my new family. I love Mr. and Mrs. Lacoeur, and I promise you that I will help them and honor them for the rest of my life."

At that moment, Julien and Aurélie returned, in time to hear the end of Angelica's prayer. Aurélie grabbed Julien's arm, and he patted her hand.

Angelica heard the door close, and she looked to see who had entered. She smiled when she saw them.

"I was just thinking about you," Angelica confessed. "You've been here for days. Please go home, where you can eat, sleep, shower, and just have more freedom." Before either of them could protest, Angelica continued. "Dr. Sutfield told me that I will be here two weeks. You can't stay here that long. Besides, what about your work?"

Julien sat on the edge of the bed. "Dr. Sutfield talked to as a few minutes ago, too. Aurélie and I want to be here as much as possible, we do. But there are things we need to do, things that cannot wait. Very important things." Julien smiled at Aurélie, who sat next to Angelica. "We will be here every day. We want to see you and be with you."

"Does that upset you?" Aurélie asked.

Angelica giggled. "None of it upsets me. I think you need to go home, get out of here, but I do want to see both of you, too."

Julien and Aurélie giggled, as well, and both of them kissed her cheeks. Just then, Dr. Sutfield came into the room, looking quite serious. Aurélie asked why.

"The police need to talk with Angelica about what happened. Since she's doing better today, I told them they could. I plan to stay in the room during the questioning, just in case. Is that all right with you?" Dr. Sutfield asked them.

"Of course," Julien answered, as did Aurélie. Angelica likewise said, "Yes, Dr. Sutfield."

"I am so sorry you have to relive that, darling. If it becomes too painful, you can stop at any second," Aurélie told the girl, concern—and fear—in her voice.

"It's all right, really. I'll be okay. But you don't have to stay and listen if it will upset you."

"No, darling, I want to stay," Aurélie said and hugged her daughter just as Dr. Sutfield and two police officers entered the room.

The police investigators introduced themselves as Inspector Beaumont and Inspector Potofi.

Inspector Beaumont asked Angelica to describe in detail everything that had happened after the Lacoeurs left the café on March 11.

Angelica did just that. "As soon as Mr. and Mrs. Lacoeur left, I got a tray and began clearing the table. I saw Mr. Lacoeur's wallet on the table, so I picked it up and ran after them calling for him. I caught up to them, returned his wallet, and wished them an enjoyable evening at the theatre. I walked back to the café slowly, still thinking about them and the afternoon. A man stood near the café door, and I thought he was a customer. I told him to go on in and I would be right in. He shook his head and kept staring at me. I asked him what he wanted, and he lifted a newspaper he held. I felt something hot in my chest, and I felt weak. He stared at me for another moment before he walked away into the crowd. I tried to walk into the café, but I couldn't. I just slid down. I tried to hold onto the building, but my hand just slid over the bricks as I kept slipping to the ground. My legs folded under me, and I just sat there, on the walk next to the building. A minute later Mr. Lacoeur was there."

"Did this man say anything to you?" Inspector Beaumont asked her. Angelica said he hadn't. "Had you ever met him before?"

"No. I'd never seen him."

"He could have come into the café before, couldn't he?"

"I never saw him there," Angelica said. She saw Beaumont's doubt. "I tend to remember faces, sir. I'm not that great with names, but I remember faces well."

"Then you can describe this man to the police artist," Inspector Beaumont said.

"I can, but it would be easier if I could draw him myself," Angelica said. "I remember every detail of his face."

Inspector Beaumont got the drawing tablet and colored pencils from the police artist and placed them on Angelica's table. Nearly half an hour later she held up the finished portrait. Julien and Aurélie studied it, but didn't recognize the man. Neither of them recalled ever seeing him.

Inspector Beaumont took the drawing and promised Angelica, Julien, and Aurélie that they would find the man. "Not only will we publish this across the country immediately, but we will compare it to all of the mugshots in the country. We will find him, I promise you that," he told Angelica and gently squeezed her hand. "I'll be in touch soon, Mr. Lacoeur."

Aurélie quickly said she would get Julien and her some coffee and practically ran from the room. Angelica looked at Julien, distress on her face. "Go after her. Please go after her. I didn't mean to upset her," she pleaded.

Julien was torn between comforting his wife and his daughter. Dr. Sutfield told him to go. He would stay with Angelica. As soon as the door closed behind Julien, Angelica began crying. Crying made her chest hurt, and she doubled forward, clenching her fists. Dr. Sutfield tried in vain for several minutes to calm the girl. Finally, as a last resort, he buzzed for the nurse and told her to administer a mild sedative. He continued to hold Angelica until she was calm, and then reclined her onto the pillows and covered her with a blanket.

Dr. Sutfield softly explained to Nurse Ramsey what had happened. "Angelica was not traumatized at all by telling what happened. Mrs. Lacoeur was highly distraught, though. You stay with Angelica. I'm going to check on Mrs. Lacoeur."

He saw Julien embracing Aurélie while she cried. "Mr. and Mrs. Lacoeur, come with me. Let's go into a private room." Julien gratefully guided his wife into a waiting room.

"I am sorry. I did not mean to cause a scene," Aurélie said through her tears.

"Ma chère, you did not," Julien tenderly reassured her. "What happened is horrifying."

"Yes, it is," Dr. Sutfield agreed. "You've only been away from this hospital for a few short hours, Mrs. Lacoeur. Have you allowed yourself to express your emotions before now? Have you cried or even gotten angry?"

Aurélie shook her head. "No. I tried to keep myself from thinking about it. I had to."

"Mrs. Lacoeur, if you don't let it out, eventually it erupts, just as it did moments ago. When something violent happens, it is normal to feel fear, sadness, and anger. Perfectly normal," Dr. Sutfield explained. "The same goes for you, Mr. Lacoeur."

"I did let it out. I had to. As soon as you wheeled her into the operating room, I stood alone in the hallway and cried. I pounded the wall, and I prayed, and I cried. I was terrified," Julien admitted for the first time.

"Oh, Julien," Aurélie moaned and began crying again. Dr. Sutfield turned away, allowing them time to come to terms with what had happened. After more than thirty minutes, Aurélie took a deep breath and stopped crying. Julien gave her his handkerchief, and she dried her eyes, blew her nose, and thanked the doctor.

"No need. Have a seat," Dr. Sutfield motioned to the couple, who sat next to one another on a sofa. Dr. Sutfield sat in a nearby chair and said, "Now you can get on with the business of adopting Angelica." The Lacoeurs looked surprised. "Nurse Ramsey told me. If you recall, I made the same incorrect assumption that Angelica already was your daughter." Aurélie smiled, which was a refreshing sight. "You can't continue to live here and expect the rest of your lives to go on without you."

"We know," Julien said. "Angelica brought it up this morning after you told her that she will stay here for two weeks. We do have a lot to do. I have to meet with my lawyer about the adoption. And we have to prepare Angelica's room in our home. We have to go get her things from her apartment. We have so much to do."

"Then do it. Angelica is safe here, and she is getting the care she needs so that she can go home. She is resting now. After you visit with her this afternoon, I want you to take your suitcases and go home. Resume life as closely to normal as possible, for her sake as well as yours. You can't help her if you exhaust yourselves. Is that clear?" Dr. Sutfield asked firmly yet compassionately.

Julien and Aurélie nodded, and then Aurélie went to the ladies room to wash her face and reapply her makeup. When she came out, she looked at her husband, smiled, and said, "Everything will be all right. Tell me it will, Julien."

"Yes, my dear. The doctors are taking care of Angelica. The police will find the man who did this. Rogier will help us adopt Angelica. Everything will be just perfect."

§§§§§

"Tomorrow, my darling, our little girl comes home. Angelica comes home."

"Yes, Julien," Aurélie said with a smile as they stood in the teenager's room. "Angelica will come home, and our family will be complete. Our human trinity will be complete. Oh, Julien, our prayer and our dream have come true."

"Everything here is ready for her," Julien said as he looked around the room they had prepared for her. "Let us have dinner with her."

When they entered her room, they were elated to see her sitting in a chair by the window, drawing in a sketch pad. Angelica looked up, saw them, and beamed. She tossed the sketch pad and pencil on the table and went to them. She grabbed their hands and smiled up at them. "You came! I'm so happy you came."

"Of course we came, sweetheart," Julien told her. "We have come every day, have we not? Why would today be any different?"

"Well, it's my last day here, and I wasn't sure if you needed to come," Angelica explained.

"We do not need to. We want to," Aurélie countered with conviction.

"Of course we want to," Julien said. "Tomorrow we will be here when Dr. Sutfield signs your release, and we three will leave the hospital together. We will return to our home, a family forevermore."

"Our home?" Angelica softly asked.

"Yes, darling, our home. Julien's, mine, and yours. We will live there together," Aurélie promised. "You will live there with us for as long as you desire."

"I can't imagine ever wanting to leave either of you," Angelica said in childlike wonder.

Three hours later, when Nurse Schwitzer entered the room and said it was time for Angelica to go to bed, Aurélie and Julien kissed her good night. "Tomorrow, my daughter, we will take you home," Julien said as he bent to kiss her forehead.

Angelica wrapped her arms around his neck, kissed his cheek, and said, "I'm so happy." She reached for Aurélie and kissed her, as well. "So very happy."

Julien and Aurélie arrived early the next morning, just as Nurse Ramsey was taking Angelica's blood pressure. She smiled and said, "It's a bit high this morning, but that's no surprise. You're obviously excited that you get to go home today."

Angelica smiled, nodded, and said, "I am, Nurse Ramsey."

"Well, you just relax, and I will bring your breakfast."

Nurse Ramsey returned with three trays, and she smiled when Julien, Aurélie, and Angelica held hands and bowed their heads. "Dear God, Thank you for your blessings, especially for bringing us together. Please protect Mom and Daddy and surround me with your light. Amen."

"That is the most beautiful prayer I have ever heard," Aurélie managed to say as tears choked her. Julien smiled and squeezed her hand.

He cleared his throat and, as they ate, said, "We are so excited for today. These two weeks have been a whirlwind of preparing for our little girl." He looked at his wife, his face expressing decades of emotion. "We finally understand what new parents feel when they bring their child home for the first time. All of the planning, praying, and waiting finally come to fruition."

"Finally, Julien," Aurélie whispered. "Finally."

After breakfast, Aurélie opened a suitcase she had brought. She removed a dress, shoes, and lingerie, and held the dress up as she smiled at Angelica. "I bought you a few things for your first week or so home, enough until we can go shopping together for a whole new wardrobe. Oh, Angelica, I always dreamed of buying pretty dresses for my very own daughter," Aurélie enthused. "I hope you like it."

"It's pretty," Angelica smiled. "I've never had a dress so pretty."

"Well, you will have lots of pretty dresses, my little princess," Julien said with a wink. "Aurélie may have dreamed of shopping for clothes with our daughter, but I dreamed of overindulging my daughter. You may have whatever your heart desires, ma petite."

"I already have what I desire most," Angelica said as a tear slid down her cheek.

"Well, I hate to interrupt, but I need to examine Angelica one last time before her discharge. This won't take long," Dr. Sutfield smiled. Julien and Aurélie stepped into the hall while Dr. Sutfield examined his patient. Her heartbeat was still irregular, although that might have been caused by the traumas to her heart. He made a note on her chart to follow up during her next appointment.

When he finished, Dr. Sutfield motioned Julien and Aurélie back into the room. "I will complete the discharge papers, but it will take an hour or two for them to process. Nurse Ramsey will go over everything with you before you leave. She will also schedule an appointment for Angelica for fourteen days from now. I don't think I have to tell you how happy I am for you." He turned to Angelica and put his hand on her cheek. "You enjoy yourself, but take things easy. Don't overdo things and make yourself ill." Turning to Aurélie, he said, "Why don't you help this young lady into those new clothes you brought her? Your husband and I will leave you ladies."

Forty-five minutes later, Aurélie opened the door and beckoned Julien into the room. Sounding like the emcee of a fashion show, Aurélie said, "Angelica wears a sky blue crêpe dress with a Chelsea collar and white patent ballerina slippers. She looks divine."

"You are my Princess Angelica," Julien whispered, overcome with emotion. She had nearly died, yet in moments she would walk through the front door of their home. Julien held his arms open, and Angelica walked to him. He held her close yet gingerly, while she wrapped her arms around him and kissed his cheek.

Nurse Ramsey tapped on the door to let them know she was there. "I just need to go through everything with you, schedule Angelica's next appointment, and soon you will be on your way." Nurse Ramsey explained Angelica's care and restrictions, scheduled a follow-up for April 10, and told one of the Lacoeurs to bring their car to the patient pick-up area. "I will be right back with a wheelchair."

Julien took Angelica's suitcase, kissed her and Aurélie, and quickly left to drive the car around. Aurélie walked alongside Angelica as Nurse Ramsey pushed the wheelchair. In moments, Julien and Nurse Ramsey helped her into the back seat, and Angelica kissed the nurse's cheek in gratitude. Aurélie sat beside the teenager and held her hand. The three of them remained silent on the drive home; there was no need for words, for their emotions enveloped them.

Angelica looked out of the car window, watching the cityscape as Julien drove along twisting and turning roads. They were in a part of Paris that Angelica hadn't known existed. It was quite provincial, evoking a village in the south of France rather than the more urban capital. Julien turned down a narrow drive, and Angelica saw the most charming three-story house. Julien parked near the front entrance, walked around to open Angelica's door, and helped her out.

"Welcome home, Chouchou," he said.

"Home," Angelica whispered. "Do you know how very beautiful that is?"

"Yes, my princess, I do," Julien answered. "Come. Let us enter our home together, as a family."

Aurélie and Julien walked on either side of Angelica, their arms around her as they climbed the steps. Julien opened the front door and held it for Aurélie and Angelica to enter. Angelica looked around the foyer and smiled when she saw a framed photograph on a table. She walked to it and ran her finger along the frame.

"Your wedding. We met on your twenty-fifth anniversary. March 11 is a very sacred day for me," Angelica happily said.

"But that man tried to kill you that day!" Aurélie retorted.

"But he didn't. And what happened kept us together. What happened led to now," Angelica said and smiled at Aurélie and Julien.

"You are amazing, Angelica. And wise. You are right, darling. As horrifying as what happened was, it all led us to here and now. It brought us together, so we can be a family," Julien said.

"I'll make sure of that. Welcome home, Angelica," Rogier said as he stepped into the living room.

"Thank you, Mr. Sandorf."

"It is my honor to help. I brought my camera. Why don't we commemorate this moment by taking your first family portrait?"

Angelica stood between Julien and Aurélie. Julien put his left arm around Angelica and his wife and with his right hand held Aurélie's left hand. Angelica placed her hand over their hands just before Rogier took the picture. He cleared his throat, touched by the evident love that existed between the three of them. He vowed to himself that the adoption would become legal and final.

"How would you like to see the rest of our home now?" Aurélie asked. "I want you to feel comfortable here right away."

Angelica nodded, and while she went with Julien and Aurélie, Rogier got the suitcase and teddy bear out of the car. He ran up to the second floor and placed the suitcase near the dresser in Angelica's room. He propped the bear against the pillows on her bed and made sure everything looked just right. Julien and Aurélie had created a room fit for a princess. Rogier smiled, thinking how very like brand-new parents they seemed. How often they had dreamed of decorating a nursery, only to be crushed by grief. Angelica may not be a new born baby, but she was their daughter in every way that mattered most. Rogier would make that legal and binding. He quickly went down the back staircase when he heard their happy voices draw nearer.

"Our bedroom and the guestrooms are on this floor," Aurélie explained. She led Angelica to the near end of the hall and opened double doors.

"This is the linen closet. The laundry chute is right next to it." She then opened another door. "This is a guest room. Ours is the next room," she said and opened the door.

She and Julien showed Angelica around their suite, which was decorated in blue and white toile and antique furniture. "This is so beautiful, like something out of a fairytale. I always imagined a king and queen would have a room just like this one," Angelica said as she touched the antique lace canopy atop their bed.

"Come. Your room is right across the hall," Julien said and took her hand. He opened the door, and at her first sight of the room, Angelica gasped. "Go on," he encouraged her.

Angelica slowly walked into the room and looked all around. The white canopy bed was covered in a white eyelet comforter. The dresser, desk and chair, nightstand, and table matched the bed—a white suite just perfect for their little princess, as Julien called her.

Angelica suddenly noticed the books on her desk, and she looked pleasantly surprised. She picked up a leather-bound book secured by a wraparound strap.   She held the book close to her chest and looked at Julien and Aurélie. "You got my books. Oh, thank you. Thank you so much," she said and hugged them each with one arm while she still clutched the book. "This journal means so much. I was so afraid I would never see it again." She placed the journal on the desk and began crying.

"This is the most beautiful room ever," she said as she stared at the wall. "You really did make this just for me," she sobbed and fingered the wallpaper pattern.

Julien stood behind her, put his hands on her shoulders, and said, "Yes, Chouchou, we did. Just for you. Our Angelica, our little angel flower," he said, referencing the flower that shared her name, the delicate white flower that filled her walls like a lovely wildflower meadow. "Archangel Michael's flower, my mother calls it."

"We could think of nothing more beautiful for your room than your flower," Aurélie added. "I was so hoping you would like it."

Angelica turned, hugged her, and exclaimed, "I do. Oh, I do."

"Well, let us take a look at the third floor, and then we can return to the main level for another surprise," Julien smiled.

He and Aurélie showed Angelica the library—filled with hundreds of books, much to her delight—the den—essentially Julien's office—and the sunroom, which had a glorious view of the back lawn and pool.

"There is one room you have not seen yet," Julien told Angelica as they reached the main floor. "I wanted to save this room for last," he smiled, took her hand, and led her to French doors. "Open them."

Angelica once more gasped at the sight before her. She had never imagined anything so glorious. "Go on," Aurélie softly told her. Angelica looked up at Julien, who nodded, and slowly walked into the room.

She lovingly moved her finger along the gleaming black finish. She traced the graceful curves. She ran a finger lightly over the ivory keys. She sat on the bench. For the first time since March 11, Angelica played one of her melodies. How could any of them have known that day what fate awaited them?

MOUVEMENT DEUX

March 27, 1964, Friday

This is the first time I've written since my life changed again, sixteen days ago.

Tonight I write this as I sit in my room. My beautiful room! In my home! I feel like this really is my home. I feel at home here. I felt it when I first walked in. I feel like I belong here. I feel—it's hard to describe, but I feel safe and protected and loved. I haven't felt that since I was a baby and my father held me.

I do remember. I remember feeling loved and safe. I remember him holding me, how warm he was. I remember his brown eyes and how they revealed his emotions. I remember his smile, so full of joy.. I remember. I remember, and I will never forget. I could never forget. I saw everything, and it's branded into my brain. That night changed everything in my life.

I won't forget, even though I am loved, happy, and secure once more. I love Daddy and Mom, I do. I love my father. I always have and always will. He made me from his love, and he is part of me. I love him.

I feel so blessed. I feel so loved. Thank you God. ♥

Angelica put down her pen and turned to the first page of her journal. She smiled when she looked at her father's face. "I do love you," she whispered. "You are always with me." She secured the journal with its strap, turned off the lamp on her desk, and knelt on her knees beside her bed.

Julien and Aurélie came to her room at that moment to tuck her in and wish her sweet dreams. They hadn't intended to eavesdrop on her evening prayer, but were grateful to hear her private feelings. "God, please tell my father how much I love him. Tell him that I am all right, and that I have a home and a family. My new Mom and Daddy are so kind and wonderful. I know Father would love them, too. I do love them, but please tell Father that doesn't mean I love him less. No one will ever make that happen, no matter how long I live. I will carry him in my heart always. I am so very sorry for what happened to him. I don't know why it happened, and there were many lonely days and nights after he went away. But please tell him that I'm not lonely any longer. Tell him that I have found love and happiness. Thank you. Amen."

Aurélie ran back to her bedroom and closed the door. She sat on the bench at the foot of the bed and cried. Julien understood. He had to stand in the hall for several moments while he regained control of his emotions. He entered as Angelica removed her robe and placed it at the foot of her bed.

He helped her turn back the sheets and comforter and helped her onto the bed. He placed the teddy bear next to her, pulled the covers up to her chin, and kissed her forehead. "Pleasant night, my princess. You are home, home with me and Mom, and we love you."

Angelica put her arms around his neck and said, "I love you, Daddy."

Julien returned to his room, sat beside Aurélie, and held her close to him while they both cried. "I never knew it would feel this way," Julien wept. "I never knew I could feel so much love and happiness deep inside me."

"I know, darling. I know. This is more than we ever expected," Aurélie said. "We did not get the baby we longed for, but we got something priceless. We got a daughter who loves us and whom we love. We got our family."

"She broke my heart, Aurélie. How sad that her father died, and that she remembers him."

"It is not sad that she remembers him, dearest. It is beautiful. That is what got to me. That is why I am crying, Julien. Any parent would feel so very loved to hear their child say that prayer. I can only hope that someday, years from now, she feels that way about us, Julien."

Julien stood, walked to his bureau, and looked at a portrait of his parents for several minutes. "You are right, darling. Love is the most important gift we can give and receive. Deep, true love is immortal. That is what Angelica's prayer was all about is it not? How can this girl fill my heart so much and teach me so much in just a few days?"

Aurélie reached for him, and Julien went to her, held her hand, and looked at her with wonder in his eyes. "Children do that, darling. They come into our lives and change them in ways we never anticipated. They change us, irrevocably and permanently."

Julien nodded. "Yes, they do. But this is different, Aurélie. This is deep inside me, part of me. I do not know how to explain this, not even to myself. I feel more than ever that I know her somehow, as insane as that sounds. I feel that she is my daughter. Angelica is my daughter." He shook his head and rubbed his temples. "Perhaps all of today's emotions are just too much for me. I do not make any sense."

Aurélie stood and held his arms. "This has overwhelmed us all, darling. But she is asleep across the hall, and when we awake in the morning, she will still be there. She will always be here with us. As incredibly happy as we are, it will take time for this to truly become real to us." Julien nodded. "And we are exhausted, dear. Come, let us get some sleep."

§§§§§

"Mother! What a wonderful surprise!" Aurélie greeted her mother-in-law the following mid-morning.

"I am anxious to meet this young girl who has captured your heart and Julien's," the elegant woman said as she placed her handbag and gloves on a table. "Where is she?"

"She and Julien are in the music room. Go on in. I will make us some tea," Aurélie smiled.

Ophelia Lacoeur stopped outside the open French doors, halted by the sight before her. She stared at her son and the teenaged girl as they sat side-by-side on the piano bench. They giggled when they finished a duet, just as Aurélie returned with the tea tray. She smiled and asked, "It is remarkable, is it not?"

"What?" Ophelia asked.

"How much she looks like Julien," Aurélie smiled. "Come on. Meet her," she said as she carried the tea tray to the table.

"Mother!" Julien happily exclaimed when Ophelia entered the room. He quickly went to her, pulled her into an exuberant hug, and said, "It is so wonderful to see you. I am so incredibly happy, Mother."

"There was only one other day when I saw you this happy, Julien. Your wedding day. Aurélie is the one who made you so happy that day," Ophelia said and patted his cheek. "Who is the cause for your happiness now?"

"Our daughter Angelica," Julien smiled while he extended his arm toward her.

Angelica went to Julien, and he introduced her to his mother. "I am so honored to meet you, Mrs. Lacoeur."

"Grandmother. You are to call me Grandmother, Angelica."

"Thank you, Grandmother," Angelica said with a smile, even though tears filled her eyes. Ophelia looked at her in concern, and Angelica explained, "That's the first time I have called anyone that. I never met my birth grandparents."

"Oh my poor child," Ophelia replied. "Well, you have one grandmother now. I dreamed of a granddaughter I could do things for and with. Sit beside me while we enjoy our tea and conversation."

Ophelia sat Angelica next to her on the sofa, while Julien and Aurélie sat on the matching chairs. Aurélie poured the tea, served the petits fours, and joined the laughter when Ophelia told stories about her son's childhood.

"Mind you, Julien was always well-behaved and well-mannered. He was actually quite serious and studious, often alone with a book or sketch pad or a piano. In fact, he garnered quite a following in his father's hotel."

"I am not surprised," Aurélie smiled at her husband. "Tell us all about it, Mother."

"Well, there was a baby grand piano in the lobby. On weekends and holidays and special events, we hired a pianist to play for the guests. At other times, the piano was unused. However, that all changed on a weekday when we all heard piano music in the lobby. Gerald, my husband, and I also heard applause and the excited voices of guests. We were never as surprised as we were that day to walk into the lobby and see our nine-year-old son playing the piano! Oh, we knew he could play. We paid for piano lessons every week, after all.

"But he was better than we knew he was. Gerald and I were stunned and thrilled by the reaction Julien received. He played for hours, entertaining guests, some of whom came and went throughout the afternoon. In fact," Ophelia turned to Angelica and said, "a photographer from the local newspaper came to the hotel and took Julien's picture while he played. It appeared in that evening's newspaper. I have a copy in my scrapbook. I will have to show it to you when you come to visit me."

"Oh, I would like that very much," Angelica said and held Ophelia's hand.

"I have many pictures of Julien to show you, Angelica. You can see him grow up right before your eyes."

"Really? Oh, that would be so miraculous," Angelica smiled.

Julien giggled and said, "Baby pictures are hardly miraculous, especially mine."

"Oh, yes, they are. Pictures are miracles to me," Angelica insisted.

"What makes you say that, my dear?" Aurélie asked.

"Your home is filled with photographs. Most homes are. It's normal for people to take and to keep pictures of their family members. But I have never had even one picture of a family member. I've only seen my father for the short time he was with me. He lives in my memory. But I don't have a picture of him. Or of my mother. I don't even know what she looked like. Except for my father, I don't know what any of my relatives look like. Pictures of my family would be miraculous to me," Angelica shared. "I want to see pictures of your relatives. I want to come to know them. I think photographs tell so much about people, not only by giving clues to when they lived and maybe where, but about who they are. Their expressions and especially their eyes reveal so much about them. Pictures are miracles to me."

Julien, Aurélie, and Ophelia sat quietly, overcome by all that Angelica had said. Rogier announced his presence by clearing his throat of impending tears. "This is perfect timing on my part."

Everyone welcomed Rogier and asked what he meant. "This," he said, and stood a framed photograph on the table. Angelica gasped and reached a hand toward the frame. "Your first family portrait," Rogier needlessly explained.

Ophelia did pick up the frame and smiled. "When did you have this taken?"

"Yesterday, Grandmother," Angelica softly said as she leaned closer to Ophelia to look at the picture. "Minutes after I came home for the first time."

Ophelia smiled, put an arm around her, and said, "It is lovely. There will be many more pictures of our family, pictures your grandchildren will treasure, Angelica."

Angelica hugged Ophelia in gratitude for her understanding and acceptance. Ophelia asked, "Who has a camera handy? I want a picture of me and Angelica."

Julien got his camera and took the first picture of his mother and his daughter. Ophelia said she wanted a copy to display in her home. "I have lots of framed pictures of my parents and in-laws, Gerald, Julien, and Aurélie. I need one of my granddaughter." She looked at Rogier. "You will make sure the adoption goes forward without any problems?"

"Yes, I will. The more information I have, the more I can discover about your family, Angelica. As soon as you are able, I do need to speak with you."

"I don't know very much, but I'll tell you everything whenever you want me to," Angelica said.

"What about today?" Julien asked. "It is Saturday. Rogier can use the information in his research beginning Monday."

Rogier agreed. So did everyone else. Aurélie stood, said she would make sandwiches for lunch, and went to the kitchen. Julien went to help her. Rogier and Ophelia went to freshen, and Angelica went upstairs to her room, where she got her journal.

"Everything is in here. My entire life is in this book. I've kept it to myself. I've guarded it. It's all I've ever had that in any way connects to my past. I've been alone until now, and now the information I do have will make my family a reality," Angelica thought before she returned to the music room.

Julien and Aurélie served sandwiches and lemonade to everyone. With Julien's and Aurélie's permission, Rogier turned on a tape recorder to capture all that Angelica told them. No matter what or how much information she revealed, it was vital to Rogier's work.

Angelica ate a few bites of her sandwich before she asked Rogier if there was anything in particular he wanted to know.

"What is your birth date, Angelica?"

"Renée told me that I was born in February 1950, but she never told me the date. I'm sorry."

Rogier shook his head. "No. That will help tremendously. That will narrow our searches of birth records. Do you know where you were born?"

"Renée never told me, but one day when I returned to her cottage, I heard her and someone else talking inside. I didn't want to intrude, so I sat on the bench by the front door. I didn't mean to eavesdrop, but I couldn't help hearing what they said. I didn't pay much attention until I heard Renée say, 'The girl and I will never return. Maldova holds too much danger for her. Reverend Soames, you are the only person who knows. I had to tell you. Someone has to know in case I die before Angelica is grown'. I don't know if Maldova is where I was born, but I did assume that."

"Maldova?" Julien pondered. "There was something in the news about it several years ago. I don't remember what."

"I'll research that," Rogier assured them. "Julien told me everything you shared with him. You know nothing about your father? A name, a birthdate, anything?"

Angelica shook her head. "No. Nothing like that."

"Then please tell us everything you do know. Any information will help, believe me. The clues will help me tremendously," Rogier told Angelica.

"All right. I have some memories of my father, but not many, I'm afraid. So many of them are similar. Then there are others that are so detailed and vivid. My first real memory is being held by someone warm and gentle. He was looking at me. He had such a beautiful smile as he looked at me. I felt so safe and warm with him. He was always there, always with me.

"He's the one who fed me. He cradled me and stared at me while he held the bottle. I remember one time I lifted my hands to the bottle. One of my hands touched his fingers, and he smiled at me. I remember that he said something and how his voice sounded, so tender and gentle. 'My little Angelica. I love you'. I hear that in my mind every day.

"I have a lot of memories like that, and they mean so very much to me. They all let me know how kind and loving my father was. But they don't help you with what you want to know," Angelica said as she looked at Rogier.

"It's all right, Angelica, really. Tell us whatever you remember."

Angelica shared several memories of her father holding her, feeding her, bathing her, dressing her, and rocking her to sleep. They all did illustrate a devoted father, a widower caring for his baby daughter. One memory, though, intrigued Rogier—Angelica's descriptions, in particular.

"One day, my father placed me in my cradle in what I now think was his office. He rocked the cradle and sang to me for a while. His voice—it made me feel so special. I can't explain how I felt. Then there was a noise, and he went to the desk. I know now the phone rang and he answered. He talked to someone for a long while. The office had a large window. I turned my head and looked out. It was white outside. Snow. It must have been snow. When he hung up the phone, my father walked to the large window. He crossed his arms and leaned against the wall as he stared out the window. I made a sound, and he turned to look at me. He looked so sad and thoughtful. That was the only time I saw him look like that, and it still makes me so sad," Angelica said, tears filling her eyes. "As I looked at him, he seemed oblivious to everything else. Then a cuckoo clock chimed the hour. He seemed to snap out of the mood he had been in, and he smiled at me again. 'My little Angelica, it's time for your supper. Come with Daddy,' he said and picked me up. I'm sorry," Angelica said as she began to cry.

Julien quickly went to her, sat close beside her, and hugged her near. "No, never apologized. Never. Your father loved you very much."

Angelica nodded and put her arms around him. "I know. I do." Angelica dried her eyes and said, "There is one more memory I have to share. The last night I saw my father. He put me in my crib and pulled the blanket over me. A teddy bear was always in my crib, and my father playfully had the teddy bear kiss my nose. He bent down and kissed my forehead, told me that he loved me, and sat in a chair right beside my crib. He reached his right arm through the rails in the crib and placed his hand over me. The nursery was dark, but there must have been a light on in the hallway. There were dark shadows in the room like always. Father softly sang to me. He sang to me a lot. Not long after he stopped singing, a shadow appeared in the doorway. Then there was a flash of light. Right after that, Father leaned forward against the crib and stared at me for a very long time. I don't know how long, but the next thing I remember is Renée picking me up, wrapping me in a blanket, and leaving. I never saw my father again."

Ophelia was crying, and Rogier handed her his handkerchief. Aurélie sat still, in stunned silence. Rogier processed what Angelica had described. Julien muttered, "Oh, dear God, no," and covered his face with his hands.

Angelica put her arms around Julien and comforted him. "Shh. Please don't cry. It's all right. It's all right. Please, Daddy, don't cry."

Julien looked at Angelica in complete astonishment. "Angelica, darling, I did not know. Oh, my darling, I am so, so sorry."

"No one knew. No one except Renée and then Reverend Soames. Both of them are dead. He died before Renée died. I've never told anyone until today. I've lived with those memories every day of my life. They were mine alone, only mine. I never even shared them with Renée. I never shared any of my thoughts and feelings with Renée. She never liked to talk about personal things. But now I can share everything with you."

Angelica looked up at Julien as he stared at her, love and sadness in his eyes. "That's the look," she whispered. "That's how my father looked after the phone call when he looked at me." Angelica finally admitted why she had stared at him in the café. "You look like him, you know," she told Julien.

Angelica picked up her journal, opened it to the first page, and offered it to Julien. He looked in stunned amazement at a face very much like his own. "This is your father?" he asked her in a whisper.

"Yes. I drew that when I was nine."

Julien then noticed the small signature and date in the corner: *Angelica 1960*. "Mon Dieu. This is remarkable." Julien stared at the drawing for many minutes.

Angelica put her hand on his cheek. "I love you, Daddy. I love you because you are kind, compassionate, vibrant, gentle, thoughtful, and passionate about what you do. I love you not because of how you look, but because of your essence, your heart, mind, and soul."

Ophelia gasped. Rogier asked her what was wrong, and Ophelia said, "That is so similar to what Aurélie said to me that day Julien proposed to her. She mentioned those same qualities. She said she knew how gorgeous Julien is, but that she loved him for his mind and his soul."

Aurélie's smile seemed to light the room. "Yes. I felt that way from that day Julien and I met." She smiled at her husband. "It is the same for Angelica. The resemblance to her father may have caught her attention at the café, but she loves you, Julien. We both love you despite those stunning looks."

Julien looked typically uncomfortable, and waved a hand as if to shush her. "It's true, Daddy. I don't love you because you look like my father. I love you because you're you," Angelica insisted as she stared into his eyes and held his hand.

Julien kissed her cheek and said, "I am grateful that you do. I love you."

Ophelia patted Angelica's shoulder and asked if she could look at the drawing. Angelica turned to face Ophelia and gave her the journal. Julien's mother looked from the drawing to her son, disbelief evident on her face. "If I did not see this, I would not believe it."

Rogier believed Angelica, but he had questions for her. "Julien's picture is often in newspapers, magazines, and on television. Angelica, might it be possible that you had seen Julien's picture and that his face became superimposed on your memories of your father?"

"No, Mr. Sandorf, that was never possible." Rogier asked her how. "Renée didn't own a television or even a radio. She never subscribed to newspapers or magazines. She homeschooled me, and we lived in a small village. I rarely had contact with the world outside her village. Renée had a record player, and we listened to classical music. I also loved to read, and Renée's one indulgence for me was to buy lots of books. I was sheltered, I know that. I know that Renée had reasons for protecting me, and I know they have something to do with my father's m— death. I had never seen you until you came into the café on March 11," Angelica explained as she looked at Julien.

Rogier had suspected that was the situation. Based on what Julien had told him and now Angelica's revelations,

Rogier knew that Renée protected Angelica from the assassins who had killed her father. More than ever, Rogier determined to find out everything.

"Angelica, I promise you that I will uncover everything about your father. Of course, the information is crucial to the adoption, but it is also important to you. You deserve to know as much as possible."

"Yes, Chouchou, you do. Rogier, please do whatever you need to do. Spare nothing. This is too important," Julien insisted, holding Angelica while she cried. "Too important."

"Thank you. Thank you all," Angelica cried.

"Angelica, honey, may I see the drawing of your father?" Rogier asked. She nodded, and Ophelia handed him the journal. "Yes, the likeness is strong. This explains why the two of you resemble one another," he said, looking at Angelica and Julien.

"Yes, but that still does not change the fact that this is all meant to be," Aurélie said. "I firmly believe that the three of us were brought together by divine providence. Angelica is the answer to Julien's and my prayer."

"Yes, she is," Julien agreed. "Angelica is our daughter, our gift from God."

§§§§§

Angelica awoke on Sunday morning to sunlight streaming into her room. She smiled, got out of bed, and went to the window. She looked at the birds in the trees, so carefree and tending to their babies. Everything was so beautiful, she thought, more beautiful than ever. Rogier would help them. The family would remain close, supportive, and loving all the days of their lives.

Angelica smiled and decided to shower and dress for church. "Oh," she uttered and went to the bench at the foot of her bed. She knelt in front of the bench and looked at her first Easter basket, filled with pretty trinkets and an antique prayer book. She stared at the basket and its contents for a long while, until she heard Julien and Aurélie wish her a happy Easter.

Angelica beamed, stood, and hugged them both. "Oh, thank you. This is the happiest Easter of my life."

"I am so happy you like it," Aurélie said, nodding toward the basket.

"Oh, I do, but that's not why I'm so happy. Easter is all about love. At least that's how I've always thought of it. I don't remember my first Easter. I wish I did. Renée and I went to church, of course, for Easter services. Every Sunday, I read the Bible while she prepared supper. On Easter, I always read about the Crucifixion and Resurrection. I never minded that. But this is the first Easter that I feel love. Your love is the greatest gift you can ever give me." Angelica kissed both of them.

Tears overflowed Julien's eyes, and he tried in vain to wipe them away. "Before I understood love, I probably would have told you not to cry. Now I know that love opens up the whole person, the heart, the mind, soul, feelings, awareness. I have cried more these past few days than ever in my life. Not because I am sad. Because I am so incredibly happy," Angelica explained as she held his hand.

Aurélie was crying, too. "Apparently, we are all incredibly happy," Ophelia said from the doorway of Angelica's room as she dabbed her eyes with her handkerchief.

"Grandmother! Oh, you came!" Angelica excitedly exclaimed and rushed to hug Ophelia.

"Yes we are," Aurélie smiled through her own tears.

§§§§§

April 10, 1964, Friday

Today was my appointment with Dr. Sutfield. He examined me for what felt like a long time. After I dressed, I went into his office. Mom and Daddy were already there, and I have a feeling that Dr. Sutfield had told them something. Something about me. The only reason this concerns me is that it made them different. They seem sad. Seeing them like that hurt me deeply. I never want them to be sad again. Never. I could not bear that. They have suffered so very much pain, loss, and sadness. They cannot suffer anymore. They can't. I will not hurt them or make them sad, and I will not let anyone else, either. I won't.

As Angelica wrote her journal entry, Julien and Aurélie sat on the back patio. Aurélie had spent the hour since dinner had ended sitting by the pool crying. Julien had spent some time with Angelica in the music room. When she had gone upstairs, he then had gone to his wife.

"Ma chère, let it out. Let the fear out," Julien said as he gently caressed her shoulders.

"I am afraid, Julien, so afraid."

"I know. I am, too. But we have to remember what Dr. Sutfield told us. He discovered the irregular heartbeat when she was in the hospital. It could very well be caused by the bullet wound and the surgery. Two traumas so close to her heart could cause that. It could resolve itself in time," Julien repeated what the doctor had told them.

Aurélie nodded. "I know, Julien. But there is still a chance it will not. What if it does not go away? Dr. Sutfield also said that irregular heartbeats can sometimes be very serious," she began to sob.

"I know, chéri. But we must have faith that she will be all right. We have to take care of her and we have to pray. We have to trust God," Julien said.

"I know, Julien. I know. But you were right. I need to let out all of this fear and anxiety. Once I do, I will try to keep them away."

"We both have to do that. We also need to trust Dr. Sutfield. He is going to examine her every three months and monitor her heart. If it is the same or worse at her July appointment, he will prescribe medication that will help her. He did tell us that Angelica is not in any immediate danger. We have to remember that, ma chère," Jillian reassured her.

Aurélie took a deep breath and smiled up at her husband. "Thank you, dearest Julien. Dr. Sutfield did tell us that. Besides, he would have done something or given her something if her condition were dangerous." Aurélie turned toward Julien and put her hands on his arms. "It is just that after everything we have been through, this was so frightening for me. I let fear take over."

"I did, too, at first. I understand. We will keep each other fearless during this. We will," Julien said and kissed her.

§§§§§

On a Tuesday in early May, the doorbell interrupted Ophelia and Angelica. Ophelia had brought some photograph albums, and she and Angelica had spent the morning looking through them. She left to answer the door, and Angelica heard her say, "Come in, Inspectors Beaumont and Potofi. Julien and Aurélie are at work. I am Julien's mother, and I am staying here with Angelica today." The officers explained that they needed to speak with the Lacoeurs, and Ophelia said she would call them and let them know to come home.

Julien in turn called Rogier and asked him to go to the house. Within the hour, Aurélie, Julien, and Rogier joined Ophelia, Angelica, and the officers in the living room. "We apologize for interrupting your work, but we have some important news about the man who shot Angelica."

"Please tell us you captured him," Aurélie said.

"In a sense, Madame Lacoeur," Inspector Potofi said. "It's a long story," he added, and everyone sat on the sofa and chairs. Ophelia served fresh coffee, and Inspector Beaumont told them everything that they had discovered and all that had happened.

"We found the man by matching various photographs and mugshots to the drawing Angelica made. Luka Blinov was part of an organization called FREE, The Federation for Russian Expansion and Escalation. They are an underground organization that operates without the support of the Russian government. Their mission is for Russia to take over the world, one country at a time." Beaumont removed a picture from a file folder he held and placed it on the table. Julien, Aurélie, and Angelica recognized the subject as the same man Angelica had drawn.

"We don't know how or why or if FREE itself is connected to Angelica, or why Blinov targeted her. He refused to tell us anything, and so have the other members of FREE we arrested when we found him. You see, we tracked Blinov to an abandoned warehouse, and when our team arrived, we also found six other members of FREE. All were taken into custody. Except for Blinov."

Julien looked horrified. "What do you mean except for Blinov? You let him escape? He can come after Angelica again?"

"No, Monsieur Lacoeur. He can never do anything again. As our officers closed in on him, he shouted that he did not regret anything he had done. He then put a gun in his mouth, pulled the trigger, and killed himself."

Aurélie placed her hands over her heart, sighed, and said, "Thank God. I am sorry if that sounds harsh, but I am so grateful that beast is dead. He will never hurt Angelica again."

"Yes, thank God for that," Ophelia added.

"We should also tell you that several other members of FREE were captured over the past two years. They were never a huge organization, but now their numbers are much smaller than when they first surfaced in 1946. INTERPOL, Scotland Yard, and the United Nations are fervently working toward the capture of all FREE members, with the goal of stopping this organization. Their crimes will soon end," Beaumont assured them.

"This is over?" Julien asked.

"For all intents and purposes, yes. However, just as a precaution, we are assigning armed guards for your home. Just as in the hospital, only approved visitors will be allowed. An officer will sign for and accept all mail and deliveries to this home, as well."

Rogier asked Beaumont for all information on Blinov and FREE. He wondered to himself if there were any connection between Angelica's shooting and her father's assassination. As Rogier stood staring out the window, lost in his thoughts, Angelica went to him.

"They killed my father," she whispered.

Rogier put his arm around her. "If they did, I will find out, and I will do all in my power to stop them. I promise you that."

§§§§§

Aurélie reached for the alarm clock on her bedside table. 6:00, plenty of time for a soothing hot shower and a family breakfast before church. As she replaced the clock, an envelope caught her attention. She sat up, opened the envelope, and burst into tears.

"Aurélie?" Julien asked in panic, her tears startling him out of slumber. He quickly sat up and turned to her. "What is it? What happened? I am calling the doctor," he said in alarm as she continued to cry.

Aurélie grabbed his arm, shook her head, and forced herself to stop crying. "No." She gasped for air, grabbed a handful of tissues, blew her nose, and handed him the card she had found. Julien instantly understood. They kissed just as Angelica entered in their room.

"Happy Mother's Day!" She kissed Aurélie's cheek and placed a tray on the bed. Breakfast, coffee, orange juice, and a white rose in a bud vase greeted Aurélie.

"You did this for me?" Angelica nodded, and Aurélie hugged her close. "Thank you, sweetheart. This is lovely."

"I'll be back in a moment," Angelica promised. Soon she did return, with another tray for Julien, much to his pleasant surprise.

"What about your breakfast?" Julien asked her.

"I already ate," Angelica answered. They asked her to keep them company while they ate, so she sat on the bench at the foot of their bed.

"When I was very young, Father bought the cards and gifts I gave Mother. But I remember the first Mother's Day gift he let me pick out," Julien shared. "He took me to Galeries Lafayette. It is huge! It was too much to see. We looked for a while, and then Father knelt and asked what kind of gift I wanted to get for Mother. I said, 'Something pretty'. He smiled, held my hand, and took me to the jewelry. I looked and looked, and finally pointed to the gift I wanted to get my mother. Father nodded, asked the sales lady to wrap it, and he let me carry the bag. On Mother's Day, I was so happy when Mother wore my heart locket to church. She still has it," Julien said with a smile.

Angelica smiled, too, and placed a gift on Aurélie's tray. "Open it," she whispered.

"Angelica, this is gorgeous!" Aurélie said and began to cry again. Aurélie lifted a sterling silver heart locket and noticed the small amethyst in the center—Angelica's birthstone. The back was inscribed *I love you Mommy*. Inside was a picture of Julien, the man whom both Aurélie and Angelica loved.

"Julien, please fasten it for me," Aurélie requested. "Now I have three very special heart necklaces—the two from you," she kissed Julien, "and this one from my beautiful daughter." She hugged Angelica, smiled at Julien, and said a silent prayer of thanksgiving.

§§§§

As soon as Julien and Aurélie left for work, Angelica excitedly grabbed Ophelia's hand. "Let's get started. There is so much to do, the day will seem to fly."

Ophelia smiled, enchanted by the girl's excitement. "All right, my dear. Let us make the cake first. Are you sure you do not want to have the bakery make the cake?" Ophelia saw the disappointment in Angelica's eyes and quickly relented. "It has been a long time since I have done any baking, but this sounds like fun. Come, Angelica, we do have a lot to do," Ophelia said as they gathered supplies in the kitchen and pantry. Over one hour later, the batter was in cake pans baking in the oven.

They decided to have the party in the music room. Since Julien enjoyed music so much, they could play some of his favorite albums in the background. Ophelia also decided that, since this was Julien's first birthday with Angelica, to keep it intimate. Only Rogier had been invited. There would be occasions for large, festive parties in the future, Ophelia thought.

After they set up and decorated the music room, they checked the cakes. Ophelia removed them and placed them on racks to cool. "Let us take advantage of the cooling time to go shopping. We still have things to buy." One of the security officers accompanied them, ever watchful as they traversed the crowded store.

Ophelia purchased a tin of Julien's favorite cookies ("To have with tea," she winked at Angelica), a new book that he had mentioned wanting to read, and two candles for the cake: a four and a six. "My little boy is not little any longer, is he dear? He stopped being little when he was eleven. He sprouted. 1.88 metres. But he will always be my little boy no matter how tall or how old he is." Ophelia hugged her granddaughter. "You will realize that, Angelica, when you are a mother. Children change us in every way, even ways we cannot imagine."

"I wonder if I will have a son who looks like Daddy and Father?"

"Oh, now, that would be just a dream, my dear. God willing, I will be alive to be his great-grandmother."

They embraced, and then shopped for birthday cards. Angelica found the perfect one for a beloved father. She also found two jazz albums that she had heard

Julien mention, so she bought them for him. As they made their way toward the elevator, Angelica noticed a silver pen that seemed perfect for Julien. She looked at the price tag: 889.31F. She had spent a huge portion of her money on the albums. Did she have enough left to buy the pen? She hadn't earned any money since the week before the shooting. Angelica quickly counted the money in her wallet. Her shoulders slumped, and Ophelia asked what was wrong. "Nothing," she answered and reluctantly returned the pen to the counter.

Ophelia picked up the pen and called for a sales clerk. "No," Angelica insisted. "I can't let you do that, Grandmother. It's not fair for you to pay for my gift to Daddy."

"Nonsense. That is how it should be."

Angelica explained the loss of her job at the café and how she hadn't received a salary since March 6. "I'll find another job and . . . . ."

"You most certainly will not. A fourteen-year-old girl does not need a job. This is not open for debate," Ophelia firmly said in response to the expression on Angelica's face. "We will take care of you in every way. Now, let me pay for this pen so we can finish the party preparations."

On the drive home, Angelica thanked Ophelia for buying the pen. "I know Daddy doesn't need it. He has pens. But when I saw it, I thought how perfect it is for him. I'll pay you back, I promise."

"No, you will not, dear," Ophelia smiled. "I wanted to buy it for you to give to Julien. It is your gift to him. Now, let us discuss our dinner menu," Ophelia changed topics

When they got home, Ophelia prepared the salmon steaks for broiling while Angelica made the cake frosting. By the time Ophelia had all of the food cooking, Angelica had finished frosting the cake. They placed the candles atop the cake, and then covered it until after dinner. They wrapped the presents and placed them on the piano, set the dinner table, and double checked the food. Everything was on schedule.

Aurélie arrived home first, followed moments later by Rogier. He quickly hid his briefcase in the music room. Its contents were extremely valuable, Rogier thought, and they would be the greatest gift he could give to Julien and his family. "Mr. Sandorf," he heard Angelica say. "Daddy just pulled up. Come on." Rogier smiled and got in place.

The house was unusually quiet when Julien entered. "Salut! I am home. Where is everyone?"

"I'm in the music room, Daddy," Angelica replied.

Julien walked quickly, smiling the whole way, never expecting the greeting he received. "Happy birthday! Joyeux anniversaire!" his family and Rogier shouted.

Julien smiled, kissed his mother, wife, and daughter, and hugged Rogier. "Merci beaucoup. You really surprised me. How did you keep this a secret from me?" he asked Aurélie.

"It was a secret from me, too," she giggled. "I think we owe this to Mother and Angelica. I found out when I got home from work."

"I didn't have anything to do with planning this, but I figured something was planned when Angelica called and invited me to dinner today," Rogier explained.

"Dinner is ready, so if you take your seats in the dining room, I will bring in the first course," Ophelia said. For more than one hour, they enjoyed the food and love that filled their bodies and their souls with nourishment. Ophelia and Aurélie cleared the plates, and when they were almost finished, Angelica went to the kitchen.

She returned to the dining room carrying the cake. Angelica placed it before Julien and then kissed his cheek.

Ophelia also kissed his cheek and then encouraged him to, "Blow out the candles, fils, and make a wish."

Julien blew out the candles quickly, and looked at Angelica. "There is no need to make wishes. My prayer has come true," he softly said, his voice thick with emotions. Aurélie put her hand on his shoulder, knowing the full import of his meaning.

Ophelia patted his back and said, "That is such a beautiful outlook, son. Well, I will cut and serve the cake now." In moments, everyone sat enjoying the cake.

"This is the most delicious cake I have ever eaten. And this icing. I have never tasted anything like it," Julien said as he ate the cake.

"Angelica and I made the cake together. She made the icing and decorated the cake," Ophelia informed him with pride. She had many times felt maternal pride for Julien, but now, for the first time, she felt a grandmother's pride for Angelica. She had long envied her friends when they shared pictures of their grandchildren or stories of their grandchildren's accomplishments. She longed to introduce those friends to her granddaughter Angelica.

Aurélie and Rogier complimented Angelica, too, which made her blush. "It's just buttercream icing. Mrs. Soames, the village priest's wife, taught me how to make it once when I visited her. She was baking cakes for a church function, and I helped her."

"Well you are going to make it quite often, Angelica. It is my new favorite," Julien said with a smile as he swiped his finger through the icing on his plate. He licked his finger as Ophelia good-naturedly reprimanded him.

"Let us take our celebration to the music room," Ophelia said. "I will make some tea and be in soon."

Aurélie put a record album on the stereo and let it softly play in the background. Rogier picked up the first picture of Aurélie, Julien, and Angelica, the one he had taken the day Angelica had been released from the hospital. They loved each other tremendously, Rogier knew that. He saw and felt that love. He knew with conviction that the adoption would become finalized without any problems or contest.

"What are you so thoughtful about?" Julien asked Rogier.

Rogier smiled, placed the picture on the table, and said, "Oh, just about how much has happened in the past three months."

"I have never been this happy, Rogier."

"I know, Julien, I know," Rogier whispered, controlling his emotions. Soon, he reminded himself. Soon.

Ophelia returned with the tea tray, which included a plate of Julien's favorite cookies. Everyone talked for a while, until Ophelia announced that it was time for Julien to open his birthday gifts. She and Angelica carried them to the table next to Julien. "My goodness, I never expected all of this," he marveled.

"But you deserve them," Angelica said with a smile. Aurélie gleefully agreed and kissed him.

Julien opened the gifts from Ophelia, Rogier, Aurélie, and lastly Angelica. "Thank you, each of you. This has been the happiest birthday I have celebrated yet."

"It's not over yet, my good man," Rogier said with a smile, knowing he still had his biggest surprise to reveal.

"No, it's not," Angelica said. "I have one more gift for you, Daddy."

"Another? But you have already given me so much. You bought something else?"

"No, I didn't buy anything else," Angelica replied. "I wrote something just for you. I hope you like it," she added, turned off the stereo, and walked to the piano.

Angelica stunned them all by playing a sonata. Julien stared at Angelica, astounded, amazed, and overwhelmed. The piece was elegant, fanciful, yet strong and forceful. It moved Julien's soul and affected him in a way no music had ever done. He felt his pulse pounding and his emotions surging. He was mesmerized, spellbound.

When she finished, Aurélie, Rogier, and Ophelia gave her a standing ovation. Julien was too overcome to move at that moment. Angelica looked at him with her love for him in her eyes, and the sight propelled him to her. Julien grabbed her in an embrace and held her close. "Oh, ma petite fille, what can I say? You wrote that for me?" She nodded as she looked up into his eyes. "I am too full of feeling, I am étourdi, stunned. So beautiful. So beautiful, my darling daughter. My heart is so happy, it feels that it is singing."

Angelica beamed. "I titled that piece *Heartsong Sonata*. I played how I see you."

"I feel so loved."

"You are," Angelica whispered and kissed his cheek. "I love you, Daddy. I am so blessed, I know that, to have two incredible men in my life. Both of you have given me unconditional love. My birth father and now you, my Daddy. You're the only two men I've composed for, the only men who have touched my heart."

"I am honored, Angelica, truly I am," Julien said. "I will never take his place. I do not want to. He loves you, and you love him, and that is how it should be. He is part of you, Angelica, and he will be part of your children and grandchildren. That is how it should be and will be." Julien kissed the top of her head.

"Thank you. You have no idea how that makes me feel, Daddy."

"Julien, I, too, have more for you," Rogier said. "For you and Angelica," he added.

"For me?" Angelica asked and placed a hand over her heart. "You found something."

"Yes, darling," Rogier said and got his briefcase while Julien and Angelica sat close to each other on the sofa. Aurélie moved closer to Angelica and put her arm around the girl. They all wondered what Rogier would reveal.

"My team and I found quite a lot of information about Angelica's family, her birth father in particular. I'm going to share everything with you this evening. There is a lot, so I want to make one thing clear now, before this becomes too emotional," Rogier said. "Angelica does not have any living relatives."

Rogier sat quietly while the full import of his statement became reality. "So the adoption will be uncontested," Julien slowly said.

"Yes," Rogier smiled. "It's Friday evening, so that means I will file the adoption application with the court on Monday. I'll bring the forms over tomorrow so you can review and sign them," he explained to Julien and Aurélie.

Rogier removed several file folders and envelopes from his briefcase. He encouraged everyone to take a short break, so Ophelia went to make coffee. Aurélie and Angelica went upstairs briefly, and Angelica returned to the music room with her journal. Soon they settled to hear all that Rogier had learned.

"Angelica, your paternal grandfather Pierre Thurmaldi died on May 2, 1934, at which time your father became the King of Maldova. Pierre's wife, Isabel Cocteau, died on July 28, 1931. Your father was their only child. Henri Pierre Maximillien Thurmaldi was born June 22, 1904 in Ringate, Maldova. He was coronated on November 2, 1934," Rogier informed them. "This is your father's coronation portrait," Rogier said and passed a color portrait to Angelica.

She stared at the portrait for several moments. "My father," she finally whispered.

Aurélie leaned closer to Angelica, looked at the portrait and gasped. "I am sorry, darling. We saw your drawing of your father, and we know he and Julien have a strong resemblance. It is just that this is like a mirror, and, well, it is like looking at my husband in a costume."

"I know," Angelica whispered. "It is emotional to see him for the first time in almost fourteen years. This is him. This is my father," she said as tears filled her eyes. She stared at the portrait for a few more minutes. "This is such a formal portrait, but I see the compassion and concern in his eyes. That's what I remember, that and seeing his love for me." Angelica looked at Rogier. "Thank you."

Rogier reached across the table and patted her hand. "Your mother," Rogier said, knowing that this information would definitely be emotional for Angelica. She held Aurélie's hand tightly, also expecting to be deeply affected. "Stephanie Josephina Duprés was born here in Paris on March 12, 1906. She and

Henri were married in Maldova's last Royal wedding on September 16, 1942." Rogier removed another portrait from an envelope. "Angelica, this is your parents' wedding portrait," he said and carefully handed her the photograph.

At her first look at her mother, Angelica began crying. Julien pulled her onto his lap, and Aurélie held the portraits protectively. Ophelia suggested they postpone the rest of the revelations until the following day.

Angelica shook her head and dried her eyes. "No, please, I'm all right. Seeing her for the first time is just too much to feel. She died giving me life, and I've always felt guilty about that. Now, to see her, brings it all up."

"Angelica, stop feeling guilty," Ophelia insisted. "Stephanie would not want you to, I know that. No matter what. I could not imagine any mother who would not give up her own life for her child. That is an act of love, ma chère. I would do that for my son in a heartbeat, without any thought. So never feel guilty, ma petite fille. Never. Feel grateful that she loved you so much that she placed your life above her own."

Angelica bowed her head in thoughtful silence for several minutes, and then smiled at Ophelia. "Thank you, Grandmother. I hadn't thought of it like that before. That does help." Angelica asked for the wedding portrait and studied it for a long while. "They are so in love. I can see it." She looked at Aurélie and then at Julien. "Just like I saw your love when you came into the café. True, lasting love, shining from their souls into their eyes. This makes me so happy, because I know they were happy."

"They were, Angelica. We found some newspaper articles about the wedding, public engagements, and even a diplomatic dinner that your parents hosted in the Palace. Also, I found a souvenir book that was published after the wedding. It contains a lot of pictures. I'll leave everything with you."

"No wonder Renée sheltered you. It would have been so easy for you to learn some of this. We had no idea that your father was such an important public figure," Julien said.

"No. I had no idea," Angelica said. "Tell me what happened," she said to Rogier. "Why was he murdered?"

Rogier cleared his throat. "Maldova was overthrown by Russia in 1946, and your father exiled. He and your mother were allowed to live if they left the country and never returned. They went to Lucerne, Switzerland, where you were born on Saint Valentine's Day 1950."

"February 14. The day of love. That should have been one of the happiest days of my father's life. Instead, it was the saddest," Angelica sorrowfully said as she looked at the portrait of her parents.

Rogier picked up a sheet of newspaper and read from it:

Angelica Anna Maria Thurmaldi was born yesterday in Lucerne, to the exiled King Henri of Maldova and his wife Queen Stephanie.

Princess Angelica is reported to be in excellent health. King Henri greeted well-wishers outside the hospital this morning. When asked how he felt, he smiled and said, "Happy. I am so happy. My beautiful little flower, my Angelica, is the joy of my life, the reason I was born. Stephanie and I loved her before we knew her. Now that I have seen her, I love her more than I can express."

King Henri's happiness proved contagious on the streets of Lucerne, where celebrations took place. Until we received the announcement issued by the hospital. With sadness, we report that Queen Stephanie died moments after her daughter was born. King Henri will return home with their daughter tomorrow, where he will, in his words, devote his life to Angelica'.

"That's from the Lucerne evening newspaper of February 15, 1950," Rogier said. "I wanted you to hear your father's own words, Angelica. Of course your mother's death was sad and painful for Henri. He loved her. Of course her death hurt him. But your birth and the happiness you brought overshadowed the sadness. There is a picture of him with the article.   Look at him," Rogier commanded and passed her the article.

Angelica saw her father the morning after her mother's death, smiling. He had said he was happy. He looked happy. "I made him happy?" she quietly asked.

"Of course you did, Chouchou," Julien replied as he smiled at her. "How could you not? You were his baby girl, the absolute love of his life. No one changes a man more than his daughter does. Believe me."

Angelica threw her arms around Julien's neck and kissed his cheek. "Thank you."

"Your father had a home in Lucerne where he and your mother had lived for four years. We learned that he had two employees, a housekeeper/cook, Renée Sabine, and, until 1949, a secretary, Stephen Poole. He never replaced Poole, which left Renée as the only other person in the home. She lived there, in a second-floor bedroom. The master suite and the nursey were also on the second floor," Rogier explained.

"Renée typically did errands in the evenings after dinner. It wasn't uncommon for her to do some late shopping or to pick up other items in the village. So it was not out of the ordinary when she left the house in the early evening of November 8, 1950. It was a Wednesday. Angelica, my dear, this is the night you described as the last you saw your father. Are you sure you want to hear this now?"

"I've always known what happened. When I was about five, I realized that someone had shot and killed my father. I saw my father murdered. I know that. I've lived with that and relived that every day of my life. Now I know the assassin was a member of FREE. Wasn't he?" Angelica asked Rogier.

"Yes, Angelica. FREE turned its attention back on King Henri when they realized that there was an heir to the Maldovan throne. Their plan was to kill both your father and you," Rogier explained.

"Oh, Mon Dieu," Ophelia muttered and clutched her throat. Aurélie looked just as disgusted. Julien clenched his hands tightly, controlling his anger and sickness. Angelica, however, stunned them all out of their own reactions.

"I killed my father," Angelica muttered, horror and disgust tinging her voice.

Julien turned her toward him, looking and sounding more hurt and angry than she had ever witnessed. "No, you did not. The people who did are sick and evil. You are not responsible for their actions. Angelica, ma fille chérie, you have done nothing wrong. Nothing."

"I'm the reason they killed him. If I had not been born, my mother would not have died when she did and my father would not have been murdered," Angelica insisted and began crying. Julien held her close and let her cry against him. She had to let go of her guilt and anger, he knew that. After twenty minutes, she stopped crying.

"We need a short break, Chouchou. Come with me, and we will freshen." Julien walked Angelica upstairs to her bedroom and helped her wash her face. He gave her one of the painkillers Dr. Sutfield had prescribed, and then he combed her hair. He smiled at her as they both looked into the mirror.

"I'm sorry I spoiled your birthday, Daddy."

Julien put his hands on her shoulders, kissed the top of her head, and reassured her she hadn't. "You could never ruin any day, let alone today. This has been one of the two happiest birthdays I will ever have. Capiche?"

Angelica smiled, nodded, and asked, "Are we ready to go back downstairs?"

Julien and Angelica entered the music room holding hands. She kissed Aurélie, Ophelia, and Rogier before she took her seat between Julien and Aurélie. "Tell me the rest, Rogier. Please."

"The shadow you saw in the hallway that night was the shooter, and the flash you described was from the gun. He did use a silencer we presume, since no one heard anything." Rogier paused. "The first bullet hit your father just behind his right ear. It killed him instantly, according to the autopsy. There was a second bullet fired. It was intended to kill you," Rogier said as he looked at Angelica. "It was found lodged inside a stuffed teddy bear that was in your crib."

"My teddy bear? My father gave him to me. It's the teddy bear I told you about," she said and looked at Julien. "That teddy bear saved my life."

"You were nowhere to be found when your father's body was discovered the next day," Rogier continued. "Neither was Renée. No one knew what had happened to you. The police searched for you and Renée for more than one year. There was no trace. The presumption was that you had either been kidnapped or killed. But there were never ransom demands. No one ever reported an infant to match your description. You seemed to have vanished.

"Of course, we know now where you were. Thankfully, Renée was very cautious and protective. She saved your life by sheltering you as she did. It wasn't until you came to Paris that you caught the attention of FREE members. One of them went into the café where you worked, and your first name alerted him. Angelica isn't an unusual name, but you appear to be the age the Princess would be. More importantly to him was a resemblance to King Henri. He reported all of this to FREE leaders, and they assigned Luka Blinov to kill you."

Ophelia muttered under her breath and poured more coffee for everyone. Aurélie lifted her cup and saucer, but her hands shook so much that she quickly returned them to the table. Angelica put an arm around her and said, "It's all right. I'm all right. It happened, but it helped bring us together."

Aurélie nodded, her throat too choked with tears to allow her to speak. Julien reached behind Angelica and squeezed his wife's shoulder in reassurance. Rogier sipped his coffee and then continued.

"Well, now we turn to your mother's family. Stephanie had one brother, Jacques, who himself had one son, Jeanluc. Your cousin Jeanluc lived in Paris. He was drafted into the French Army and fought in the Korean War beginning in 1951. We found one picture of him," Rogier said and handed the photograph to Angelica. She looked at a smiling young man with blonde hair and green eyes. "Jeanluc was killed in battle on April 25, 1953. His body was returned to his father and buried in Père Lachaise Cemetery. He was nineteen years old. I'm sorry, Angelica.

"Your maternal grandparents were Michel and Jacqueline Duprés. I found this picture of them at your parents' wedding." Angelica smiled when she looked at the happy, handsome couple.

"Jacqueline died of a heart attack in 1946. Michel lived with Jacques after Jeanluc's death. He died in his sleep in 1960. His death certificate says he died of natural causes."

"My uncle? He's dead, too?"

"Yes, darling, I'm sorry. Jacques died while saving a young boy from a car that had swerved and plunged into a river. Before Jacques could escape the car, it filled with water and trapped him. He is buried alongside his son and wife. I found a picture of him at your parents' wedding, as well."

"Jeanluc had his green eyes," Angelica said. "Jacques must have been a wonderful person, so kind, to risk his life for someone else. He was a hero." She looked at her maternal relatives. "I'd like to visit them."

"Of course, sweetheart. Anytime you want to," Aurélie softly promised.

"Where are my parents buried?"

"Henri and Stephanie lay side-by-side in the small crypt he had built when she died. It's private, kept locked, although people still visit and pay their respects. The day I went, there were fresh flowers outside the locked entrance. I did not go in, but I did take some pictures for you. Your parents are in the St. Nicholas of Flüe Church Cemetery."

Rogier gave her the pictures of her parents' crypt. "My parents. My beautiful, loving parents." Angelica held the pictures to her chest and bowed her head. "I love them so much."

"They know that, ma petit," Ophelia cried. "They know."

"Yes, they do, Angelica darling. They have always known and they will always know. They will love you forever," Aurélie said as she leaned close to Angelica.

"They love you, and you love them. Aurélie and I love you," Julien added. Angelica nodded, smiled, and kissed them both. "After your next doctor appointment we will go to Lucerne, the five of us."

"You would do that for me?," Angelica softly asked, her voice filled with incredulity.

"Of course we will, Chouchou. We will plan to spend at least two weeks there, longer if possible. We can plan for August if that works for all of us."

Ophelia was retired, so she would be able to travel anytime. Aurélie would take vacation time from her job. Julien's assistant would run the foundation, and the hotel manager had run the hotel for nearly twenty years. Rogier was the only one who had a full schedule of clients and court cases. He promised he would try to clear the time. He was certain that his partners could handle his workload.

"You have all done so much for me. I can never thank you or repay you. I love you all so much, and I am so grateful to God for bringing us together. Today is your birthday, Daddy, but I am the one who has received the greatest gift today. Thank you."

§§§§§

Sunday morning, Angelica arose early, looking forward to celebrating Father's Day. She had honored her birth father every year. She prayed for him, lit a candle in the church, left flowers at the statue of Saint Mary, played the piano for him, and talked to him. She remembered him. She loved him. She would honor him this Father's Day, as well.

She would also honor Julien. Angelica wrote a message to him on the card she had bought. She tiptoed into the master suite and placed the card on his nightstand. Julien gently took hold of her hand just at that moment. She appeared utterly surprised.

Julien sat up and pulled her onto his lap. "You did not wake me, Angelica. I have been lying here awake for a while. What is so important for you to be up and dressed this early?"

"I have something to do."

"Can I help?" Julien asked

Angelica shook her head. "No. You stay here and relax," she said, kissed him, and stood. She blew him a kiss as she left.

As Angelica went downstairs, Julien wondered what was going on. He shrugged his shoulders and picked up the envelope she placed on the nightstand. The *Daddy* written on the front made him cry. His sob woke Aurélie, who asked him what was wrong. He handed her the envelope. Aurélie smiled.

"Oh, darling. Open it," Aurélie said.

Julien smiled and cried simultaneously as he read the card, especially Angelica's note. They heard Angelica's footsteps as she slowly climbed the stairs. "I better help her," Julien said. Aurélie stopped him, and he looked puzzled.

"She wants to surprise you, darling," Aurélie smiled.

Sure enough, Angelica entered with a breakfast tray. "Happy Father's Day, Daddy," she said and kissed his cheek. He settled against the headboard and kissed her forehead when she placed the tray over his lap. "I need to get Mom's tray. I'll be back soon."

Angelica returned to the kitchen, leaving Julien awestruck. Aurélie kissed him passionately and then said, "We are the most fortunate parents in the entire world."

"We are. Rogier files the adoption application tomorrow. This will make our family legal. I want nothing more, mon amour. Nothing."

"Neither do I," Aurélie said just as Angelica returned with her breakfast tray. "This is so lovely, my dear. You are the most thoughtful daughter," Aurélie said and hugged and kissed Angelica.

A few hours later, the three of them entered the church together. During the service, Angelica thanked God for her two fathers, Henri and Julien. Both men filled her life with love, and she treasured them so. After the hymn *In My Father's House*, Angelica stood on her tiptoes and kissed Julien's cheek. "I love you, Daddy."

After the service, Angelica, Julien, and Aurélie remained in the church. Angelica lit a candle for her father, and then bowed her head. "Dear God, Please hold my father eternally in your loving embrace. Please let him feel my love for him, as well. I remember him, and I think of him daily. He surrounded me with love, and that stays with me always. Thank you for gifting me to him. Amen."

Julien, too, offered a prayer. "Dear God, I thank you for the life of Henri Thurmaldi. I never met him, but I have come to know and to respect him. Henri left this world many gifts. The most important of them is his daughter Angelica. I love her as he does. Please assure him that Aurélie and I will love and protect her all the days of our lives. Amen."

§§§§§

The following morning, Angelica was again up quite early. The smell of brewing coffee brought Julien and Aurélie to the kitchen. Ophelia arrived not long after that. All were very aware of the day's importance, although none of them mentioned it. Until Rogier arrived at 6:35.

"The court opens at 9:00, and I will be there when they do. I will file your application for adoption, including the evidence, death certificates, and letters from the Swiss officials. The judge will send me a directive when the first hearing is scheduled. There is nothing more for us to do until then."

"Nothing can go wrong today?" Ophelia asked.

"Nothing. I promise you. But I will call here as soon as the application has been filed. Everything will be all right. I'll talk to you in a few hours," Rogier said as he walked toward the door.

Angelica followed him and stopped him in the foyer. "Rogier, I wrote this letter to the judge," she said and held an envelope.

"I will add it to the file." He put his hand gently on her cheek. "This will happen, darling. I'll call in a while."

"Thank you," Angelica said. "This has to happen. It has to. I can't lose another father."

"You won't, I promise you that."

Julien, Aurélie, Angelica, and Ophelia sat quietly in the third floor sunroom all morning. The telephone ringing startled them. Julien rushed to the hall telephone. He listened for a moment and then said a relieved, "Thank you."

Julien returned to the sunroom. "That was Rogier. The adoption file and application have been submitted. The clerk said everything was in order and formally filed the application. They will be reviewed by the judge. Now we await the summons, the request for an interview with the judge."

"It is in God's hands, mon fil. We must continue to pray as we wait," Ophelia said.

Aurélie agreed, and mentioned she would do some laundry before lunch. Ophelia said she would help, and both women left to go to the first floor. Angelica walked to the window and looked out at the clear sky.

"I need to get some things at the shops. Come with me," Julien invited her.

"All right," Angelica replied.

Several minutes later, Julien parked on a street peppered with sundry shops. "It should be ready. Let us go to the bakery first."

Angelica smiled up at Julien, held his hand, and enjoyed the smile he gave her. Julien asked the clerk if his order was ready, and she went to the back room for it. She returned and placed a large cake box on the counter. She opened it for his approval. Julien nodded and softly said, "This is perfect. Thank you."

The clerk tied the box with string. Julien paid, and left holding Angelica's hand. "Let us go to the florist now," he suggested.

Inside the flower shop, Julien requested one dozen white roses. "Is all of this a surprise for Mom?" Angelica asked while the florist prepared the order.

"No, Chouchou, not today," Julien truthfully answered, yet never said for whom he bought the sweets and the flowers. Angelica didn't ask for further explanation, realizing that he would have told her if he wanted her to know.

Julien paid for the roses, which were wrapped in green paper, and handed them to Angelica. She carried them in her arms, and Julien put one arm around her. They walked down the sidewalk slowly, stopping to window shop.

They were unaware that people paused to watch them. They were striking with their similar coloring and features, especially their emotive brown eyes. They charmed people when they stopped at a toy store window. They laughed joyfully when two wayward toy robots fell onto a train track and caused the train to derail. Suddenly, Angelica's hand covered her mouth.

"What is it, Chouchou?" Julien asked, alarmed.

"Nothing," Angelica replied.

"Something caused that reaction. What was it?"

"There are just so many beautiful dolls, that's all. They look like they came out of one of Mom's fashion magazines," Angelica explained.

Julien smiled. "You like dolls? All girls do."

"I don't know," Angelica said and began walking away. Julien stopped her and asked what that meant. How could she not know? "I never had any dolls. Renée didn't believe in them. But I did cut paper dolls from scrap paper, and I drew their faces and clothes."

Julien felt like crying, but he forced himself not to. Instead, he took her hand and went into the toy store. "Which doll do you like best?"

Angelica's eyes were huge. "I don't need a doll. I'm too old for one anyway."

"No, you are not. Which one do you want?"

After quite a lot of persuading, Angelica pointed to a doll in a red and white velvet and organza gown. Julien asked the sales lady to wrap it for Angelica.

Julien carried the bags and held her hand as they left the store. Several people who had stopped to watch the scene play out felt tears in their eyes at what happened next. Angelica put her arm around Julien's neck and stood on her toes to kiss his cheek. "Thank you. I love you, Daddy."

"I love you, too, Chouchou," Julien said.

They walked to their car, where Julien helped her in, and they were soon on their way home. When they entered with their packages, Aurélie greeted them with questions in her eyes. "Chouchou, why not take your doll up to your room," Julien smiled.

"All right. I really didn't need her, but thank you for her," Angelica smiled at him and then went upstairs.

"What have you been up to? You bought her a doll?" Aurélie asked with a smile.

"Dolls were not on my agenda when I took her shopping. Today is June 22." Julien saw the confusion on his wife's and his mother's faces. "It is her father's birthday. She has never known this is her father's birthdate before. This is the first year she can celebrate his birth on the actual date. So I decided that we would have a birthday party for Henri," Julien explained.

He opened the cake box. Aurélie hugged him when she saw *Happy Birthday Father* on top of the cake. "This is so amazingly kind and thoughtful, Julien. Not many men would be as generous," Aurélie said. "I love you more each day," she kissed him.

"He is her father. She loves him and remembers him. She should. I cannot and will not replace Henri. I can and will do what he cannot do. That is all," Julien clarified. He picked up the roses. "White roses are his flower, so I got them. Angelica can keep them in her room after the party. Do we have a vase for them?"

Aurélie's smile was huge when she got a vase from the cabinet and sat it on the counter. "White roses are your flower, too, mon amour," she said. "Your birthday was just three days ago. You and Henri have a lot in common," she added as she filled the vase with water.

"I guess we do. Angelica is our most important connection. We both love her."

"I know. All right, let us get this surprise party ready," Aurélie said and arranged the roses. Ophelia was so proud of her son and her daughter-in-law for their compassion and understanding. She kissed them both and got a cake plate. Julien gathered dessert plates, forks, and a cake knife, as well as glasses of lemonade on a tray which he carried to the music room.

As the three of them arranged everything on the table, Julien remembered the doll. "You asked about the doll. We stopped to watch the displays in the toy store window. She happened to see the dolls and said how pretty they are. She told me she had never had a doll. Renée did not believe in dolls, she told me. She said she cut paper dolls from scraps of paper. She drew their faces and clothes. That broke my heart. It hurt. Then Angelica told me she was too old for dolls. She is only fourteen. She has never had a doll. I wanted to buy her one."

"Oh, Julien, what a beautiful thing to do. Only a father, a real father, would do that for his little girl. You are one incredible man, mon mari."

Ophelia dabbed her eyes with a handkerchief just as they heard Angelica's footsteps. Julien called out to her to come to the music room.   He, Aurélie, and Ophelia stood smiling when she entered. She appeared puzzled, and Aurélie nudged her husband to explain.

"Chouchou, today is a very special day.   Yes, Rogier filed the adoption application today. This is the perfect date for that," Julien said.

"Today is my father's birthday. I wrote a letter to him in my journal this morning.   It's the first time I can commemorate his birth on the date."

"I know, Chouchou. I know what this means to you. That is why we are celebrating your father's birthday today," Julien said, stepping aside to reveal the cake and the roses.

Angelica had never suspected Julien's plans. She stared at the cake for several minutes, overcome with emotions. Suddenly, she grabbed Julien in a hug. "You are too much, Daddy. I had no idea. Thank you for understanding."

"We will celebrate Henri's birthday every July 22. This is a perfect year to start. Your father was born sixty years ago today," Julien said as he hugged Angelica

"Sixty. I know we can never change what happened. But he was so young when he was taken from me," Angelica softly said. She smiled and continued, "I do believe what the Bible says. I believe that he is alive. I believe that I will meet him again someday. I know he is always with me. I love him. I love you more for accepting that."

"Your love for your father is beautiful, Chouchou," Julien said as he kissed the top of her head.

Aurélie cleared the tears from her throat. "Angelica, dear, a few days ago you told us that you had written a composition for your father." Angelica nodded, memories flooding her mind. "Please, will you play it?"

"All right," Angelica said and sat at the piano. The piece was elegant, happy, and melodious. Aurélie, Julien, and Ophelia listened, entranced and enchanted. A daughter's love for her father, expressed so exquisitely, touched them to their cores. When she finished, she sat with her head bowed for several minutes.

When she stood, they embraced her in a family hug. "That is so lovely, my dear. Thank you for sharing it with us on this very special day," Aurélie gently said as she smoothed Angelica's hair.

"I wrote that on my ninth birthday. I didn't know it was my birthday, but that's the day it came to me. I went to the village church and used the piano there. I see my father as he was nearly all of the time I knew him. Smiling, happy, loving, gentle. I saw him, alive and smiling and singing to me as I played this that day. This came from my love for him," Angelica told them.

"Your love for him fills and seems to come from the music. It is a magical, beautiful gift from you to him. I know how much he loves you, and I know how this piece makes him feel. He feels your love for him, Chouchou, and you feel his for you. That is such a beautiful love for us to witness and now to share, Angelica," Julien said with tears in his eyes. "We love you."

MOUVEMENT TROIS

July 10, 1964, Friday

Today has been very full. This morning, Daddy and Mom took me to my appointment with Dr. Sutfield. He examined me, and he finally told me something that is wrong with me. He said he first noticed it in the hospital, but since it could have been caused by the traumas to my heart, he took a wait-and-see approach. It's an irregular heartbeat, and Dr. Sutfield decided that it would be prudent (his word) if I start on medication today. I have to take it every day, and he will check my condition at my October appointment. I asked him to please not tell Mom and Daddy. I don't want to upset them. He said he had to, and in fact that he had already told them after my last appointment. I hated to see Mom cry, but she said that is what moms do because they love their children so much. I understand that.

The three of us went to lunch at Daddy's hotel. It's such a beautiful building, dating from the 1840s. The restaurant is at the top of the building and overlooks Paris. How thrilling to see the Eiffel Tower and the Arc de Triomphe from 55 stories high. Daddy was greeted by everyone, staff and guests alike, and asked to pose for pictures and sign autographs. People admire him for his work. He told me some about his foundation, but I want to learn more. I would enjoy working for Donner du Coeur with Daddy. I want to help people. I know how fortunate and blessed I am.

In these few months, I have learned a lot from Daddy. He grew up in a wealthy family and heir to the hotel and fortune. But he is not greedy and self-centered. He knew how fortunate he was. Just like his 10th birthday that he told me about, when he didn't want gifts. The party was for the other children at the hotel that day. The foundation helps people who are suffering terminal illnesses. The foundation helps with hospital bills and other expenses related to their care. Daddy told me he was inspired during his father's illness. His father was diagnosed with inoperable liver cancer, but the treatments, care, and medications were very expensive. Daddy realized that many people could not afford the expenses, so he established the foundation. That is so benevolent. I want to follow in his footsteps.

I am sure my father would do this kind of work. He was kind and compassionate. Everything I have read about him mentions his concern for people. I know he would approve of my working with the foundation.

Speaking of Father, we are going to Lucerne, Switzerland in a few weeks. Rogier and Grandmother came to dinner this evening, and we made the plans. Rogier consulted his calendar, and said the case he has during that time can be handled by one of his partners. We are leaving after church on August 2. My heart is so full of love and gratitude. I love them all—Father, Mother, Daddy, Mom, Grandmother, and Rogier. This journey will be the most meaningful of my life. I am so incredibly blessed.

§§§§§

Julien's private airplane landed at Zurich Airport at 2:10 on the afternoon of Sunday, August 2, 1964. A car was waiting for the Lacoers, Angelica, Rogier, and an armed body guard. A courier followed in a second car with their luggage. Angelica watched the scenery during the forty-five minute drive to Lucerne. Soon she would be in her birthplace for the first time since November 8, 1950.

Finally, they arrived in Lucerne, and Julien drove to their hotel, Palace Luzerne. Julien stepped out of the car, as always eliciting stares and attention, and opened the back door. He assisted his mother and his wife before Rogier stepped out. Julien helped Angelica from the car and put his arm around her.

A woman on the sidewalk gasped and put her hands over her heart. "My God, it can't be! It just can't be!" Her shocked comments drew others' attention to Julien and Angelica, at whom she stared. "It is," a man said. "King Henri and Princess Angelica! You have returned!" Soon, other people clustered around them, bowing to Julien.

After several awkward moments, Julien finally understood the cause for their presumption. "I am Julien Lacoeur. I came here with my family from Paris. My wife Aurélie. My mother Ophelia. Our friend Rogier Sandorf. Aurélie's and my daughter Angelica," Julien introduced his party.

"You are not King Henri?" an elderly man asked Julien.

"No, sir, I am not. I do realize that I bear a striking resemblance to him."

"Striking resemblance? You are identical to King Henri," the first woman insisted, still uncertain who she actually saw. "This is your daughter? Her name. It's the same as the Princess' name. And she looks like King Henri."

The woman's comments caused a furor. "This is Princess Angelica!" "Our Princess has come home!" "We wondered for many years what happened to you, Your Royal Highness." "God bless you, Princess Angelica." "We love you, Princess."

A woman stepped forward and looked closely at Angelica for many minutes. She gently took the girl's hand in both of hers. "I know you, Princess Angelica. I was the nurse who took care of you in the hospital when you were born. It is you."

Angelica looked up at Julien, unsure what to say. The woman was correct, of course, but Angelica did not want to say anything without Julien's approval. Rogier noticed her reticence and whispered to Julien that he would say something. "I am the Lacoeurs' friend and lawyer. We have just arrived in Lucerne, and as you can imagine, this is overwhelming for all of us, particularly Angelica. She has not been here since she was an infant. Therefore, I ask that you please give her and the Lacoeurs time to settle in and adjust. Thank you."

Angelica smiled at everyone and then requested Rogier to ask the nurse if she would come with them. The woman nodded and went to Julien's and Aurélie's hotel suite with the party. After the porter left, Ophelia ordered tea and sandwiches from room service. Soon everyone settled comfortably on the sofas and chairs.

Angelica began with the request she most wanted to ask the nurse. "Ma'am, please tell me about my parents. I never saw my mother. I knew my father so briefly. Please tell me what you remember about them. Anything at all. Please."

"Of course, my dear. My name is Gerta Brandt, and I am still a pediatric nurse at Holy Cross Hospital. I have cared for hundreds of newborns over my career, but I remember your birth and you quite clearly. There was a lot of attention surrounding your birth. Many photographers and reporters stood outside the hospital as soon as word spread that Queen Stephanie had been admitted.

"King Henri stayed beside her. Queen Stephanie had been closely monitored throughout her pregnancy. She was forty-three, almost forty-four, years old. Her doctor had no cause for concern, but nonetheless examined her when she was admitted. She never minded. I was in the room during the examination. She smiled the entire time. She even looked at me and said with pure joy, 'I want to hold my baby. I love her so'. I remarked on her pronoun—*her*. She said she knew her baby was a girl. The doctor laughed and remarked we would all know soon.

"Queen Stephanie was in labor for ten and a half hours. She was brought to the hospital early on Valentine's Day. She and King Henri kissed and said how meaningful and symbolic that their beloved baby be born on that day. King Henri held her and said, 'Our precious angel lives because of our love. She will share our love, and our lives will be perfect'.

"Queen Stephanie smiled and said, 'She will be surrounded by love every moment of her life. I am happier than ever, Henri'. I almost felt guilty for intruding upon these moments, but I am glad that I did. After everything that had happened to them, being forced to leave their country and live in exile, it was so nice to see them so happy and in love. You were all that mattered to them. That was obvious." Miss Brandt paused to sip her tea. She asked Angelica if she really wanted to hear everything.

"Yes, I do. I have to. I want to know. If it isn't an imposition on you, I really do want to know everything," Angelica assured the nurse, understanding that she would hear details of her mother's death.

Miss Brandt continued. "Queen Stephanie began delivery at 4:30. King Henri stayed with her. He had insisted all along that he would stay with her. He held her hand, wiped her forehead, talked to her, and sang love songs to her. Finally, at 5:52 your birth began. Queen Stephanie pushed several times, and finally at 6:13, she made the final huge push, and the doctor had you in his hands.

"Queen Stephanie began hemorrhaging. The doctor quickly cut the umbilical cord and handed you to me. King Henri stood next to his wife, holding her hand and telling her that he loved her. I was cleaning you, Princess, but I heard Queen Stephanie weakly say, 'I love you, Henri. Tell her I love her heart and soul. Always'. King Henri kissed her at the moment she died. His kiss was the last thing she felt." Miss Brandt took her handkerchief from her purse to dry her eyes. Aurélie and Ophelia were crying, too.

"That is so sad and beautiful," Angelica softly said. "My mother left this world surrounded by her husband's love. I'm grateful for that." Angelica put a hand on Miss Brandt's arm. "Thank you for telling me."

"King Henri asked me to stay in the delivery room with you. He stayed with Queen Stephanie's body until the undertaker came for her. I had wrapped you in swaddling clothes and a blanket. You were a quiet baby and did not cry. King Henri asked me to give you to him, so I carefully placed you in his arms. He kissed you on the forehead and told you how much he loved you. He then smiled at you and said, 'Your mother loves you so, my precious girl. She always has and always will. You are very loved, little one. You always will be'. The undertaker arrived, and he was willing to allow King Henri as much time as he needed. But King Henri said he needed to take care of you. He kissed Queen Stephanie's lips one last time and told her he loved her.

"Then he told me that he wanted to feed and dress you. I took King Henri to a private hospital room. A crib was brought in for you. I brought a bottle of formula so he could feed you. I stayed in the room to assist if needed. A short time after your feeding, your father dressed you in a gown of white angora that Queen Stephanie had bought for you. He wrapped you in a silk blanket and sat in the chair holding you and singing a lullaby to you until you fell asleep.

"He nodded at me, which I understood was the signal for me to leave. He wanted to be alone with you. You were asleep in the crib, and King Henri sat in a chair beside the crib watching you. He looked happy as he watched you. I want you to know that. He had a small smile and a peace about him. I know how dreadfully sad Queen Stephanie's death was, as sudden and unexpected as it was. I had seen the horror and sadness on his face when she died. But I also saw his love for you, Princess Angelica.

"When King Henri greeted the well-wishers outside the hospital the next day, many of them had no idea that the Queen had died. All they saw was a father's love and happiness for his baby girl. He was happy because of you, because he had you in his life.

"I was one of the medical staff who escorted him and you to his car when he took you home. He smiled and waved at those waiting to see you both. People saw his happiness. There were many pictures taken of that day. King Henri's happiness is immortalized in those pictures. I have a book at home about your birth. I want you to have it."

Angelica looked stunned by all she had heard and by Miss Brandt's offer. She shook her head. Miss Brandt hugged her. "I want to give it to you. I will bring it to the hotel on my way to work in the morning. I have often thought of you and wondered what had happened to you. I prayed for your safekeeping. I am so grateful to see you, my dear. I hope to see you again while you are in Lucerne, but if I don't, you have my prayers and wishes for happiness all the days of your life." Miss Brandt kissed Angelica and thanked the others before she left.

The adults sat quietly, processing everything that Miss Brandt had told them. Angelica walked to a window and looked out at the city of her birth. Angelica suddenly began crying fervently, which immediately stirred the others from their thoughts. Julien rushed to her and held her close to him. He and the others understood how incredibly emotional and upsetting Miss Brandt's memories had been for Angelica. They knew she had to cry and release her feelings. However, they grew concerned when she still cried after nearly forty-five minutes.

Aurélie went to her, as well, and suggested they take her to their bedroom, where she could rest. Rogier carried Angelica's suitcases into the bedroom, and Aurélie asked him and Julien to leave. Aurélie helped Angelica change into her nightgown and then helped her onto the bed and covered her. She tried in vain to soothe the teenager's crying.

Aurélie ran into the sitting room and told Julien to send for the hotel doctor. "She has not stopped crying, and

I am worried. Please tell him to hurry," Aurélie requested and rushed back to Angelica. Julien made the call, alerted the guard who stood in the hall, and also went to Angelica.

She lay on her side, still crying. Aurélie and Julien looked at each other, feeling helpless and worried. The doctor entered and quietly spoke with Julien and Aurélie. He had heard that the Maldovan Princess had arrived, seen in Lucerne for the first time since her father's assassination. Julien briefly explained Miss Brandt's visit. Aurélie informed the doctor of Angelica's irregular heartbeat and showed him the Amiodarone that had been prescribed for her.

The doctor nodded knowingly, but asked the Lacoeurs to leave so he could examine Angelica. They waited, restless and anxious, for nearly thirty minutes before the doctor entered the sitting room. "Angelica is physically all right. She is calmer now and resting, though she refused a sedative." Julien and Aurélie looked confused and concerned. Something had happened. But what? "She has finally allowed herself to do what she never has before. She told me that the woman who raised her did not approve of tears, so she never cried for any reason."

Julien appeared disgusted. "Apparently, Renée did not approve of a lot of things," Julien reacted angrily. "I am sorry," he told the doctor.

"Well, the explanation is understandable, resulting from a chain of events. First was meeting you, Mr. Lacoeur. Angelica told me that when she saw you for the first time, you looked like a reincarnation of her father. And I have to say, your resemblance to King Henri is shocking. Second was the information and photographs from Mr. Sandorf. That was the first time since his murder that she had actually seen her father's image.

"Third was the filing of the adoption application. She loves you both, and this is a happy, positive event. She went out of her way to tell me that," the doctor smiled. "But you know that happy life events cause stress, too.

"Lastly was today, first the immediate and instant reaction of the people on the street and then the appearance of Miss Brandt. Angelica is grieving her parents. All of the feelings, the grief, have remained inside of her for fourteen years. What you saw today was her releasing all of that."

"Oh, the poor child," Ophelia said in dismay.

"What can we do to help her?" Aurélie asked.

"Be here. Support her. Love her. Grief is a personal experience, I know that. Those who love us can be here for us. They cannot stop the pain or erase what happened. No one can. Angelica needs time to go through this process. She needs time to adapt to everything. We must do like always, just surround her with our love," Julien replied.

"That is exactly what you do," the doctor agreed. "The grieving process was delayed for so long that she even feels guilty for grieving. Her guilt is the other thing to not make an issue about. Angelica does not need to be told her guilt is wrong. Do not even mention it. Just let her grieve. Sometimes she will want to talk. Let her. Listen and love her. She will emerge from this. But there is no timetable for grief. Call me if you need me, day or night."

By then, it was just after 6:30. The day had overwhelmed everyone. Rogier took charge. "Listen, you three go freshen and relax for a while. I will order dinner for us all and have it delivered here." They thanked him, more grateful than he knew. Ophelia went to her suite across the hall, where she relaxed in a hot bath before changing for dinner.

Julien and Aurélie went into their bedroom and stopped when they saw Angelica. She had washed her face, combed her hair, and changed into a dress. She had just packed her nightgown, and she smiled at them. She walked to them, hugged them, and said, "I love you. I'm sorry for causing all of this trouble."

"We love you, too, darling. We were just coming to tell you that Rogier has ordered dinner for us all. We need to freshen and change," Aurélie said, intentionally not mentioning what had happened. She kissed Angelica's temple and went into the bathroom to shower.

Julien put his arms around Angelica, kissed her forehead, and smiled. "You are going to put us to shame. Here we are in our rumpled traveling clothes, and you are fresh and neat for dinner.

Scoot so I can be as presentable," he teased, which caused Angelica to giggle. What a beautiful sound, he thought.

The evening remained pleasant and enjoyable. The dining area overlooked a view of Lucerne, lit by streetlamps in the darkening evening. They all slept soundly, anticipating all that that the following two weeks would bring. The next morning's newspaper alerted Rogier to one difficulty with which they would have to contend.

Princess Angelica Returns! Fourteen Years After Her Disappearance, Teenager Reemerges

The headline heralded her return to her birthplace. Public scrutiny in the midst of her grief and emotional journey was more than any of them had expected.

Julien emerged from the bedroom while Aurélie finished her shower. He picked up the newspaper from the entry hall table, only to stare in shock at Angelica's picture. Julien barged across the hall and pounded on Rogier's suite door. Rogier instantly knew why his friend was there.

"Rogier, what are we do to? She cannot visit the places connected to her father with people always around. She deserves privacy. I understand that the people of Lucerne are surprised by Angelica's appearance. They respected and loved King Henri. They want to see his daughter. I understand that, Rogier. But she needs some time and space without the intrusions."

"I know, Julien. I've thought of this all morning. Here's what I think we should do." Rogier outlined his plan, and during breakfast the men shared it with Aurélie, Angelica, and Ophelia.

The first thing Julien did was hire more security to protect them, particularly Angelica. He refused to take chances as long as FREE existed. The second recommendation Rogier made was that Angelica issue a written statement. She was the one people longed to see and hear. Julien, Aurélie, and Ophelia agreed that a written statement was a fair compromise. Angelica trusted them, and she agreed to write a statement.

Ninety minutes later, Ralf Farner, the editor-in-chief of the major daily newspaper in Lucerne, sat in the Lacoeurs' suite. They told him why they had come to Lucerne and of the danger Angelica faced. "Angelica only recently learned her parents' names and that she is a princess. This is all so new and quite emotional for her. We had to ask for your assistance," Julien explained.

Mr. Farner looked down at Angelica's handwritten statement. "Of course. The only problem is that the evening edition hits newsstands in several hours. You need a more immediate release." He noticed the worried expressions and said, "I am going to do something that has rarely been done. I am going to release a special edition of the paper within the hour. Basically, I am doing a one-sheet special bulletin of this statement and a few pictures."

Mr. Farner took pictures of Angelica, alone and with the Lacoeurs, and rushed back to the newspaper office. Within the hour, Angelica's statement was on newsstands and in the hands of dozens of Lucerne citizens:

I am dazed by the reaction to my return to Lucerne. I never expected to receive any attention. I am filled with gratitude at the abundant respect and love people here feel for my father, Henri Thurmaldi. I am overcome by the affection for my father, but I understand it. He was so easy to love.

My father died when I was nine months old, but I do have memories of him. All of them are filled with love and joy. I do love him tremendously, and I always will. My own respect for my father has grown over the recent months as I have learned of his work, his concern, and his benevolence. As the King of Maldova, his primary focus was his fellow Maldovans, He strove to make their lives as secure, comfortable, and abundant as possible. When he and my mother were forced into exile, they chose to come here.

They made Lucerne their home. They were happy here. My father continued his work, establishing a foundation that helped people in need. He was active in the church he and my mother attended, St. Nicholas of Flüe Church, and he established a food pantry and a kitchen at the church so that those who needed food would have somewhere to go.

My father filled my first nine months with his love for me. I saw it in his eyes when he looked at me. I felt it when he held me. I still feel his love. I always will, I know that. His love and his benevolence are the legacy he leaves me, and I shall share that with my children in the future.

Likewise, his legacy continues to shine on Lucerne.   The work begun by my father endures, helping the people who welcomed him and his wife. I thank you for that. I vow that I will carry on my father's work.

Through his legacy, Henri Thurmaldi remains immortal. As long as people remember him and continue his work, he remains alive and vibrant.   Thank you or loving him and for welcoming me back to the city of my birth as I endeavor to learn more about my parents.

Rogier had contacted the current owners of the Thurmaldi home, and they were more than agreeable to a visit from Angelica and the Lacoeurs. They had scheduled the visit for that morning, so with the six security officers accompanying them, they set off in a rented car.

Rogier turned off the main street and drove down a narrow road up a hill. He parked in front of a house atop the hill, and he helped Ophelia and Aurélie from the car. Angelica tightly held Julien's hand and looked at the house as she stepped out of the car. "This is my father's home," she whispered.

At that moment, a couple came outside to greet them. They looked at the young girl who stood there with her wide, sad eyes and realized that she had spent the first nine months of her life in that home. Rogier had told them that Angelica remembered seeing her father murdered in that house. How horrifying.

"Welcome," the woman smiled. "I am Lucretia Warne, and this is my husband Fedor." Mrs. and Mr. Warne shook everyone's hands and invited them inside. The security officers remained outside.

Mrs. Warne put her arm around Angelica and smiled at her. "We thought we would show you the entire house, and then we would love for you all to join us for lunch. After that, I thought Angelica would like to explore the house on her own."

"I don't know what to say. I don't want to intrude. This is your home now," Angelica said, dazed by their kindness. They reassured her that their offer was sincere. As they began, Mr. Warne informed them, "The architecture of the home has not been altered. All of the furnishings were bought new when we purchased the home in 1952. All of the furniture and possessions that belonged to

King Henri were placed in storage. There are books, papers, and photographs among his possessions. They belong to you, Angelica."

Angelica appeared on the verge of tears, so Julien spoke up. "Thank you, Mr. Warne. We will have them picked up and taken to our hotel." Angelica looked at him in gratitude. He held her hand as they walked through the sitting room, the dining room, and the kitchen, all on the first floor. She had no vivid memories of those rooms, although she enjoyed seeing the entire house where her parents lived.

Mrs. Warne led the group into the fourth room on the main floor. As soon as she entered, Angelica gasped and covered her heart. "Chouchou, what is it?" Julien asked her in concern.

Angelica walked slowly to the large window, looked out, and stared at the sky for several minutes. She finally revealed, "This was my father's office. This is where he stood after the telephone call that night I told you about."

Angelica slowly walked to the middle of the room. "This is where my cradle was. It was from here that I watched him look out that window with sadness on his face, in his eyes. That was the only time I ever saw him look like that. I remember it so vividly. It breaks my heart. My father's sadness breaks my heart." Julien went to her, put his hands on her shoulders, and kissed the top of her head. "I wish I knew what that call was about. I wish I knew what made him sad. He was fine before that call." Angelica looked at the wall where the cuckoo clock had been. "I suppose it doesn't matter now. It can't be undone or changed." She realized that the Warnes, Aurélie, Ophelia, and Rogier stood silent and unmoving. "I'm all right, really. This is just the scene of one of my most important memories."

"Are you sure, Angelica?" Aurélie asked. Angelica assured everyone she was, and so the Warnes led them upstairs.

"The master suite is through here, and this would have been your parents'," Mrs. Warne explained.

Angelica stood in the bedroom for a long while, thinking and feeling. "I know that my parents deeply loved each other. I am certain they talked in the darkness, about their dreams and plans and hopes, about life, love, and everything. I know they were happy here, in this house, despite the circumstances that forced them here."

There was a third bedroom which the Warnes used as a guest room, a linen closet, a sitting area in the loft, and finally the most meaningful room of all.

"We have never used this room," Mrs. Warne explained. "As we said, all of the furnishings have been placed in storage. There may be some pieces from this room that you want, Angelica. You can decide what you want, everything or certain pieces. We have left the wallpaper and curtains in the room. When you are ready, you may open the door."

"My nursery," Angelica whispered. She bowed her head and said a silent prayer before she opened the door. Aurélie gasped and grabbed Julien. The wallpaper! It was pale green with delicate angelica blossoms scattered over it—so similar to the custom wallpaper they had commissioned for Angelica's bedroom.

"My crib was here," Angelica said as she stood on the spot. "Father kept a rocking chair next to the crib, where he fed me at night, sang to me while he held me, and where he sat watching me. This is where it happened," she said, and Ophelia began to sob. So did Mrs. Warne.

"It was dark. The hall light was on. Father sang to me. I can still hear him." Her voice was dreamy, but then changed. "A shadow appeared in the doorway," she said as she looked toward the door, "and a flash of light exploded. Father fell forward, against the crib rails, his eyes open. He stared at me for the longest time, but he never said anything or moved. He was dead.

"I never thought I would be in this room again," Angelica marveled as she looked around.

Mrs. Warne went to her. "Angelica, why don't you stay here while we go downstairs and prepare for lunch?"

"May I? I'd like that very much."

Julien and Aurélie understood. They both kissed her before they followed the Warnes. Ophelia helped Mr. and Mrs. Warne; she wanted to keep busy. Rogier stood looking out a sitting room window, while Julien and Aurélie talked in the corner.

Angelica had few memories of the house, but she did remember her nursery. No, she didn't remember the décor and minute details. She did remember the love she felt there. She did remember her father's face, how he smiled, how he sang to her, how he looked at her, how he loved her. She remembered him with love. Yes, he was murdered viciously and without provocation, and yes, that was sad and heartbreaking. However, as she stood on the spot where her father died, Angelica now knew that the tragedy of his death would forevermore be overshadowed by the greatest gift of all— his love for his daughter.

"Father, I thought this room would cause me great pain. I thought being here would make that night come crashing down on me in brutal horror. It hasn't. I stand here now, and I feel only love and peace. Being here has only made your love for me more vibrant, alive, and real to me. Being here has begun my healing, not prolonged my pain. How do I tell you what that feels like? It's a miracle. I love you, Father."

Angelica looked around the room, her nursery, one last time before she went downstairs. She walked to Rogier and hugged him.   He appeared stunned. "What is this for?" he asked her.

"Thank you for arranging this, Rogier. Thank you."

"I was happy to do this for you. I did worry that coming here would be too painful for you," Rogier admitted.

"I expected it to be. But is hasn't been. There is so much inside of me. I need time to live with it before I talk about it. Is that all right? Does it even make sense?"

"Sure," Rogier gently replied.

Julien went to Angelica and put his hand on her cheek. "Oui, Chouchou. It makes perfect sense. You take the time you need. We will be here for you when you need us." Julien kissed the top of her head.

Mrs. Warne announced that lunch was ready, so they all went to the dining room. After lunch, Angelica went to the room that had been her father's office. There, she looked out the window one last time. She pulled a sheet of paper and a pencil from her purse and sketched the view—the view her father had looked at after that unsettling telephone call.

Angelica rejoined everyone in the sitting room. "Mr. and Mrs. Warne, there is one piece of furniture of my parents' I would like." They asked her which one, and she surprised no one when she replied, "The white rocking chair that was in my nursery."

"Of course, dear. I will have it wrapped and packed. It will be taken to your hotel suite. So will the papers, letters, and documents. We wish you only happiness," Mr. Warne said.

That afternoon, in her hotel suite, Angelica poured her feelings and thoughts into her journal. She taped the drawing she had done earlier into the journal. She spent hours in her suite, alone with her memories and her emotions. She prayed to God, and she spoke to her father.

Angelica joined her family and Rogier for dinner. When they convened in the Lacoeurs' sitting room for coffee, Angelica went for her journal. She sat beside Julien on the sofa. "Today was long and emotional for me. I wrote about it in my journal. I want you to read it, if you want to."

"I am humbled that you trust us to do so," Julien said.

Angelica opened to the most recent entry and handed the journal to Julien. He held it so that Aurélie could read it at the same time. When they finished, Ophelia and Rogier read it.

August 3, 1964, Monday

Today has been such an immensely important day. I only recently learned that I was born in Lucerne, Switzerland. Yesterday, we arrived in Lucerne. Yesterday, as soon as we arrived, was amazing with the unexpected appearance of Nurse Brandt, the nurse who took care of me when I was born. This morning brought a trip that Rogier arranged when he was here a few months ago, at least the preliminary planning.

My parents' house! I went inside the house for the first time in almost fourteen years. Of course, I didn't remember most of the house. But two rooms are part of my memories, and I have seen them, or parts of them, all of my life. But to stand in those rooms—it was unlike anything I have ever experienced. I never thought I would ever return there, and I admit that I was reluctant to enter. I feared that being there would open the floodgates of pain and heartbreak. I was not afraid to go into the house. I was afraid of what being in that house would do to me.

Yes, there were sad, bittersweet feelings. After all, that house is where I spent the first nine months of my life. Those were extremely happy months, during which I felt only love. I didn't exactly realize at nine months of age that what I saw my last night there was my father's murder. I realized that later. Still, I know now that I saw my beautiful, loving father murdered. Of course going back to the scene of that is bound to be very sad.

However, I also realize that I finally released my pain and sadness yesterday. It was Miss Brandt who opened the door to that, and for the first time in fourteen years, I grieved my parents.

So rather than pain, the visit to my parents' house brought peace like I have never known. I was happy, safe, and loved in that house. I felt that today, especially in the two rooms I most remember—my father's office and my nursery.

I feel my father's love; I always have. I know that his soul surrounds me with love, just as he did when I was a baby and he held me close to him. He is real to me, and the more I learn *about him, the man he was, the more I love and respect him. I will always love him, and someday, when I am dead and my soul goes to Heaven, I will finally be able to say those words to him.*

I also know—I feel it—that my father is now completely at peace. Most of my life I was essentially alone. Renée gave me a home, food, clothes, and an education. She protected me, and only now do I truly know how much she did protect me and from whom. She was a godly woman, and she provided for me. But she never showed me love and tenderness. She never talked to me or with me about anything other than lessons, the Bible, and house work. She never talked with me about my family, and I do understand why. She never wanted to talk about love or life, such as the purpose each of us has for being alive.

She wouldn't allow me to go to town alone. She rarely let me visit anyone, and I never understood why. I could never have lunch or dinner at anyone's home. I realize now that she shielded me from television, magazines, and newspapers, from anything that might reveal information about my father. I was never allowed to go to someone else's home to play. The other children had to come to Renée's house, and even then we were limited in what we could play. No dolls, no cards, no board games. Renée was very strict.

Now my life is different. I have a family who once again fills my life with love and happiness. I can talk with them about anything. I feel free and fully alive. Despite everything from the past, I am content, and my life is full of love. That is why my father is finally at peace. That is why I can move forward in peace of my own. I will always remember my father, but not in sadness and grief. I will hereafter remember him in love and joy only.

My life began in love and joy with my father. My life continues now in love and joy with Daddy, Mom, and Grandmother. I have come full circle. The circle of love is complete.

Julien, Aurélie, and Ophelia surrounded Angelica in an embrace. Rogier smiled, recognizing the symbolism of the embrace.

"The shop is just ahead on the corner," Julien told Rogier, who was driving the family on Wednesday morning. "I shall be only a moment," Julien promised as he got out.

He did return soon, holding two bouquets of flowers. He turned to Angelica. "You said you wanted to get some flowers, so I got these. Forget-me-nots were Queen Stephanie's favorite flower," Julien explained and gave her one of the bouquets. "It was no surprise to discover your father's favorite flower. He named you for them," he tenderly said and handed her a bouquet of white, delicate angelica blossoms.

Angelica looked up at him with tears shining in her eyes. "Thank you, Daddy. These are beautiful," she said and smelled the flowers.

A short time later, Rogier parked near St. Nicholas of Flüe Church, the church Henri and Stephanie had attended and where they were buried. Rogier had arranged for the caretaker to meet them, and an elderly gentleman warmly welcomed the Lacoeurs. He bowed and kissed Angelica's hand.

"Princess Angelica, it is a miracle to see you. A lot of us feared for you all of these years. It is my honor to escort you to your parents."

"Thank you, Mr. Stokes. Please, call me Angelica."

"Your parents were just as down-to-earth as you are. I knew them, and they told everyone to call them Henri and

Stephanie. Not everyone did. To all of us they were always King Henri and Queen Stephanie, and not everyone addressed them so informally. I never could. Forgive me if I find it impossible to be so informal with their daughter," Mr. Stokes told Angelica. "Are you ready, Princess Angelica?"

"Yes, I am."

Julien and Aurélie walked on either side of Angelica, while Rogier held Ophelia's arm. The Thurmaldi crypt was surrounded by trees and wildflowers, in a secluded area of the cemetery. The crypt itself was simple and classic, with the THURMALDI surname carved above the entrance. The setting was quiet and peaceful.

Angelica smiled. "Flowers. There are fresh flowers here."

"Flowers are left every day, Princess Angelica. People remember your parents. They lived here almost four years, and they were happy here. They bought a home, nothing like a palace, but it was a place of happiness and love. People could feel it, as if it traveled on the wind like the smell of apple pie on the window sill. King Henri and Queen

Stephanie chose Lucerne as their new home. They loved the people who welcomed them, and the people loved them. I suppose some people call that a mutual love affair," Mr. Stokes shared.

"Thank you for telling me about them and their lives here, Mr. Stokes. The more I learn or hear about my parents, the more I understand why people still respond to them," Angelica told him.

"This is for you, Princess Angelica. It is a key to their crypt. I have the only other key as cemetery caretaker. This has been my job for forty years. When I retire, the new caretaker will have charge of the key. You come any time you desire. I hope you visit us often, Your Royal Highness," Mr. Stokes said with a bow. "I will leave you in privacy now. I am honored to have met you, Princess."

Angelica held the two bouquets with one arm and hugged Mr. Stokes with the other. She thanked him and kissed his cheek. He stood a bit taller as he walked away.

Angelica took a deep breath and stepped closer to the locked entrance. Julien helped her unlock the entrance, and she smiled up at him before she went in alone. Sunlight streamed in through the stained glass windows set high in the four walls. She looked at the two marble tombs and the tombstones set into the wall above each.

Angelica stood beside her mother's tomb first and bowed her head to pray. She whispered Amen and placed the bouquet of forget-me-nots atop the tomb. She looked at the tombstone for several moments as she thought of the beautiful woman who had died giving her life.

Stephanie Josephina Duprés Thurmaldi

12 March 1906

14 February 1950

Forget me not for all the love we shared

"I will never forget you, Mother. I love you." She gently traced the letters of her mother's name, and then kissed her fingertips and touched the tombstone again.

Angelica slowly turned to face her father's tomb. "Oh, Father, my precious father, I love you so." She bowed her head and prayed for several moments. She whispered Amen and opened her eyes. Like her mother's tomb, her father's was a simple and plain white marble tomb. His tombstone was likewise set into the wall above his tomb. Tears of love filled her eyes when she read it.

Henri Pierre Maximillien Thurmaldi

22 June 1904

8 November 1950

Walk by faith, not by sight.

--2 Corinthians 5:7

"Faith. To me that means trust and confidence. Despite everything that happened to us, we both had faith that God would stay with us. The people who hurt us did not live according to God's commandments. Not everyone does. But you did. That was your choice. That is my choice, too.

"I choose to live a life that honors you and mother, God, and now my new parents. If I do that, I will be rewarded with eternal life in Heaven. I will finally meet Mother and tell her I love her. I will reunite with you and finally tell you the words I wish I could have said so long ago. I love you, Daddy.

"You and Mother made me. You are part of me. We have an eternal connection that no one or nothing can weaken. God gifted me to you and Mother. He planned for us to be a family. He planned for me to inherit and to learn from the two of you. I am only recently learning about you both, and I am learning so much about what it means to live a life of service. I was born your daughter, and I vow to live my life as the heir to your benevolence and charity.

"My new father is very much like you. He looks like you, and his character, his soul, is like yours. He is kind, giving, gentle, compassionate, and not ashamed to share his feelings. He works to help people, just as you did. He adores art and music, and I share that with him. You would love him, and he would love you. I know that. You are both godly men, and you share so much in common.

"I love you forever, Daddy. You know that. My life may be in Paris now, but I will do as much as both you and Julien. I will help people. He has a foundation, and I would like to be part of that. In doing so, I will carry on your work and legacy. I know you would approve of that."

Angelica kissed her father's tomb, placed the bouquet of her namesake flower atop it, and smiled. She opened the entrance and motioned the Lacoeurs and Rogier to enter. "My father and my mother," Angelica said, as if she were introducing them. "I'm so grateful they are here together in such a peaceful, quiet spot. They were together in life, and their souls are together eternally. Their bodies lie here, side by side, together forever. Isn't that beautiful?" she asked, her brown eyes huge and full of love.

Julien's voice was soft and laden with tears when he held Angelica's hands and replied, "Yes, Chouchou, very beautiful. I can only pray for the same ending to my and Aurélie's story."

"Oh, but this isn't the ending," Angelica enthused. "There is no ending. Their story and your story are never-ending. Their love and your love are never-ending. Life is eternal. Love is eternal. There is no ending."

"Your faith is so marvelous, Angelica, so firm and strong. I can learn so much from you," Aurélie sobbed and dabbed her eyes.

"Read my father's tombstone," Angelica requested.

The four of them did. Aurélie recited the Bible verse aloud. "Incredible," she gasped.

"You are indeed your father's daughter," Julien smiled, hugged Angelica, and said a silent prayer of gratitude to Henri for this remarkable girl and for entrusting him with her.

They returned to St. Nicholas of Flüe Church on Sunday morning. The parishioners were stunned but delighted, and all of them greeted the teenaged princess. Some of them had last seen Angelica on the morning of Sunday, November 5, 1950. King Henri carried his baby daughter into morning worship every Sunday of her first nine months. He held her during the services.

Many people shared their memories with Angelica and the Lacoeurs. "You were such a quiet, well-behaved baby, so happy, too, always smiling and laughing. It was pure joy to watch you and your father together. King Henri clearly loved you, Princess Angelica," one woman, Heidi Rohr, told Angelica.

"Oh, yes, Princess Angelica. You were the sunshine of your father's life. Oh, it was so sad and tragic that Queen Stephanie died in childbirth. She and King Henri were so in love. But you, Princess, kept the sadness away. I stood outside the hospital when you were born, and I remember how King Henri smiled. I remember the joy in his eyes when he spoke to us the next day. Oh, he did love you very much. We all looked forward to watching you grow up into a fine, beautiful young lady. We never got to see you grow up. Fate prevented that. But you are such a beautiful, godly young lady," an elderly woman shared.

A man took Angelica's hand and kissed it. "God bless you, Princess Angelica. It is a miracle to see you here. So many of us feared what fate had befallen you that dreadful night. There was no trace of you. We prayed for you all of these fourteen years. Our prayers have been answered. Long may you live."

The most enchanting greeting came from someone who wasn't even alive during Henri's and Stephanie's lives. "Princess Angelica," someone said and tugged her dress hem. Angelica smiled broadly when she looked down and saw a young boy. "These are for you," he said and handed her a bouquet of wildflowers. Angelica thanked him and patted his head. "I learned about King Henri. I'm sorry your parents are dead. When my grandmother died, people said she went to Heaven, with God and the angels. My aunt said people who go to Heaven become angels. That means King Henri is an angel. He must be your guardian angel. He protected you when you were a baby so you could grow up. I'm very glad he did."

Many of those gathered near Angelica echoed the boy's last sentiment. They kissed or shook her hand before taking their seats in the pews. Julien put his arm around Angelica's shoulders, kissed the top of her head, and softly said, "So am I."

That afternoon, Mr. and Mrs. Warne arrived with King Henri's items for

Angelica. A porter brought the items on a luggage cart: boxes of papers, letters, documents, and photographs, and the rocking chair. Angelica thanked and hugged the Warnes. "Thank you, oh thank you. I shall read everything in the boxes. I have learned so much about my father, but I want to learn as much as I can. And seeing his handwriting and his thoughts will be extraordinary. And I will keep the chair in my room. I never dared dream I would own anything of his."

"We are so happy to do this for you. These belong with you," Mr. Warne said.

"So does this, dear. I found it while I was repacking the papers. I thought you would like it," Mrs. Warne told Angelica and handed her a gift box. "Open it."

Angelica gasped when she saw the gift. "Oh! I can't believe it! This is such a surprise! Thank you, Mrs. Warne." Angelica hugged the woman while she sobbed.

"Oh, you are most welcome, Angelica. It was a surprise to me when I found it among your father's papers. I just had to have it framed for you."

"This will look so sweet on the wall in my bedroom," Angelica smiled as she held up the frame. Julien and Aurélie saw it for the first time, and they, too, gasped in surprise. "My new bedroom has similar wallpaper. I know it's just wallpaper, but to me this is another sign that this was all meant to happen. It's like my life has come full circle, from the loving, happy time with my father and now with Daddy and Mom."

Angelica, the Lacoeurs, and Rogier had received an invitation to lunch with the Swiss Federal Council. Julien had accepted for Monday, August 10, 1964. The drive to the Federal Palace in Berne took seventy-five minutes, so the Lacoeur party set out at 9:00 that morning. Rogier drove, and four security officers accompanied them. Angelica stared out of the window for many minutes, observing the picturesque scenery and pondering recent events.

"Why does the Federal Council want to meet with me?" Angelica suddenly asked.

"There are several reasons, Chouchou. Foremost, your story is one of miracles. No one knew whether you were alive or dead for nearly fourteen years. Suddenly, you are back in your birth country. Second, you are the last Princess of Maldova, and a daughter of Switzerland as well as of two much-respected people. Third, you never sought public attention, but you have reacted to people with kindness and honesty. Your public comments are wise, intelligent, and thoughtful. Of course they want to meet you," Julien smiled.

"You're too kind. But I have not done anything exceptional to warrant any attention. I understand how much people still admire my parents. I also know that I am the only living person connected to them. That is why people are interested in me, and I understand that," Angelica said.

"That is true, but Julien is right. You have proved yourself calm, graceful, and gracious in the face of this sudden attention and interest. You are a princess by birth, and you are a princess by nature," Aurélie added.

Angelica shook her head, speechless by their comments, just as Rogier pulled up to the Federal Palace. Word of Angelica's visit had leaked, and a throng of people and photographers greeted her arrival. The security officers were on high alert, watching for any minutely suspicious signs. Rogier helped Ophelia and Aurélie from the car, and Julien assisted Angelica. As soon as she stepped from the car, people screamed and yelled her name.

Angelica waved at the crowd, which thrilled them. Many of them held bouquets toward her, and she asked Julien how much time they had. He told her they could spare ten minutes, so she went to the crowd and greeted as many people as she could. "Thank you for welcoming us to Berne. We are honored and humbled. I wish I could stay longer, but we have an appointment."

Angelica's arms were filled with bouquets, which Julien and Aurélie helped her put in the car trunk. Angelica turned and waved once more before they entered the Federal Palace.

Inside, they were welcomed by a staff member and escorted to an executive meeting room. The seven members of the Federal Council were already standing, waiting to receive Princess Angelica and her party. One at a time, the men bowed and introduced themselves to the Princess: Friedrich Traugott Walhlen; Willy Spühler; Paul Chaudet; Hans-Peter Tschuldi; Hans Schaffner; Jean Bourgkhecht; and the current President of Switzerland, Ludwig von Moos.

"Princess Angelica, on behalf of the citizens of the Swiss Federation, I and the members of the Federal Council are delighted to welcome you back to the country of your birth," President von Moos told Angelica.

"Thank you, Mr. President. I am honored to meet you and your esteemed Council members. I am very honored that you wished to meet me," Angelica said.

"Your Royal Highness, there is someone else who wishes to meet you," President von Moos announced as another gentleman entered the room. "May I present President Karl Kobelt."

"It is a pleasure to see you again, Princess Angelica. I visited your father and you at the hospital the day after you were born. You have grown into a beautiful, kind-hearted young lady," President Kobelt said as he clasped Angelica's hand.

"Thank you, President Kobelt. Thank you most of all for welcoming my parents to Switzerland when they had to leave Maldova. I now know that they chose to come here over anyplace else, and they were very happy here. Thank you for making that possible," Angelica responded.

"King Henri and Queen Stephanie were very good people, kind and compassionate, and their residence in Lucerne was a blessing to the people of Switzerland. If fate had but been different, King Henri would still be doing his humanitarian works, with you now alongside him."

"I know that, President Kobelt. But fate cannot be changed, and I have had to reconcile myself to everything that happened. I will carry on my father's humanitarian works, Sir. I want to help people as he did. And as my new father does," Angelica said and smiled up at Julien. "Your Excellency, I am delighted to introduce Monsieur Julien Lacoeur."

President Kobelt stared at Julien as the men shook hands. "Incredible," President Kobelt said. "I've seen pictures of you, and I thought you looked similar to King Henri. Seeing you in person, however, is like seeing King Henri all over again. You are his veritable doppelgänger, Monsieur Lacoeur. Forgive me. It is my extreme pleasure to meet you."

"Thank you, President Kobelt. I never realized myself how much I resemble King Henri. I suppose if I am to resemble anyone, there is no one more admirable," Julien replied.

"Yes, that is true," President Kobelt smiled. "May we convene to lunch?"

They went to the state dining room, where they enjoyed a meal of Zürcher Geschnetzrltes, rösti, zopf, and fondue, all national dishes. After lunch, they assembled in a sitting room for coffee and conversation.

"I remember your parents well, Princess Angelica. After they were forced to leave Maldova, King Henri and Queen Stephanie came here, to the Federal Palace. They wanted my approval before they made their permanent home here. King Henri feared repercussions toward the country in which he and Stephanie lived. He was quite concerned about Switzerland and the citizens of

Switzerland. That concern impressed me tremendously. I and the other Council members heartily welcomed King Henri and Queen Stephanie to Switzerland. This country considered them ours, citizens and active members of their community.

"Your birth was an extraordinary event, Princess Angelica. The Royal baby was exceedingly anticipated. There was excitement in the air when Queen Stephanie neared the end of her term. When she was admitted to the hospital, people began celebrating. It was a great celebration, indeed, when your birth was announced, quickly followed by grief when the news of Queen Stephanie's sudden death was soon thereafter announced. She was greatly admired and respected.

"As tragic as Queen Stephanie's death, what happened to King Henri just nine months later was most shocking and horrifying. I am not one prone to emotional reactions. I pride myself on my cool, level-headed nature. However, I had come to know King Henri well, and I considered him a friend. His murder sickened me. It saddened me. He was too kind and charitable for all he had to face and how he was treated by that FREE organization.

"Forgive me if my comments were too insensitive, but I have not discussed that day for a very long time. Sharing my memories with King Henri's and Queen Stephanie's daughter is, I admit, beyond any experience I ever dared imagine I would have. I never anticipated seeing you again, let alone discussing your parents with you," President Kobelt confessed as he looked at Angelica.

Angelica shook her head and smiled. "No forgiveness is necessary. Thank you so very much for telling me about my parents. You have been most kind and thoughtful, President Kobelt."

"You are so very like King Henri. Your kindness, of course, and your concern for others. And your eyes. I do not mean to stare at you, but I have not seen those brown eyes since late October 1950 when I had dinner at your father's home. You have the exact same eyes as did King Henri." President Kobelt looked at Julien. "So do you, Monsieur Lacoeur."

Angelica smiled up at Julien. "Yes, President Kobelt, my new Daddy looks like my father and has a similar character. I love them both, and I'm so fortunate to have them both in my life and in my heart," Angelica beamed.

On Wednesday morning, Rogier once again drove them to St. Nicholas of Flüe Church. They arrived early, as Angelica had told Julien and Aurélie that she wanted to help at the food kitchen that King Henri had established at the church.

"You all can go and do other things today. I can take the bus back to the hotel when I'm done," Angelica told them all.

"Nonsense, Chouchou. We want to stay and help. There is nothing else we want to do today," Julien assured her with his beautiful smile. Angelica kissed his cheek, and then hugged the others before they headed into the kitchen.

There, they helped to prepare the food before people entered at 8:00. They lined up to be served their plates of food. The first person in line was stunned when he looked at the person who handed him his plate. "Thank you, Princess Angelica.

I never expected to see you here. I am not surprised by it, but I am touched. Thank you."

"You are most welcome, Sir. I hope you enjoy your meal," Angelica said.

Each person at the food kitchen that day shared the sentiments: none were surprised that Angelica spent the day serving them. The food kitchen had been founded by her father, after all, and King Henri had served the food on several occasions. They each thanked Angelica before they left, many telling her they remembered her father well.

"I recall one day about two months after your birth, Princess Angelica. Your father was here that day, serving us just as you have done today. After we all got our plates of food, he sat and talked with us. He talked a lot about you, how beautiful and happy you were. He pulled his wallet from his back pocket and opened it. He showed us pictures of you that he had taken. He was so in love with you, Princess Angelica," one man told her as her eyes filled with tears.

Angelica leaned up and kissed the man's cheek. "Thank you. Thank you for telling me such a beautiful memory. I love my father so much."

Back at the hotel, Angelica wrote about the day in her journal, what it meant to her to continue her father's work. She also recorded everything the men and women who had come to the food kitchen had told her about her father. She treasured each and every recollection people told her. The more she learned about her father, the more she loved and respected him.

After she finished, she went to her parents' suite. Julien was sitting alone in a chair, his head leaned back and his eyes closed. Angelica tiptoed back toward the door, not wanting to disturb him. Just as her hand touched the doorknob, she was startled to hear Julien's soft-spoken, "Come here, Chouchou." When she didn't move, he said, "I was not asleep. I was thinking. Come here."

Angelica walked to him and stood beside the chair. Julien gently pulled her onto his lap and kissed her cheek. "I am so proud of you, Chouchou."

"Whatever for?"

"For being such a kind, thoughtful young lady. For putting other people's needs and feelings above your own. For being the daughter of my prayers. For being you," Julien smiled.

"Oh, Daddy, I love you." Angelica put her arms around him and laid her head on his shoulder. After a few minutes, she asked, "Where is everyone?"

"Oh, Rogier went out for a while. Grandmother is taking a nap before dinner, and Mom is relaxing in a hot bubble bath. It was a long day's work, but I feel wonderful for it. There is nothing else to compare to seeing gratitude and appreciation in people's eyes. Nothing."

"No, there isn't. I, too, feel all warm and peaceful inside. It felt important helping people today. I mean, what we did is important, not I. I can't imagine not helping people after today. No wonder Father did this and you do, too. Helping other people feels right," Angelic told him.

"Mm, yes, it does, ma petite. Helping others is the right thing to do, especially if one has the means to do so, physical, financial, or otherwise."

"Daddy, I've thought a lot about this over the past several weeks. I wanted to ask you if it would be all right if I help you with your foundation. It's what I want to do," Angelica said as she still leaned her head on his shoulder.

"Of course it is all right. It is more than all right. I am extremely happy, and my heart is so full that you want to work with me. You, my darling daughter, have just made a long-term dream of mine come true."

"I have?"

"Yes. I have dreamed since I started it that our child would want to continue the work of the foundation. At last, that dream has come true." Julien put his arms around Angelica and kissed the top of her head. "I love you, ma fille. I love you."

They all began packing after Saturday breakfast, for they were returning to Paris the next day. Angelica's telephone rang midmorning; Aurélie asked her to come to the Lacoeurs' suite. When Angelica entered, she was surprised to see Mrs. Warne there.

"Hello, Mrs. Warne. It's so nice to see you again before we leave."

"Hello, dear. After my husband and I brought the other artifacts to you, I seemed to remember something I hadn't seen or thought of in years. I searched through some of the boxes that are in storage before I remembered this piece wasn't there. I remembered that my husband put it in our bank safe deposit box, so I went there a couple of days ago to get it. I wanted to give this to you, Angelica. It belongs with you," Mrs. Warne explained. She handed a black velvet jewel box to Angelica.

Angelica opened the box and inhaled sharply. Inside was a gold engraved heart-shaped locket. She turned it over and read an inscription: *To my S with eternal love, Your H.* "My mother's locket. My father gave it to her." Tears pooled in the corners of her eyes. "Thank you, Mrs. Warne," Angelica choked and hugged the woman.

"Open it," Mrs. Warne whispered.

"Oh!" Angelica gasped at her first look at the two pictures inside the locket. "My father. She carried my father with her. This is the most beautiful and special locket ever. I will wear it every day of my life." Angelica looked up at Julien. "Will you fasten it around my neck, Daddy?"

Julien obliged with a smile, and Aurélie admired the locket. So did Ophelia, who then said, "It is beautiful, dearest girl. Now we three Lacoeur women each have our own very special heart lockets."

"Yes, we do, Mother. Oh, Angelica, this really is a most meaningful locket," Aurélie said as she hugged Angelica. "Julien gave Ophelia her locket when he was a child. You gave me my locket on Mother's Day. Your father gave this one to your mother. All three were given in love. What beautiful gifts we have."

"We do. Love is our greatest gift," Angelica said and hugged her small family.

After church the next morning, Angelica, the Lacoeurs, Rogier and the security officers walked to her parents' crypt. Angelica kept the key on a long gold chain she wore around her neck. She pulled the key from under her dress, unlocked the entrance, and went in. She bowed her head in prayer, and then she looked at her parents' tombs for several minutes.

"Mom. Father. I love you both so much, more than my words can ever let you know. I don't know when I shall return to Lucerne, but if God allows, I will visit you again. Someday, though, when my life on earth ends, I will be with you both in Heaven. You will also get to meet Mr. and Mrs. Lacoeur, who are my parents now. I know you will love them. They know how much I love you. They are the ones who brought me here to Lucerne. I am so incredibly blessed to have all four of you in my heart. Until we meet again, know that I do love you."

§§§§§

The remainder of the summer passed calmly. Julien and Aurélie had their interview with the judge in late August. The interview was exhaustive and lasted more than three hours. The judge requested an interview with Angelica, and it was scheduled for September 4, a Friday. Julien and Aurélie drove her to the courthouse, where Rogier met them.

"I'm going into Judge Moore's chambers with Angelica. I don't plan to say or to do anything. I'm just going in because Angelica is a minor. I will leave this young lady to her own answers to Judge Moore's questions, with no guidance or advice from me."

"I'm not worried. As long as I speak from my heart and I'm honest, everything will be fine," Angelica smiled.

"Yes, it will, Chouchou," Julien smiled. "Everything will be fine."

"Of course it will," Rogier agreed. "Judge Moore just needs to hear from Angelica how she feels about this and about the two of you. We know how she feels. She's said it often enough. There is absolutely nothing to worry about." Rogier looked at his watch. "We best go in, Angelica. We will come here after the interview," he told Julien and Aurélie.

As promised, Rogier sat silent during the interview. Angelica remained calm, polite, and well-spoken. She answered each of Judge Moore's questions honestly and thoughtfully. The first question was very easy for her to answer.

"Angelica, do you want to be adopted by Julien and Aurélie Lacoeur?"

"Yes, Your Honor, I do."

"Why?"

"Both of them are kind, giving, compassionate. I love them both more than mere words can tell you. They love me, too."

"How do you know they love you?"

"I feel it. I see it. Every day they tell me that they love me. More than that, though, is that everything they do proves their love. Before I was released from the hospital, they created a suite in their home just for me. They not only give me a home, and meals, and clothes, but so very much more.

"They teach me by example how to live a godly, benevolent, unselfish life. They have taught me by example how important it is to help other people. They have shown me what it truly means to give back, to share the blessings I have been granted.

"Daddy and Mom have taught me in six short months to be giving and compassionate. I will follow their example for the rest of my life, no matter how long or short it is. In fact, I have already told Daddy that I want to work with him in his Donner du Coeur Foundation. I want to make that my life's work. I will do so even if you do not approve the adoption, Your Honor.

"But I hope you do approve it, most of all because we already are a family. No piece of paper can ever change that."

When the interview ended, Angelica thanked Judge Moore and shook his hand. Rogier nodded to the judge and also shook his hand. When Rogier and Angelica left Judge Moore's chambers, Angelica hugged her parents. "I told him the truth, how much we love each other and how much you have both taught me. Now this is in God's hands. He knows our hearts. He will make this happen. I know he will."

§§§§

Julien arrived home after work on Thursday, October 8. He heard Aurélie in the kitchen, so he put down his briefcase and went into the kitchen. Aurélie was peeling potatoes at the sink. Julien put his arms around her and kissed her neck.

"What a wonderful greeting after a busy day," Aurélie said as she turned her head to smile at him.

"I missed you all day," Julien said and kissed her again. "Do you need some help?"

"No, mon cher. I find preparing dinner relaxing. I scooted Angelica away, too."

"Where is she?"

"She said she was going to read in her room," Aurélie answered.

"All right. I want to talk with her. I will be back down later," Julien promised. He kissed her yet again before he skipped up the stairs to the second floor.

Julien stood in Angelica's doorway watching her. She sat in her father's white rocking chair reading a book. He smiled as he watched her, so studious and focused—so much like himself. She paused in her reading to write notes in the margin of the page. Julien shook his head in pleasant wonder. He, too, annotated the books he read, and he had since childhood.

Angelica suddenly noticed Julien standing there, and she smiled up at him. "Good afternoon, Daddy. How was your day?"

"Good afternoon, Chouchou. Today was busy but productive." Julien moved her desk chair and sat facing her. "I want to talk with you about tomorrow."

"Tomorrow? I have my appointment with Dr. Sutfield."

"I know. I thought after that, you might want to accompany me. I plan to do some work after your appointment. Since Dr. Sutfield's office is in the hospital, it will be the perfect day to make my weekly visits to some of the patients that the foundation assists. I thought this would be the start of your work with me and the foundation," Julien explained.

"Really? Oh, Daddy, that will be just wonderful. Thank you for trusting me enough to ask me," Angelica enthused and leapt from her chair to hug him.

The next morning, Dr. Sutfield gave Angelica a thorough cardiac examination. The irregular heartbeat persisted, which he noted in her chart. He also gave her several tests, including an exercise electrocardiogram. "Simply walk on the treadmill until I tell you to stop or until you feel you cannot walk anymore. That's all there is to it, Angelica."

Dr. Sutfield kept close watch of the EKG, which showed the changes in Angelica's heart activity. Highs and lows were normal, but Dr. Sutfield became alarmed when the reading showed that her ST segment was longer than normal. Her heat essentially flat-lined for a long moment. At that instant, Angelica stopped and panted, "I can't."

Dr. Sutfield rushed to her and held her against him while he asked the nurse to place the oxygen mask over Angelica's nose and mouth. Dr. Sutfield helped Angelica to a bed, where he made her lay down for several minutes. When she said, "I'm okay now," he insisted on giving her another examination.

"Angelica, you cannot risk physical exertion. Your heart is not strong enough. Is that clear?"

"Yes, Dr. Sutfield. I promise."

"All right, dear. You get dressed, and Nurse Lynley will bring you into my office."

Dr. Sutfield asked Julien to come into the office, where he informed Julien of Angelica's condition and the necessity to avoid any exertion on her heart.

Julien clenched his fists in an effort to control his fear. "What can we do? Will this get better?"

"We can make sure that she obeys my orders. No exertion at all. No running, dancing, exercise at all. None. She has to realize the restrictions she must live under. You, Aurélie, and your mother, must understand. You must so that the three of you can help her."

Julien nodded. "I do. I will talk to Aurélie and Mother. They will understand. We will help Angelica. We all will. We have to. We have to."

"Good. Angelica's heart condition won't get better, but we can keep it from getting worse. That is our goal. Keep in mind that it has not been one year since the shooting and the surgery, so she is still recovering from those traumas and the shocks her body received," Dr. Sutfield told Julien. "I want to see her again in two months, on December 9."

"All right. So we take care of her and we wait."

"Yes, we do," Dr. Sutfield said just as Nurse Lynley knocked on the door.

Angelica entered and smiled when she saw Julien. "You're still taking me with you today, aren't you, Daddy? That hasn't changed, has it?"

"Of course not, Chouchou. Since I rotate the hospitals I visit each week, it has been a couple of weeks since I have been here. The patients will get a treat today—a pretty girl, not this old mug."

Angelica giggled. "You aren't old, Daddy. And you make people happy and feel better. Your smile is wonderful medicine. Trust me. Just seeing you has made me feel just perfect," Angelica smiled.

"That is mutual. The only antidote is for us to spend as much time as possible together. Papa et fille, ensemble toujours. Oui?"

"Oui," Angelica answered and hugged him. "Are we ready? To visit the patients?"

"Yes, we are. Thank you, Dr. Sutfield. Thank you." Julien shook the doctor's hand and left holding Angelica's hand. As they walked, Julien prepared Angelica for the rest of the day. "Chouchou, do you know exactly the work that Donner du Coeur does?"

"Yes. You help people who are very sick with their medical bills."

"That is true, Angelica. But the foundation helps certain people whose conditions are very serious."

"I know, Daddy. You help people who are terminal, people who are dying," Angelica stated as they continued walking. "I think what you do is so brave, so kind, and so loving. It takes a strong person to do this work. I want to be as strong as you. I want to do the work that you do. Today is my first day on the job. Let's go. We've spent enough time already."

Julien smiled, amazed at his little girl and the inner strength she already possessed. Julien thought as they took the elevator to the geriatric floor. There were so many meaningful activities that Angelica could do without overworking her heart: drawing, composing music, meeting patients, and helping him. If she kept busy with those accomplishments, there would be less risk to her.

Julien stopped when they left the elevator. "Chouchou, we will visit Monsieur Pierre Fortner. He has been a patient here before, but his condition became worse, so he returned a few weeks ago. He is rather lonely, a widower with one grown daughter. She works, but visits him at least once each week."

"That is so sad. Let's cheer him up," Angelica said. "Which room is he is his?"

"Up ahead, the second on the left," Julien explained, surprised that Angelica marched into the room on her own. A doctor stopped Julien at that precise moment, so by the time he got to Mr. Fortner's room, introductions proved unnecessary. Angelica and the gentleman were laughing, a sound which pleasantly surprised him. Typically, Mr. Fortner had been rather apathetic during Julien's prior visits. Angelica had brought joy and laughter into his life in mere minutes. Yes, these visits would benefit both her and the patients.

"Am I interrupting?" Julien asked good-naturedly from the doorway.

"Not at all, Sir, not at all. Are you responsible for this little lady?"

"I must admit that I am. I see she has charmed you, too, Mr. Fortner."

"She has indeed. You must bring her every time you visit. Such a pretty, engaging young lady is better than any medicine or treatment the doctors can give me. In just a few minutes, I feel better than I have in many months."

"I haven't done anything," Angelica countered, a look of perplexity clouding her face.

"She did something quite special. She came in with a smile, greeted me by name, and kissed my cheek. I cannot tell you the last time a girl kissed me," Mr. Fortner told Julien. "Most people avoid me. I'm old and sick. No one wants to bother."

"Nonsense," Angelica said, pulled the chair closer to the bed, and sat facing the man. "I want to talk with you, get to know you, learn from you. I want to visit you as much as I can."

Julien smiled as Angelica asked Mr. Fortner about his interests, hobbies likes, and dislikes. Angelica practically jumped in joy when he said he enjoyed poetry. "So do I, Mr. Fortner. I can bring a book of poetry the next time I visit and read to you. If you don't mind."

"Mind? Why would I mind? You come any time you want to. You can read the telephone directory for all I care. I just want your company, Angelica."

"I promise, Mr. Fortner. Daddy and I will come as often as we can," Angelica promised and kissed his cheek before she and Julien left his room. They visited three more patients in the ward before Julien suggested they go to the pediatric ward.

"Angelica, darling, are you sure you want to do this today? Some of the children are very sick. Some of them are very weak. One little boy, Sam, is connected to machines. He cannot talk. These visits are difficult, sweetheart. You do not have to go with me."

"I want to, Daddy. I know how hard this is. Illness and death are difficult. But that means these visits are even more important. Like Mr. Fortner said, many people avoid him because he is sick. That is not right. Everyone deserves love and attention. Everyone."

Julien put his arm around her and said, "I am so proud of you, my little girl. I love you more each day."

"Your love is one of the strongest inspirations I have." Julien looked down at her, his brow furrowed. "You love me. So does Mom. You both stayed with me when I was in the hospital. Without you, I would have been alone. Not all patients have someone to be with them. But even if they do, visits from other people who care will help them. You do this because you care and you love people. Your love is the strongest force in my life, Daddy."

Julien stopped walking, put his hands on his hips, and bowed his head. Angelica watched him, concerned for a moment—until Julien suddenly turned toward her and lifted her into an embrace. "You are my prayer come true, ma petite. Je t'aime, my Angelica. I love you." Julien kissed her cheek and gently stood her on the floor. "Let us go visit some children."

"We are an awesome team, Daddy," Angelica smiled up at him as they neared a private room.

"Yes, we are, Chouchou. This is Nicky Schumer. He is seven years old and he has leukemia," Julien explained as he knocked on the door.

A nurse opened the door, and when she said, "Good day, Mr. Lacoeur," Nicky shrieked with delight.

"Goody! Julien! You came!"

Julien beamed from the doorway and said, "Of course I came, Nicky. I promised I would. I have a surprise for you today," he winked and pulled Angelica next to him. "My daughter Angelica wanted to come with me today."

"You never told me you have a daughter. How come? You've been coming to visit me for over a year," Nicky pouted. Angelica noticed that he looked sad, as if he were upset that Julien hadn't been honest with him. She quickly walked to Nicky's bedside.

"Nicky, he couldn't have told you one year ago, because I wasn't his daughter then." When Nicky asked how that was possible, Angelica explained the adoption. "So we will be a family legally once the judge finalizes the adoption. We already are a family in all of the ways that matter most, Nicky."

"Wow. That's really neat. I've never known anyone who's adopted. But I thought most people adopt babies. What made you choose Angelica?" Nicky asked Julien.

Julien told Nicky about his and Aurélie's prayers for a child, how they had asked God to bring the child into their lives, and how they had met Angelica that very afternoon. "So, you see, Nicky, Angelica, Aurélie, and I are meant to be a family. Angelica is the answer to our prayer." Julien smiled at Angelica and added, "Besides, I fell in love with her the moment we met."

"And I with you," Angelica whispered. "The only thing I want for Christmas is for the adoption to be final."

"Well, today is October 9. How many days until Christmas?" Nicky asked.

"Hmm, let me think," Julien answered as he calculated the number in his head. "There are seventy-six days until Christmas Day."

"That's a lot of days. Maybe it will happen by then. I hope so, Julien. I want you to be happy," Nicky said and hugged his friend.

"You are very kind, Nicky, my boy. I am happy, but yes, knowing that we are legally a family will be the best Christmas gift of all."

Several minutes later, Julien and Angelica left Nicky's room and spent the next two hours visiting quite a few other patients. Finally, Julien told her, "We have time for one more visit. I think you will really like Thomas. He is seventeen, and he likes music," Julien smiled. So did Angelica, although her smile disappeared when they entered his room. He wasn't there.

Julien and Angelica asked at the nurse's station where Thomas was—tests, perhaps? "Oh, no, Thomas is in his favorite place, the music room. Go on in, Mr. Lacoeur."

"The hospital has a music room? I never knew about it when I was here," Angelica stated.

"You will make up for it now that you will know Thomas. He comes here often," Julien explained as he held the door open for her.

Angelica stood still and quiet, listening to Thomas' violin music. When he finished, she gushed, "That was superb. Chopin never sounded so sonorous yet gentle."

Thomas quickly stood, startled, and turned to see who had spoken. A beautiful girl with large brown eyes, pink lips, and dewy skin smiled up at him. He suddenly couldn't speak.

Julien fought his smile and introduced Angelica and Thomas. Angelica walked to him and extended her right hand. "Hello, Thomas. You play beautifully."

His fingers tangled in the violin strings, and he awkwardly managed to free himself before finally taking her hand. "Thank you, Angelica."

The silence resonated as Julien and Angelica allowed time for Thomas to say more. Finally, Julien cleared his throat and said, "Angelica plays the piano."

"She does?" Thomas shook his head and then looked at Angelica. "You do? How magnificent. Please play something."

Angelica looked up at Julien, unsure how to respond. He gently nudged her and softly said, "Go ahead. It is all right."

"I'm not prepared for this," she said as she went to the piano. She looked at Julien for confirmation, and he nodded. Angelica took a deep breath and began playing a piece she had composed a few years before.

Thomas slowly walked close to the piano, all the while listening intently. Without warning, without missing one note, Thomas accompanied Angelica. Julien watched and listened, stunned at how Thomas instantly and intuitively blended with Angelica, especially since Julien knew that it was an original composition that Thomas could never have heard before.

When the piece ended, Angelica, Thomas, and Julien were surprised to hear applause and cheers. Other patients and some staff had heard the music and been drawn into the music room. Several of the patients gathered around Thomas, all talking at once, voicing their appreciation and admiration.

"I've never heard you play like that before," one young boy said.

"I've never played with someone who is so inspiring," Thomas admitted and then smiled at Angelica.

Some of the patients had met Angelica earlier, and they were delighted to see her again. They pleaded with Angelica and Thomas to play another piece, so after a nurse said there was time for one more song, they relented. They decided to play a portion of Mozart's *Moonlight Sonata*. Afterward, Angelica hugged each patient before they had to leave for dinner. She promised to visit again soon with her father.

"This was really nice, Angelica. It's been a long time since I've had someone to perform with. A lot of the other patients try, and I know they have fun, but it isn't the same as playing with a real musician. I do hope we can do this again," Thomas said to Angelica as the three of them walked to Thomas' hospital room.

"I'd like that, even though I'm not a real musician," Angelica responded with a giggle.

"You had me fooled," Thomas instantly replied.

"One of the first things that I realized about my daughter is how incredibly talented she is. She composes most of the music she plays. That piece back there, for example. She composed that years ago," Julien informed Thomas with paternal pride.

"I wondered about that since I had never heard it before. I'd love to hear more of your compositions, Angelica. Maybe, just maybe, you could spend a few hours here, you know, so we can play music. Since I can't come to your home, this is the only place we can see each other," Thomas suggested, his eyes pleading with Angelica.

"Sure, I can do that. Can't I, Daddy?"

"Of course, you may. I can bring you on my way to work, and Grandmother can pick you up. But for now, Thomas has to eat dinner, take his medicine, and rest. It has been a pleasure," Julien smiled and shook Thomas' hand.

"Yes, it has. I look forward to your next visit. And yours, too, of course, Angelica," Thomas smiled at her.

"Thank you. So do I."

As Julien and Angelica walked to the elevator, he smiled and said, "I knew you and Thomas would like each other."

"He is nice. And it is so wonderful to know someone who plays music," Angelica said. A moment later, she asked, "Daddy, what is wrong with Thomas?"

Julien sighed, having anticipated her question but dreading it nevertheless. "Thomas is a sick boy, Chouchou, very sick. He was diagnosed with lupus several years ago. That led to kidney failure, so he needs a kidney transplant. He receives dialysis three times each week."

"He will get a kidney, won't he?"

"We hope so. He has been on the registry for more than fourteen months," Julien answered as they got in his car.

"He has to, Daddy. He has to. He can't die, not now, not before he has a chance to live the life that's meant for him."

Julien awoke suddenly in the middle of that night. He lay very still, listening for what he had heard in his sleep. He heard faint sobs. Angelica. He quickly stood up, put on his robe, and walked across the hall. By the light of the moon, he saw Angelica sitting on the floor before her window seat, her head resting on the cushion as she cried.

Julien sat beside her and softly asked, "Ma chère, what is wrong? Why are you crying?" When she kept crying and never answered, he knew. "Today? The hospital visits?"

Angelica nodded, and Julien gently raised her against him. "Oh, Daddy, why? Why do people get sick, suffer, and die? Why?"

"I cannot answer that except to say we each face trials and tribulations. For many people, that is illness. It is never easy to share or to watch. I know that. I knew today would be too much for you, Chouchou. I should not have asked you to do this. I am so sorry, my sweetheart."

Angelica shook her head. "No. Don't be sorry. I'm glad I went."

"But it upset you. I feared this."

"I'm not upset, really I'm not. I'm very sad, because everyone I met is so kind, sweet, and friendly. They are so wonderful. And they are dying. It's not fair. It doesn't seem right."

"I know, sweetheart. I know," Julien whispered and patted her back.

"How do you deal with all of the pain, Daddy? How do you stay so strong?" she asked as she looked up at him, her large brown eyes filled with tears.

Julien took a deep breath and looked out of the window. "I have to. I have to keep it inside so that the patients and their families do not get upset or fearful. I have to for them." Julien looked down into her eyes. "There are times when I go to the library upstairs, alone at night, and cry. I get angry. I let it out. That is healthy. It helps me to stay strong. So you cry as often as you need to, my darling. There is nothing wrong in that. Capiche?"

Angelica nodded and hugged Julien. "Thank you, Daddy. Thank you."

§§§§§

Angelica spent two days each week at the hospital over the next three weeks. She read poetry to Mr. Fortner and asked him to tell her about his life. His doctors remarked on his improved outlook, which in turn helped stabilize his condition. Nicky received a lot of Angelica's attention, as well, which pleased him. The two of them played board games and drew pictures, and when Nicky was tired, Angelica held his hand while he slept.

Angelica's visits with Thomas were truly enjoyable, for they spent most of their time in the music room. Aside from playing music together, the two spent considerable time talking. Thomas confided in Angelica his greatest fear.

"I know that I will die if I don't get a kidney transplant soon. I don't want to die. I don't. But what I'm most afraid of is what this will do to my parents. They try to hide it from me, but I can see it. I know how scared they are. My mother especially. I hate what this has done to them. I wish I could take it away, Angelica."

"I know, Thomas," Angelica softly said. "It's the pain it causes others that makes illness even more unbearable. I pray for you every night, Thomas. I pray that you get a kidney and become healthy."

"If friendship and love count for anything, I will," Thomas said and looked into her eyes. "I don't mean to sound egotistical, but I feel loved and supported, Angelica. I mean, I know my parents love me, and my aunts, uncles, cousins, and grandparents, too. But then your father came into my life, and he cares. I know he does. And now you. Love does so much. I know that sounds sappy, but it's true. You know that."

"I do, Thomas." She told him how Julien and Aurélie had stayed beside her after the shooting, how the three of them had bonded and fallen in love, and how they were a family. "So, yes, I know what love does for someone whose situation seems dire and hopeless. Love is the greatest gift I've ever been given, Thomas."

"I don't know what to say. I had no idea you had been through so much, Angelica. You came so close to death. Were—were you scared?"

"No. I thought I would die soon after I was shot. I felt my strength go. I felt weak. It was so hard to breathe. But there was nothing I could do. I just accepted it. I just remember thinking that I would die. There was no panic or fear. Just resignation," Angelica admitted.

"Mr. Lacoeur was somehow beside me, though, and as he looked at me and tried to stop the bleeding, I felt it, Thomas. I felt love. I felt so sad. I finally found love, and yet I was dying. But Mr. Lacoeur went in the ambulance with me, and he was beside me when I opened my eyes after surgery. Love. His love gave me the will to live. I can't explain that, but it's true, Thomas. Love saved me."

"I believe you, Angelica."

"Love will save you, too, Thomas. I know it will. I know it in my heart."

Thomas held her hands and said, "I believe you, Angelica. I believe you."

ʃʃʃʃ

On the first Sunday afternoon of November, Angelica helped Aurélie clean up after lunch. "Mom, may I use the kitchen this afternoon?"

"Of course, darling. You want to make something?"

"Yes, I do. Something very special."

"Why not check that we have everything you need? If there is anything you need, I can go into town for it," Aurélie said. Angelica smiled and looked in the pantry and refrigerator. She informed Aurélie that they had all she needed. "All right. I am going to the sunroom with Daddy for a while. Call for me if you need any help."

A couple of hours later, Julien entered the kitchen just as Angelica removed a pan from the oven and turned it upside down on a rack. He smiled when he saw two pans, and he had an inkling what she was making. As she began measuring ingredients into a mixing bowl, he got a bottle of carbonated water from the refrigerator, and then kissed the top of her head before he left.

Two hours later, her confection was completed and encased in a covered plate. She washed and put away the dishes, pans, and utensils. Angelica likewise returned all of the containers to the pantry or the refrigerator. Then she went to the third floor and informed her parents that she was done. Aurélie smiled up at her and patted the seat next to her. "Join us. It is so relaxing to just watch the birds and the breeze."

"And just being together," Julien added.

Aurélie sighed contentedly and snuggled closer to Julien, while Angelica sat beside Aurélie. Angelica reached over and gently held Aurélie's hand. Aurélie squeezed Julien and then put her arm around Angelica and pulled her close. Julien kissed his wife's head, and smiled in contentment. His life was, at that moment, all he had prayed it would be.

§§§§

The next morning, Ophelia arrived as the family ate breakfast. She got a cup of coffee and joined them. Julien kissed his mother's cheek, wished her a happy birthday, kissed Angelica, and then walked to the driveway with Aurélie. Angelica excused herself and followed her parents.

"Daddy, Mom, what time will you both be home today?"

"Around 5:30, I suppose," Aurélie replied.

"I should be back at the same time, ma petite," Julien said with a smile.

"That's perfect," Angelica enthused. "We will have a wonderful evening," she said, kissed them, and returned to the kitchen to help Ophelia clean up.

"What was that all about? What has Angelica got planned?" Aurélie asked.

"A birthday party," Julien grinned.

"Of course! The baking yesterday. She is planning a surprise party for Mother. Well, we best not be late this afternoon, darling. Aurélie and Julien kissed before they got in their respective cars and drove to their offices.

Angelica and Ophelia went for a walk after they washed and put away the breakfast dishes. As they strolled at a leisurely pace, followed by an ever-present security officer—who always remained alert but discreet—Ophelia became reflective. "You are so very young, my dear, but so very wise, wiser than most adults I have known. It may seem odd for an elderly woman to share these thoughts and feelings with a child, but you above all people will understand."

"You aren't elderly, Grandmother."

Ophelia smiled and patted Angelica's arm. "Yes, I am, darling. I am 68 years old. I have been alive nearly seven decades. I have seen a lot of changes, not all for the better. I have had quite a lot of happiness. And heartbreak. My childhood was very pleasant. My marriage. My son. Julien's marriage. My husband's illness and death. Aurélie's numerous miscarriages and her stillbirth. Each time she became pregnant, we three fell in love with the baby and looked so forward to the life we would share. But each time, that was dashed. Our hearts were broken so many times.

"To tell you the truth, I had given up all hope of ever having a grandchild. I would see my friends and so many other women with their grandchildren, and it would hurt dreadfully. So very much. It was hard to be happy for other people when I was brokenhearted. I've never told that to anyone before, Angelica. I am ashamed to tell you, to admit my resentment. It is so wrong to resent others' good fortune."

Angelica remained thoughtfully silent for a few minutes. Finally she responded, "When it is part of the grieving process, it is not wrong."

"Grieving process? I had never actually thought of what the three of us went through as grief. I am not sure why I never did actually. We were grieving.

The babies. . . . The babies died. I have never said that before, Angelica. I never thought of them dying. They were never born. That is how I thought of them. Never born. Not dead. But they did die. I never faced that truth before," Ophelia said and wiped a tear from her cheek.

Angelica put her arms around Ophelia and sobbed. "Oh, Grand-mère, I am so sorry, so very sorry. I wish I could undo it all, I do. I wish none of it had happened. I wish you, Daddy, and Mom did not hurt so much. I hate that you and they hurt."

Ophelia hugged Angelica close, her eyes clenched tightly to staunch her tears. "Yours is such a sensitive and compassionate soul, my little one. But as brutally painful as each loss, I have to believe that there is a reason why those children were not born. Maybe they were already ill with some condition. I can't know that, and I suppose the reasons do not really matter.

"But as Julien and Aurélie have said, everything that happened led them to you. The three of you were brought together because they had gone to that church to pray to God for a child. They even talked about adoption before they left the church. Then they found the café, met you, and here we are. So, you see, Angelica, changing what did happen would also change the present. None of us wants that, do we?"

Angelica looked up at her grandmother, shook her head, and said, "No. Never. I love you, Daddy, and Mom. You are my family."

Angelica set up the party in the music room while Ophelia helped Aurélie with dinner. Julien watched Angelica quietly from the entry and smiled. One year earlier, he, Aurélie, and Ophelia had celebrated—just the three members of their small family. Oh, there were distant cousins elsewhere in Europe, but Julien had met only a few of them when he was a child. For all intents and purposes, his family consisted of four members: himself, Aurélie, Ophelia, and Angelica. Dear God, he prayed silently, let her remain with us. Let her be our daughter legally. That is all I want.

"Hello, mate. I came to wish your mother a happy birthday," Rogier suddenly greeted Julien. "You look very pensive. What about?"

"Bonjour, Rogier. I was just watching Angelica arrange Mother's surprise party and found myself praying." Julien walked to a window and stared out, his fists in his pants pockets. "About the adoption. It has to be finalized. It has to. She is ours, more than I know how to say."

Rogier put a hand on his friend's shoulder. "The adoption will be finalized. Judge Moore has a trial in session for the next week, and once this trial is over, Judge Moore will get back to his cases. I was told that if Judge Moore were going to deny the adoption, he would have done so already. Relax. Everything will be fine."

"Thank you, Rogier."

Aurélie summoned everyone to dinner, after which Angelica smiled, took Ophelia's arm, and walked with her to the music room. Aurélie and Julien smiled at one another and beckoned Rogier to follow.

When she saw the cake, presents, and flowers on the table, Ophelia began crying and collapsed onto a chair. Angelica appeared horrified and on the verge of tears herself.

Julien looked from his mother to his daughter. Knowing the reason for his mother's tears, he pulled Angelica to him. "No, no, ma petite. There is no need to be upset. Grand-mère is overcome with happiness. She is not sad or upset. I promise."

"She's not?"

"No, my daring, I am not," Ophelia assured as she sat up straight and dried her eyes. "Come," she said and held her arms outstretched. Angelica went to her, and Ophelia held her close. "My dear petite-fille, you are the most precious, thoughtful, kind grandchild I could have hoped to have. Today has been a most marvelous birthday. This beautiful surprise party. Our walk and talk this morning filled my soul with peace. I pray we have decades of such talks awaiting us. I love you, Angelica."

§§§§§

Five weeks later, on Monday December 9, Dr. Sutfield examined Angelica's heart. As she dressed, he talked with Julien in his office. "Well, Angelica has surprised me. She is getting stronger." He noticed Julien's hopeful expression. "This does not mean the restrictions are lifted, however. Her heart is getting stronger because she is prudent, takes the Amiodarone, and because her body is healing, truly healing. She must remain cautious in what she does. For the rest of her life, most likely. If she is, there is no reason she cannot have a normal life."

Julien exhaled and smiled. "That is the answer to our prayers, Dr. Sutfield. Thank you."

At that moment, Angelica asked if she could come in. "Of course," Dr. Sutfield exclaimed.

Angelica looked at Julien, saw his wide smile, and beamed at Dr. Sutfield. "You told him."

"Yes, darling, I did. Just remember what I told you. This is not license to overdo things. The best way to maintain this improvement is to keep the physical limitations in place."

"I will, Dr. Sutfield, I promise." Angelica turned to face Julien. "May I visit Thomas for a while, Daddy?"

Julien stood and answered, "I do not see why not. I will pick you up on my way home." He thanked Dr. Sutfield and headed for Thomas' room. "I want to say hello to him before I leave."

A nurse smiled when she saw them and told them that Thomas was in the music room. Angelica smiled up at Julien, grabbed his hand, and walked quickly to the music room.

Thomas was alone, sitting on the piano bench. Angelica stood still, watching him. Thomas kept running his index finger back and forth slowly along the piano's sidearm. His back was to her, but Angelica could tell that he was unhappy.

"Thomas?" she softly asked.

He looked up and gave her a small smile in response. She asked what was wrong, and he admitted, "I'm tired of being here. My life is on hold, at a standstill, and I want to live. I'm just feeling sorry for myself. I'm sorry."

Angelica went to him and sat beside him. "No, Thomas, don't apologize. I understand. I was in the hospital for only a few weeks, but I, too, felt that life had stopped. I know what I went through is nothing compared to your situation, but it does help me to understand what you feel."

Thomas turned, looked at her, and took her hand between both of his. "I know you do, Angelica. You understand all of my thoughts and feelings as no one else does."

Julien inwardly smiled, but cleared his throat. He had no qualms about their friendship, but Angelica was far too young for romance. Thomas looked at Julien, who stated, "Thomas, I have every faith that you will be home for the new year."

"But it's already December," Thomas lamented. "I want to believe you, Julien, I do, but I can't. I've tried to remain positive, but it gets harder every day."

"I know, Thomas. But faith means believing, no matter what happens," Julien explained. "Aurélie and I could have long ago lost all hope of ever having our child. And then we walked into Angelica's life, and we found our child. God does not operate on our timetable. He does what is best for us when he decides the time is right. Do not lose hope, Thomas. Do not give way to fear and doubt. You are strong. Stay strong, physically, mentally, and spiritually."

Thomas sat silent for a few moments as he pondered and considered all the truth in Julien's words. Finally, he smiled at Julien and hugged him. "You are right, Julien. I need to think positively. Thank you."

"Good man," Julien said as he gently squeezed Thomas' shoulder. "I will see you later when I come for ma petite," he promised. He stood, kissed Angelica, and added, "Just do not overtax yourselves, either of you."

"We won't, Daddy. I love you."

Soon, the two teenagers were alone. "I just want to play music. I feel that I was born to do that. I have to play music. I have to. Music is the one thing that makes me feel whole and happy. I could never live, truly live, without my music, Angelica."

"I know, Thomas," Angelica whispered. "Your passion for music comes through when you play. You are like an actor. You bring life to the emotions in a piece. You make people connect to the piece, you help them feel it and understand it. You will have your music all of your life, Thomas. People will listen to your music. They will enjoy it, but more than that, they will fall in love with it."

Thomas looked into her large brown eyes. They were so sincere and earnest. He felt his heart pound strongly against his sternum. He felt his body tremble and begin to sweat. He had never felt that way, and he had to wonder what was wrong with him. Angelica noticed and looked at him in concern. She leaned forward, put her hands on his arms, and, in a voice tinged with worry, asked, "What is it, Thomas? What's wrong?"

As Thomas struggled to regain his composure, he suddenly realized what was wrong. He could not let Angelica know, not yet. She was only fourteen years old. He somehow had to hide his love from her for the next few years. He could not dare to jeopardize their friendship.

"I'm all right, Angelica. I was just thinking about everything. I do hope you are right. I hope I have a long life filled with my music and everything else important to me. I don't want to die before I have a chance to do all I long to do."

Once more, Angelica grasped his arms. "Oh, Thomas, that is my prayer, too. I want your life to be long and happy."

"Thank you, Angelica," Thomas muttered through the lump in his throat. He swallowed hard and suggested, "Let's make some music." Angelica smiled, turned to face the piano, and Thomas stood and picked up the violin and bow. They played several pieces over the next ninety minutes, lost in their emotions.

Both of them were suddenly startled when a man called Thomas' name. "Dr. Corland," Thomas said, surprise in his voice and on his face. "Is anything wrong?"

"No, Thomas, nothing is wrong. We have to prep you for surgery. Your kidney is on its way here by helicopter."

"My kidney?"

"Oh, Thomas!" Angelica gleefully exclaimed. She grabbed him in a hug and held him tight. "Oh, Thomas, this is the answer to our prayers."

"I-I know. But I'm scared, Angelica."

"I know. But the doctors will take the best care of you, and I will pray for you. Now go. Go get healthy," she gently commanded and kissed his cheek. He nodded, kissed her cheek, and left with Dr. Corland.

Angelica bowed her head for several minutes. The quiet in the room was deafening, which only elevated her excitement and fear. She was thrilled that Thomas would become healthy, but she also knew the risks of the surgery. She began walking slowly around the perimeter of the large room. She had to move. Moving would at least make the time feel as if it were passing quicker.

More than one hour later, two young patients entered the room. "Hi, Angelica," one of them called. "Where's Thomas? I wanted to show him the comic book my father brought me."

"Hello Wally. Thomas probably won't be able to look at your comic book for a day or two. He is in surgery right now."

"Surgery? For what?"

"He got a kidney!" the other boy shrieked.

Angelica smiled. "Yes, he did, Kevin." When the boys asked when they could see Thomas, Angelica explained, "I don't know exactly, but probably not for a couple of days." She glanced at her watch. "The surgery will last another two or three hours. After that, Thomas will be in recovery for a few hours. His parents will get to see him, but he won't have visitors at least until tomorrow afternoon I would think."

"Is it a very serious surgery?" Wally asked.

Angelica knelt in front of the little boy and touched his cheek. "Yes, it is. But Dr. Corland is the top kidney transplant surgeon in Paris, and Thomas has the best care. He will be fine. We must believe that, Wally and Kevin. Someday we will see Thomas on a concert stage," she enthused.

"That will be wonderful, Angelica," Kevin replied. "We're going to tell our friends about Thomas. They will be so happy," he said and hugged her.

"Yeah, happy," Wally agreed and also hugged Angelica—and kissed her cheek—before the boys left with the exciting news.

Angelica was alone again in the quiet room. She wasn't in the mood for casual conversation, though, so she actually preferred the solitude. To fill the time, she sat at the piano and played, losing all sense of time. She heard footsteps as someone entered the room, and she nearly jumped from the piano bench.

"Daddy, it's you."

Julien's brow was furrowed when he asked, "Who were you expecting? Thomas?" She shook her head, and tears filled her eyes. "Angelica? Where is Thomas?"

"Surgery."

"Surgery? What happened?" Before she could tell him, Julien understood. "His kidney transplant?"

"Yes, Daddy. It's been almost three hours. I've been praying ever since Dr. Corland came and got Thomas. This is what we all hoped for, but I can't help worrying," she cried.

Julien wrapped his arms around her, held her close, and kissed the top of her head. "I know, Chouchou. I know. We do worry about family and friends." Julien looked at his watch. 4:00. "Speaking about worrying about people I love, have you been in this room all day?" Angelica nodded. "You have not eaten lunch, and it is getting late in the afternoon. Come."

"Where?" Angelica asked as Julien picked up her coat and began leading her from the room.

"To a private waiting room." Julien told the nurses at the desk that he and his daughter would be in the waiting room and asked that they be informed as soon as there were updates on Thomas. Julien helped Angelica settle comfortably on the sofa, covered her with her coat, and kissed her forehead. "I am going to the cafeteria to get us some food. Rest here until I return."

Angelica leaned her head back, stared at the ceiling, and silently prayed until Julien returned with a tray of food. Angelica slowly nibbled her sandwich, oblivious to the taste. She obediently ate it all, though, so that Julien would not worry about her when Thomas was the one who needed prayer and concern. She glanced at her watch. 4:42. Nearly four hours. When would they get any news about Thomas?

One tap on the door caused Angelica to jump and grab Julien's hand. A nurse entered and announced that Thomas was now in recovery. "He is still under anesthesia, but the surgery was a success."

"When will they know if the transplant is a success?" Julien asked.

"I can't say much, but the donor is an exact match to Thomas," the nurse replied. "Mr. and Mrs. Bertrand are with their son in recovery, and Dr. Corland is there, too, constantly monitoring Thomas. In fact, he will be awakened from anesthesia soon. He will probably stay in recovery for another hour or so before he is moved to his private room."

"Thank you," Julien told her. "This is the best news."

After the nurse left, Angelica looked concerned. "How can the kidney be an exact match, Daddy? I was told that only a blood relative would be an exact match."

"I am not sure, Chouchou. We may never find out, though. Donors are often kept confidential." Julien put his hand on her shoulder and gently squeezed it to reassure her. "The important thing is that Thomas will be well."

"I know, Daddy. But I can't get rid of the sick feeling I have." Julien looked at her quizzically, and she answered his unasked question. "About the donor. If only a close relative can be an exact match, then the donor must be related to Thomas. That means. . .that means. . . . . And he does not know yet. Oh, Daddy," Angelica moaned as she began crying.

Julien pulled her close to him, holding her while she cried. After several minutes, there was a knock on the door, and Julien told whoever it was to enter. He quickly stood when he saw who it was.

Angelica looked up and her sobs became more frantic.

"Mr. and Mrs. Bertrand," Julien greeted Thomas' parents and went to hug them.

"Julien," Mrs. Bertrand said as she hugged and kissed him. "This would not have happened without you, Julien. You kept our son alive so that he could have this transplant and have a full life. Thank you," she wept.

Julien shook his head. "I did nothing. The doctors are the ones who brought Thomas' lupus into remission through their treatments. Dr. Corland performed the transplant. I simply became Thomas' friend. And that is my pleasure."

"Julien, no," Mr. Bertrand interjected. "None of this could have happened without you. You, your foundation, made this possible. Despite everything, this is a blessing. Thank you, Julien." Mr. Bertrand's tears fell down his cheeks as his feelings overwhelmed him. Julien put his arms around the man's shoulders and supported him, both physically and emotionally.

"I'm so sorry."

"Angelica?" Mr. Bertrand asked, his confusion over her condolence snapping him out of his tears. He looked at Julien in concern, and Julien immediately went to her.

"Chouchou," Julien cooed as he sat beside her and put his arms around her.

"I'm sorry," Angelica muttered while she cried. "I don't mean to upset anyone." She looked up at Thomas' parents. "I am sorry."

"For what, dear? Thomas will be fine," Mrs. Bertrand commented.

"I know. I am grateful for that. I am. But he doesn't know, and. . . . ."

"How did you know?" Mrs. Bertrand asked, stunned.

"I can explain," Julien answered. "When the nurse updated us on Thomas, I asked when Dr. Corland would know about rejection. She could only tell us that the kidney is an exact match. Angelica had learned that an exact match is almost always a close blood relative."

Mr. Bertrand sat beside Angelica and took a deep breath. "You are correct, Angelica. My nephew Daniel died this morning, and my brother gave his son's kidney to my son. Daniel was twenty-three years old. He was a student at the university in Lyon, in his last year. He wanted to be a doctor. Daniel would be pleased that his kidney saved his cousin Thomas. He would, Angelica.

"Yes, Thomas will be sad and mourn Daniel, but he will understand Daniel's desire to help someone, especially a member of his own family. Thomas knew that Daniel wanted to be a doctor because of Thomas' disease. Daniel wanted to heal people. He has done that, Angelica. Daniel's death is not in vain."

The following morning, Julien drove Angelica to the hospital. Julien escorted her to Thomas' ward and asked for an update. Thomas was awake but resting comfortably at the moment. He had awakened early that morning, talked with Dr. Corland and his parents, and had sat up for a few minutes. Angelica smiled up at her father.

Julien asked the nurse if Thomas could have visitors that day, and was told that Dr. Corland had left instructions that Julien could visit. "You may go in, Sir."

"Go on, Daddy. Tell Thomas that I'm praying for him," Angelica told Julien with her big brown eyes full of hope.

Julien knew that Angelica wanted to see Thomas, and he felt wretched that she couldn't. But when she once more urged him to go, he smiled at her and entered Thomas' room.

"Julien," Thomas greeted his friend, his voice tired yet clear.

"Thomas, I was so elated for you when Angelica told me the news. You look well, my boy. How do you feel?"

"Tired and a bit sore, but I am all right, Julien. Dr. Corland says I'll be up walking the day after tomorrow. He says I am doing well so far. Thank you, Julien. You made the surgery possible. I owe you my life."

"No, Thomas, no you do not. You live your dreams. That is all I ask of you," Julien countered.

"I will, Julien. How is Angelica? Where is she?"

"She is fine. She is right outside."

"Why didn't she come in?" Thomas asked, his disappointment evident.

"She wanted to visit you, Thomas, but her name was not on the visitor's list. She told me to tell you that she is praying for you."

"Not on the list? Why? I want to see her," Thomas retorted. "Tell her to come in."

Mr. Bertrand went to the door and motioned for Angelica. "Come in, dear. Thomas asked for you." When she hesitated, he held her hand and gently pulled her in.

"Angelica," Thomas whispered while tears filled his eyes. "Stay with me."

"If it's all right, I'd like to."

"Of course it's all right," Mrs. Bertrand reassured Angelica.

The five of them talked for almost one hour, until Julien noticed that

Thomas was tired. He explained that he would go to work but visit again after work. Thomas smiled, said that would be nice, and asked if Angelica could stay until then.

"On one condition," Julien offered. "If Dr. Corland asks her to leave, she is to call me or her grandmother to come get her. Capiche?"

"Yes, Julien," Thomas responded.

Dr. Corland had no problem with Angelica's visit, especially when he noticed that her presence, her company, made Thomas feel better. So it was that Angelica stayed until Julien came late that afternoon and returned the next two mornings when Julien went to work. On Thursday, Thomas was still confined to bed. Blood was drawn and urine collected for tests. He had his first post-surgery food at lunch, which he ate with his parents and Angelica. Julien and Angelica stayed for dinner.

Friday proved exciting and productive. In mid-morning, a therapist helped Thomas out of bed and take his first steps. Mrs. Bertrand began crying, and Thomas went to her, hugged her, and consoled her. "Don't cry, Mom. I know you're crying because you're happy for me. I also think the stress of everything is wearing you down. Go home, Mom and Dad, and get some sleep." When his mother protested, Thomas pleaded, "Look at me, Mom. I'm fine. My lupus has been in remission for almost two years. I have a healthy kidney. I'm fine."

Thomas finally convinced his parents to get some rest and return for dinner. Angelica would keep him company. And that she did. Thomas and Angelica sat side by side on the sofa in his room. "The world is more beautiful than ever, Angelica. I just want to get back out there and live in it," Thomas commented and looked out the window.

Angelica thrilled at his joyous expression and grabbed a tablet of paper and a pencil. After a few moments, Thomas withdrew from his reverie and looked at Angelica. "What are you writing?"

"I'm not writing. I'm drawing." When Thomas asked what, she clarified, "Not what—who. You, Thomas. You look so very happy that I wanted to capture that moment."

"May I see?" Angelica handed him the drawing, and Thomas stared at it for several minutes. "This is like looking in a mirror. Are you sure you're not Julien's biological daughter? He's an incredible artist. If this is any indication, so are you."

"Thank you. Oh, Thomas, I feel like Julien's daughter. I am his daughter. A piece of paper can never change that, but I want so much for the adoption to be final."

"Have faith that it will. It will be fine, just like you and Julien told me."

"I know. But that would be the best, most magnificent Christmas gift for all of us. Daddy, Mom, Grandmother, and me. I want this for them most of all."

At that instant, the therapist returned. "It's time for our walk. I just need to check your blood pressure and temperature, and then we can begin." Thomas' vitals were normal, so he put on his robe and asked if Angelica could join them. "Of course."

The three of them walked to the end of the long hallway, and the therapist explained, "I thought we would go to the first floor, to the gift shop, and then back here." They took the elevator from the fourth floor to the first floor. On their way to the gift shop, they passed the chapel.

"Is it all right if we go in for a bit?" Thomas asked. The therapist nodded, stood at the back of the chapel, and the two friends went to the altar. Thomas and Angelica held hands, bowed their heads, and prayed. When they finished, they smiled at each other and hugged.

Minutes later, they entered the gift shop, and Angelica grabbed Thomas' arm when they came to the shelf of teddy bears. "This is where Daddy got me my teddy bear when I was in the hospital. We had just met, but we felt a connection, a bond, immediately. I love him and Mom so much."

Thomas held her hand. "I know. I see it in your soul—your eyes—and I see Julien's love for you in his eyes."

Thomas picked up a small white teddy bear and smiled, "I want to get this for you, Angelica. My first gift to you."

"That's very sweet, Thomas, but I don't want you to spend money on me."

"Nonsense. I want to. Let's see if there is anything else we want."

Angelica bought Thomas a book he wanted to read, and they took the elevator back to the fourth floor. The therapist took Thomas' blood pressure when they got to his room; it was 121/70, which was excellent.

"May Angelica and I take a walk in the hallway?"

"I don't see why not. You're doing remarkably well, Thomas."

After lunch, Thomas and Angelica walked the length of the hallway, up one side and down the other, at a leisurely pace as they talked.

"Dr. Corland says I should be able to go home next Wednesday. I'll have to take medicine every day for the rest of my life and have regular tests and check-ups, but I will have my life back. I owe that to my cousin." Thomas cleared his throat. "Daniel was such a swell guy, so serious and studious. I will miss him, Angelica, but I feel that he still lives. In me. It's his kidney that has saved my life. I will not waste one day that I have been granted. Life is too unpredictable, and I do not want to die with regrets."

"I know, Thomas," Angelica whispered. "I know your music is important to you. I know it feeds your soul. Please never stop your music no matter what else you do."

Thomas smiled at her. "I promise, my angel girl. I promise. Oh, I have no illusions about music earning me a living, but I have to play. I have to, and I will. I want you to promise me the same thing. Promise me that you will make music forever."

Angelica leaned against Thomas and giggled. "I can't promise that. Forever is impossible. The best I can promise is the rest of my life."

"Fair enough. But you are just fourteen, so you have many decades ahead of you. We will make lots of music together, Angelica," Thomas predicted with a wide smile.

"I look forward to that. I want my main work to be with Daddy's foundation. It's too important. Besides, he is such a kind and gentle soul and teacher. There is nothing else I want to do."

"You are, too. A kind and gentle soul, I mean. You really are so much like Julien," Thomas pronounced and put his hands on her shoulders.

"Angelica!"

"Rogier. Is something wrong?" Angelica asked in panic. What was he doing there?

"No, not at all. I've called Aurélie and told her, but Julien is in a meeting. I thought you would want to go with me and tell him as soon as the meeting is over."

"Tell him what?"

"Judge Moore's secretary called me. He wants the three of you in his chambers at 9:00 Monday morning. The adoption will be finalized at that time. You will legally be Julien's and Aurélie's daughter, Angelica."

"Rogier? This is for real?"

"Oui, enfant. It most definitely is real."

"Thank you, Rogier. Thank you," Angelica cried and hugged him. She turned to Thomas and hugged him, too. "Thank you for your friendship, Thomas. You are my best friend. Thank you. I am so very happy. You are healthy, and the adoption will be final. All of my prayers have been answered."

§§§§§

Promptly at 9:00 on the morning of Monday, December 14, 1964, Julien, Aurélie, Angelica, and Rogier entered Judge Moore's chambers.

"Monsieur and Madame Lacoeur, Angelica. I am certain that Juriste Sandorf informed you that I am approving the legal adoption this morning. I have carefully and conscientiously considered your application. Juriste Sandorf's evidence proved important in establishing Angelica has no living family members. That would have made her a ward of the state. But she is one of the very fortunate orphans in that she has a couple who wants to adopt her. The most convincing evidence came from my interviews with the three of you. I saw for myself the love you have for Angelica and she has for you.

"Yes, with your wealth, you can provide the best of everything for Angelica. Love, however, is far more valuable and important, and, Monsieur and Madame Lacoeur, you provide a vast wealth of love to Angelica. She possesses great love and respect for both of you. Independently, all three of you declared that you are a family regardless of the legal adoption.

"Therefore, I am truly honored to sign the adoption decree and to proclaim you a family according to the laws of France. I have but one question for Angelica." Judge Moore looked directly at her and asked, "I trust that you desire your legal name to be Angelica Anna Maria Lacoeur?"

Angelica pulled a sheet of paper from her purse, handed it to Judge Moore, and smiled. Judge Moore nodded, completed the adoption decree, signed it, and looked at Angelica. "My dear, you are now and forevermore Angelica Anna Maria Thurmaldi Lacoeur, daughter of Julien and Aurélie Lacoeur."

Angelica's eyes filled with tears. She looked at Julien, on the verge of asking him if he minded the inclusion of her birth surname, when he hugged her tight. "Chouchou, what a beautiful tribute to your birth father. I feel a connection to Henri, through you, and I am so immensely honored to be your father now. I am sure Henri is as elated as I am, ma chère. Je t'aime. I love you."

Outside, on the courthouse steps, Julien and Aurélie hugged Rogier. "Thank you, Rogier, for everything. Your tireless research and work made this happen. Angelica is our daughter because of you," Aurélie said through her tears and then kissed his cheek.

Julien smiled at his friend and hugged him again. "I can never truly show you my gratitude. You made my life complete and indescribably joyous. Thank you. Thank you, Rogier."

"All of this has been my pleasure. I wanted this for all of you. I had to do this. I'm just glad that I was able to do all of this. Now, go celebrate. Go get Ophelia and celebrate."

"Come with us," Julien invited.

"I would, but I have another court case early this afternoon. Dinner tonight?"

"Of course. Just come over when your work is through," Aurélie smiled.

"Thank you for making our lives so happy and complete, Rogier," Angelica smiled, stood on her toes, and kissed his cheek. "Thank you for everything."

"I love you, little girl."

They watched Rogier walk back to his office. "Daddy, can we go to the hospital before we go to Grandmother's? I want to tell Thomas."

Julien looked at Aurélie, who smiled and responded, "Of course, ma fille. I can finally meet Thomas."

A short while later, they exited the elevator on the fourth floor. Angelica saw Thomas at the far end of the hall and smiled up at her parents, happy to see him so active and healthy. Julien smiled, too, held his wife's hand, and said, "Let us surprise him on this beautiful day."

Surprise him they did. Thomas nearly bumped into Angelica when he turned from the window. "Angelica. Julien. I didn't expect to see you today."

"Thomas, my wife Aurélie and my daughter Angelica Lacoeur."

"It's over? It's legal? Angelica is your daughter?" Thomas asked Julien.

"For all time," Julien softly replied.

"I'm so happy for you, all of you. Your prayer was answered just as you hoped it would be. Oh, Angelica, what a week this has been for us," Thomas enthused and hugged her.

"I know. This is the most wonderful gift. I'm happy for both of us, Thomas," Angelica said, her big brown eyes full of light and wonder.

"Forgive me. It's so nice to meet you, Mrs. Lacoeur. Of course, I've heard quite a lot about you. It's a pleasure to meet Julien's true love."

Aurélie smiled, blushed, and glanced at Julien. "Thank you, Thomas. Julien and Angelica have told me about you, too. I'm so happy and grateful for your recovery, Thomas." He thanked her, but was somewhat surprised by her next comment. "Angelica tells me that you are a violin virtuoso. I must hear you play sometime."

"Oh, thank you, Mrs. Lacoeur." Now Thomas was blushing. "I don't know about that. But I do love music. No matter what else life may put in my path, I will always play music. Some people don't understand that. They think music should be just a pastime or a hobby. But it's my life. I know Angelica understands. She feels the same way." Thomas and Angelica smiled at one another, their friendship evident.

However, Aurélie suspected more than friendship, at least on Thomas' part. She gave Julien a knowing look, and he nodded once in answer to her silent question. Aurélie nervously cleared her throat, smiled, and agreed. "She certainly does. Julien and I heard her playing piano the day we met her. That was nine months ago today."

"And now we are a forever family in every way," Angelica beamed.

"Yes, we are, Chouchou," Julien confirmed. "Thomas, we hate to, but we must leave. We are taking my mother to a celebratory lunch."

"Of course. I get released Wednesday, so soon, I hope, I can visit Angelica."

"That will be wonderful, Thomas. Congratulations," Angelica said. As she and her parents rode the elevator down, she stated, "I hope it's soon. That Thomas can visit, I mean. He is the first friend I have ever had. He's my only friend, really, but I think of him as my best friend. We do have an understanding, an empathy that connects us. No matter where life takes us, Thomas will remain a lifelong friend."

"That's lovely, darling. I am so glad you have a friend you can talk to, share with, and trust. That kind of friend is very special," Aurélie remarked and winked at her husband.

"True. It seems our little girl is more like we than we realized," Julien stated. "You and I began as best friends, mon amour."

Julien rang his mother's doorbell, and a moment later, when Ophelia opened the door, was greeted with her confusion. "Did you forget your key, Julien?"

"No, Mère. I need to introduce you to your granddaughter Angelica Anna Maria Thurmaldi Lacoeur."

"It is final? She is truly, completely ours?"

"Oui, Mère. Angelica is ours in every way."

"Oh, my darling petite-fille," Ophelia wept and hugged Angelica.

"I love you, Grand-mère," Angelica softly said, which made Ophelia cry more.

"Angelica called us a forever family. I like that. We are. We may be a small family, but our love is huge," Aurélie commented.

"I like that, too. A forever family. That is exactly what we are for all time," Ophelia agreed. "Come in. Why are we standing in the doorway?"

"We came to take you with us. We are celebrating. Get ready, Mother," Julien commanded with a smile.

Shortly, the four of them were seated in Julien's car. Many minutes later, Julien parked in front of the Hotel du Raphael. Julien was instantly recognized as he and his family entered his hotel. After all, he was there several times each week, splitting his time between the hotel, the foundation, and his art. Angelica radiated delight at the respect and admiration shown to her father.

Guests took Julien's picture with their cameras, the flash bulbs making the hotel lobby seem like a Hollywood red carpet. One young woman even approached him with a piece of paper and a pen and asked for his autograph. Julien smiled, thanked her, and went with his family to the elevator.

They exited at the rooftop restaurant, and once again, Julien was the object of adoration. Diners shook his hand, greeted him, or asked him for autographs. Finally, they were escorted to their table, one which overlooked Paris. A waiter took their order, served their drinks, and made sure the Lacoeur family had everything they needed.

Angelica looked at her grandmother and parents, a smile illuminating her face. "I have everything I need and want. All of my hopes, dreams, and prayers have been answered. I am filled with peace and contentment. My life is perfect."

"My little princess, today is the second happiest day of my life. You are the answer to my prayers. My life is absolutely perfect. I love you, Angelica." Julien looked at Aurélie and held her hand. "I love you, ma chère." He then smiled at his mother and put his hand on her cheek. "I love you, Mère." He looked at the three women in his life and declared, "I love you, ma familie."

Angelica leaned over and kissed his cheek. "I love you, Daddy." She turned, kissed Aurélie's cheek, and said, "I love you, Mom. Grand-mère, I love you," Angelica added as she reached across the table and clasped Ophelia's hand.

The waiter returned just then, served their meals, refilled their drinks, and smiled as he walked away. It was such a joy to see Monsieur Lacoeur and his family so happy. Every employee of the hotel held him in the highest regard. Some of the employees had been hired by Gerald Lacoeur, Julien's father, more than three decades earlier. They remained loyal and dedicated. Both Gerald and Julien inspired that in people.

Angelica knew that; she saw it whenever she was anywhere in public with Julien. She took hold of Julien's and Aurélie's hands and bowed her head. They and Ophelia did likewise, and Angelica prayed. "Dear God, Thank you for giving me a family. They are the most perfect and wonderful family. I never dared to hope that I would be part of such a splendid family. I love them each, Daddy, Mom, and Grandmother. No matter what else happens in my life, I am so very happy and grateful. Thank you for your blessings. Amen."

"That was beautiful, Angelica," Ophelia wept.

"It was beautiful, Chouchou. I am grateful for you, that you are with us and truly ours," Julien declared. Aurélie echoed his sentiments, and smiled as they enjoyed their food.

"Angelica, what do you want to do? Your hopes and dreams, the things you want to do?" Julien asked her.

"When I worked at the café, college students often came in, and I used to watch them. Some of them sat alone reading text books or doing homework while they ate. Others sat together and talked about their classes. I never knew anyone who had gone to college, except for Reverend Soames.   It seems so exciting, a chance to learn from experts and to meet people."

"College is exciting, Angelica. But you are only fourteen. What about high school?" Ophelia asked.

"I completed the high school requirements of the Education Board," Angelica replied.   She noticed their confusion, so she explained.   "Renée followed the curriculum, and she tested me regularly.   When I completed the curriculum, she arranged for my comprehensive final examinations.   An official for the Education Board came to the village. For three days in a row, I met her at the church. In a meeting room, I completed the examinations. Three weeks later, Reverend Soames brought a large manila envelope that had been addressed to me and mailed to the church. It contained my high school diploma."

"You received your high school diploma before most people start high school!" Aurélie exclaimed. "That is incredible. You are incredible, Angelica."

"Our little girl is remarkable," Julien added and smiled at her. "I will take you to the university soon, and we will find out about registering you."

Angelica looked at Julien with an expression of astonishment. "Really?"

"Oui, Chouchou. I think we should go this week. The next term begins in February, so you need to complete registration and then enroll in classes."

"I never thought college would be possible. Thank you, Daddy."

"I am your Daddy, and I want to take care of you and give you everything I can. I want to share life with you for many decades to come. I waited all of my life to be a father. Now I am. I love you, ma fille."

"I love you, Daddy. I will remember this day forever."

$$SSSSS$$

"Where are we going?" Thomas asked his parents when they turned in the opposite direction from their home. He had expected to go straight home after his release.

"Oh, we need to go somewhere," Mr. Bertrand replied. From his backseat vantage point, Thomas couldn't see the smiles his parents exchanged. Thomas looked out the car window for clues to their destination. There were none as the car traversed streets of Paris that Thomas had never seen. When his father parked in front of a beautiful three-story house, Thomas was more confused than ever. Until Angelica opened the front door.

Mr. Bertrand assisted Thomas from the car, and smiled and hugged his wife at their son's reaction. "I can't believe it! I never suspected this is where you were going," Thomas marveled and hugged his father.

Thomas turned toward his friend and wept, "Angelica." He walked up the steps, took her hand, and continued, "I'm so happy, happier than I've ever been."

"So am I," Angelica choked. A moment later, she regained her emotions and held the front door open for Thomas and his parents.

Julien and Aurélie greeted them warmly, and Julien winked at Angelica. "I thought we could relax in the music room," he said and motioned for everyone to follow him and Aurélie.

"The music room?" Thomas whispered.

Angelica could barely contain her excitement when the Bertrands entered. Thomas looked around the room and smiled at Julien and Angelica. "The piano is incredible. I haven't heard you play in a long time, Julien. Will you?"

"Perhaps later. I thought you would like to play for us," Julien suggested.

"I would love to, but I don't play the piano," Thomas giggled.

"Oui, that is true.   Would that violin on the corner table do?" Julien revealed.

Thomas loudly gasped.   He walked to it, carefully opened the case, and suddenly jumped back. Mrs. Bertrand appeared alarmed, until Julien smiled at her.

"Go on, Thomas.   It is yours," Julien softly encouraged.

"Mine?   How?   Why?   What?" Thomas was dumbfounded, overcome with a wave of emotions on this most emotional of days.

"Every violinist should have the best.   This is our gift to you, Thomas," Julien explained.

"I   can't.   This   is   far   too extravagant for me.   You've already done so   much   for   me,   Julien," Thomas protested, to no avail.

"Nonsense.   The violin is yours, Thomas.   Would you christen it here, today?" Julien implored.

"I never thought I would see a Stradivarius, let alone play one. This is so beautiful, I just want to let it sink it for a few minutes," Thomas said as tears of joy filled his eyes.

"Julien, this is extravagant. These violins are rare and almost priceless. We can't. . . .," Mr. Bertrand countered, only to have Julien gently interrupt him.

"It is not extravagant. Thomas longs to be a concert violinist. He deserves this. The violin is his."

"Do you know its history?" Thomas asked Julien, still staring in reverence at the violin.

"This particular violin was made in 1699. It is called the Lady Tennant. Antonio Stradivari made it. It was once owned by Charles Philippe Lafont. There were two owners after Lafont. You, Thomas, are the fourth owner. Bring life to it once more, Thomas," Julien coaxed.

Thomas inhaled deeply and gingerly picked up the violin. He rested it on his left shoulder, exhaled, and placed his chin on the chin rest. He lifted the bow, closed his eyes, and began playing Mozart's *Violin Concerto No. 5 in A, Second Movement*. When he finished, everyone applauded.

"Oh, Thomas, that was as majestic as I am sure Mozart intended it to be. I have never heard it played this way before. That violin belongs with you. You have brought it back to life." Angelica gushed.

Thomas blushed, but he did feel a connection to the beautiful violin. "Maybe I have. But I feel that it has brought a piece of life back to me that has been missing for too long." Thomas carefully placed the violin in its case and went to Julien. "Thank you," he wept and hugged Julien.

After Thomas dried his eyes, Julien suggested, "Thomas, Angelica, I am the only one who has heard you play together. Why not do so for all of us?"

"Well, but we haven't rehearsed," Thomas answered.

"You did not rehearse that day in the hospital, either," Julien disputed with a smile. "You simply began playing with Angelica as if it were the most natural thing in the world."

"I suppose we can. Angelica?"

"Sure," she smiled and sat at the piano. Thomas once more picked up his antique violin and signaled to Angelica that he was ready.

Angelica began playing a melancholy piece she had composed four years earlier as she sat in the village church. She had had a dream about her birth father the night before and missed him more than usual that day. Thomas' violin joined Angelica's piano in a piece that evoked sadness and mimicked the lonesome wailing of the wind through the leaves.

Mrs. Bertrand fumbled for a tissue in her purse, and her husband handed her his handkerchief. Julien leaned forward, his head bowed as he fought back the torrent of tears that threatened him. Aurèlie put her hand on his back and wiped tears from her eyes as well.

When the teenagers finished, Mr. Bertrand cleared his throat and spoke first. "That was very beautiful, children. Very emotive, too, I must say. I've never heard that piece before, Thomas. Who composed it?"

"I'd never heard it before, either, Dad." Thomas looked down at Angelica. "Angelica," he stated.

"Angelica what, son?"

"Angelica composed it.   She composes most of the music she plays."

"And you had never heard this before today?" Thomas confirmed that he hadn't. "Then how. . . . How on earth were you able to accompany her?"

"I don't know really. I feel the music, its heart, its meaning, its emotions. I don't know how else to explain it," Thomas struggled to express.

Julien dried his eyes, sat straight, and added, "This is similar to that day in the hospital music room. Thomas asked Angelica to play the piano, and she played a piece she had written. He joined her, and it was magical. It was perfection. I could never have told you what I heard that day. I do not know how to explain it."

"I don't either," Mr. Bertrand admitted.

"Angelica is my musical soul mate," Thomas stated. "I can read her. We are in synchronization. I have found my life partner," he said and smiled down at her. She returned his smile. Their parents looked at each other, fully aware of Thomas' meaning.

§§§§§

The next morning, Julien drove Angelica to École Normale Supérieure (ENS), one of Paris' premiere universities. Angelica completed the admission application and produced her diploma and birth certificate. The Admissions counselor made mention of Angelica's young age, but also noted the honors distinction on her diploma.

"All of our applicants must take a very competitive admission examination. This examination helps us determine the depth of your knowledge. After we complete your paperwork, you may take the examination. It lasts three hours, and is given in a room with an official of the university acting as proctor."

Angelica declared her major as art history, and as such would be a student of the Département Hisroire and Théroie des Arts. Julien smiled and said, "That was my major when I was a student here, Chouchou. Tel père, telle fille," he grinned. Angelica giggled and held his hand.

Soon she was led to a small room, where she would take the three-hour examination. A man, who introduced himself as Dr. Richert, Assistant Dean, entered with a large manila envelope. He provided Angelica with a pen and the examination book. Dr. Richert sat at a table while she worked. She reread her answers prior to the deadline, and felt confident—but nervous—when Dr. Richert collected her examination.

He escorted her back to the Admissions counselor, who informed her they would contact her the following week. Angelica and Julien thanked the counselor and went to his car.

"I am sure we are both hungry. We will eat a late lunch nearby before we go home," Julien suggested. Angelica's smile filled his heart with elation. "You better get used to being what is called a Daddy's Girl, Chouchou. I waited my life for you, and I will relish every moment with you. I want to spend time with you. I want to give you all I can. I want to enjoy you."

"Oh, Daddy, that is just what I want, to spend time with you. You don't have to give me things. All I need is you and Mom."

"I know I do not have to. I want to. I used to dream of having a daughter for whom I could buy lots of pretty things. Now I can. And I will," Julien countered as he parked at a restaurant.

The father and daughter duo garnered attention when they entered, attention which maintained its fervor throughout their meal. Neither Julien nor Angelica noticed, though. They remained engrossed in their conversation about art. It wasn't until they walked toward the door that the other diners caught their notice.

"Excuse me, Mr. Lacoeur, may I have your autograph?" a woman asked. Julien obliged, smiling all the while. The request was repeated several more times before they exited.

Angelica smiled up at her father. "People admire and love you so, Daddy, for everything you do. You are a true Renaissance Man."

"Chouchou, you are blinded by love. Do not put me up high. I am not all that you seem to think I am," Julien protested, his discomfort showing.

"Yes, you are. You know so many subjects, and you do so many things well," Angelica insisted as they crossed the street. She looked at him, noting his revulsion. "Mom is right. I know you don't like to talk about yourself. I'm sorry, but I still believe what I said."

"We will go shopping now," Julien diverted the subject as they neared a shop.

The shop overflowed with high-end one-of-a-kind objects, from figurines to framed prints. Angelica scanned the walls and shelves after they entered. "Are you looking for a Christmas present?" she asked Julien.

"No, just something special."

Angelica dutifully followed Julien while he browsed some shelves. As he looked at decorative boxes, she stepped to the next aisle lined with beautiful figurines. She gingerly fingered a figurine of a ravishing woman with flowing dark hair, blue eyes, and a white gown.

When she walked away, Julien looked at the figurine. He instantly knew that it reminded her of her mother Stephanie. He picked it up, took it to the counter, and purchased it before she could see. The saleswoman wrapped it carefully. Julien went to Angelica, who was near the back of the shop. "Is there anything you want, Chouchou?"

Angelica shook her head. "No. I don't need anything."

"No one needs anything in this shop, Angelica. But is there something you would like to have?" She hesitated. "Angelica?"

"Well. . . . . There is a figurine I like," she finally admitted and led him to the shelf. When he asked which one, she shook her head. "It isn't here. It's been sold." She smiled up at Julien. "It doesn't matter. The money you would spend on that can be used for more important things."

"You are important, ma fille. You. You, Mom, and Grandmother. Come. Let us go home."

Aurélie was not yet home from work, so Julien seasoned a roast and placed it in the oven. Angelica helped him peel and dice the potatoes, which he boiled in preparation for mashing. "There is nothing more to do yet. What shall we do now?" he asked Angelica.

"Play the piano for me? Please."

"All right, but you will play for me, too."

They went to the music room and sat side by side on the piano bench. Julien played a few of his favorite classical pieces, and Angelica felt her senses fill with splendor and joy.

"Oh, Daddy, you play exquisitely, with such emotion."

"As do you. Play for me," Julien requested with a tender smile. Angelica obliged, playing a few of her compositions. "Your compositions are so elegant. I do have a special request, the one you composed for me. *Heartsong Sonata.*"

Angelica smiled at him and played the piece composed from her immense love for the man she called Daddy. Neither of them noticed Aurélie standing in the music room doorway, her eyes filled with tears as she watched her husband and her daughter. When Angelica finished,

Julien kissed her and asked if she knew Schubert's *Ava Maria*, and when she said she did, suggested they play a duet.

"What an absolutely stunning treat to come home to," Aurélie said as she went to them. She kissed them both and added, "I love you, my darlings. How did everything go at the university?"

Julien and Angelica told Aurélie, ending with the Admission Counselor's assurance of a telephone call the following week. "I remember Julien telling me about that comprehensive examination. He did not find it too difficult, so I am sure you did well, too, Angelica."

"It wasn't difficult, but I don't know how the university officials will evaluate my answers. I reviewed my answers before I submitted the examination, and I was satisfied. I did the best I could."

"That is all anyone can do, and I am positive your best is excellent," Aurélie told her daughter. "Do I smell dinner cooking?"

"Yes. Daddy put a roast in the oven. The potatoes are ready to mash, and the vegetables are ready to simmer. It smells wonderful."

"Your father spent lots of time in the hotel kitchen when he was a child. He is an excellent chef."

"I was right. He is a Renaissance Man," Angelica said and smiled up at him. She then went to help Aurélie set the table while Julien finished the meal.

After dinner, Angelica and Aurélie cleared the table, loaded the dishwasher, and cleaned the kitchen and dining room. While they were occupied, Julien took the bag from the gift shop upstairs and placed the figurine on top of Angelica's dresser near her parents' wedding portrait. He smiled, knowing how much she wanted the figurine and pleased he was able to buy it for her. He had longed for a daughter he could indulge and surprise. Angelica would likely notice the figurine when she got ready for bed.

Julien was still smiling when he joined his wife and daughter in the kitchen. Aurélie made a pot of hot chocolate, and they snuggled on the sofa in the living room. Julien opened the television cabinet, and they watched a movie. When it ended, Aurélie washed the pot and mugs, and then walked upstairs with her family.

In the hallway, Angelica kissed her parents and said, "Thank you for today, Daddy. I do enjoy spending time with you."

"And I with you. Sweet dreams, Chouchou," Julien responded and kissed her.

"Good night, daring. You had a busy day. Sleep well."

"I will, Mom. I love you."

They parted ways, and Angelica removed her watch in preparation for her shower. She placed it on the tray atop her dresser and saw the porcelain figurine. Her eyes filled with tears. "Oh, Daddy. You knew." She picked it up and looked at a likeness very similar to her mother's. She carefully replaced it, sprinted across the hall, and knocked on her parents' bedroom door.

Julien beckoned her in, and she entered to see him hanging his suit jacket on the oak valet. She ran to him and grabbed him in a hug from behind.

"Thank you, Daddy. You knew the whole time."

Julien turned, embraced her, and admitted, "I saw you looking at it, and when I saw the figurine, I knew why. It resembles your birth mother. I wanted to surprise you."

"You did. Thank you, Daddy."

Less than one week later, on Tuesday, December 22, the Lacoeurs' telephone rang. Aurélie called Angelica to the telephone. Fifteen minutes later, she hung up. She went to the kitchen, where Aurélie was cleaning the oven.

"Mom, that was Mrs. Garner, the Admissions Counselor at the university. I have been accepted. Mrs. Garner wondered if I could come today to obtain my student identification card, course schedule, and to purchase my text books. If not, I will have to do it the Friday before classes begin."

Aurélie stood, her mouth open, as she listened to her daughter. She quickly untied her apron. "Of course we can go. Just let me freshen, and we will go."

A few hours later, when Julien arrived home, Aurélie told him, "Darling, our daughter is officially a university student. She got the call today. She did very well on her examination. She had her picture taken for her identification card, got her course schedule, and bought her text books. Oh, Julien, you should have seen her. She held the books like they were treasures. She began reading one on the drive home. She is upstairs at her desk still reading."

"What wonderful news just before Christmas. I had no doubts that they would accept her." Julien kissed his wife. "I am going to congratulate our daughter."

Julien watched Angelica as he stood in her open doorway. She sat, with perfect posture, at her desk, a large book open. He tapped on the door and asked, "May I come in?"

"Daddy!" she exclaimed and leapt from the chair. They met in an embrace. "I'm so glad you're home. I missed you."

"And I you. I was told you are a university student, Chouchou. Congratulations. I am so very proud of you."

"I would have never done it without you and Mom. It isn't just the money, your money, that pays for the tuition. I feel safe and free and loved, and that gives me courage."

"Chouchou, I can never in any way take credit for your courage. The day we met, I was shocked by your story. You had turned fourteen the month before. You are so young, yet you moved to Paris, got a job, and lived alone. I am in awe of you, my astonishing little girl."

§§§§§

Angelica tapped on the library door while Julien sat reading in a chair by the window. "Chouchou, come here," he smiled when he looked up and saw her. She walked to him and looked down at him. "Is something wrong?" he asked, appearing alarmed.

"No, Daddy. I want to ask if I may do something tomorrow."

"Tomorrow? Last minute shopping?" he smiled.

"No. I have all of my Christmas presents. It's important."

Julien was concerned and sat up straight. "Go on, Angelica."

"I want to go to the jail tomorrow."

"The jail? Whatever for? Tomorrow is Christmas Eve."

"I know. That's why." She saw his confusion, so she quickly continued. "We spend a lot of time each week visiting hospital patients, and like Mr. Fortner, many of them do not receive many visits. There are other people who will be alone tomorrow. The people in jail. A lot of them don't receive visits, either. They are forgotten and alone at Christmas. Yes, they did things they should not have done, but that is no reason to forsake them. How can they return to a society that forgets them and ignores them?"

Julien's first instinct was to forbid such a visit, but he saw the earnestness in her eyes. He stared out of the window at the snow-covered trees and thought for several minutes. "What made you think of visiting a jail?" he asked her as he still looked at the trees.

"Matthew 25:36."

"I was in prison, and ye came to me," Julien softly recited. He looked up at his daughter and pulled her onto his lap. "And, yes, Chouchou, I remember what Jesus said right before that: *I was sick, and ye visited me.* All right, my wise little girl, we will go to the jail tomorrow. We will show them human kindness and love. You are completely humbling."

"I was inspired by you, Daddy. You have shown me to share my blessings and love with all people."

The following afternoon, Julien and Angelica drove to the local jail. Julien had telephoned the warden the day before and arranged their visit. An officer escorted Julien and Angelica to the cells and stood nearby while Angelica introduced herself to the man in the first cell.

The man stood from his seat on his bunk and went to the bars. He looked at the young girl who smiled up at him. He then looked at Julien and recognized him from newspaper and television. "You came to visit me? Why?"

"I didn't want you and the other people here to be alone at Christmas," Angelica told him.

"Why? You don't know me or anyone here."

"That doesn't matter, Sir. You are no different from anyone else, and you deserve the same acknowledgement and kindness that we all desire. No one deserves to be alone at Christmas."

"You're serious," the man said to Angelica. He looked at Julien and asked, "Why did you bring her here? I know you have a nice, big house to celebrate Christmas in. What is this, some publicity stunt?"

"I brought my daughter because she asked me if she could come today. I admit that I was against this until I asked her where she got the idea," Julien honestly stated.

"Well, where?"

Julien and Angelica told the story, which attracted the attention of the other prisoners in the block.

"You are serious," a middle-aged man remarked.

"Most people avoid me," a young man admitted. "I've been in here five times this year. Every time I get a job and try to get my life in order, someone says or does something and I lose my temper. This time I beat up the guy. You don't need to be here. Go home and forget us."

"I can't forget you," Angelica told him. She went to his cell door and took his hand in hers. He pulled it away brusquely. Angelica forced her hurt feelings aside. "I won't hurt you."

"What?"

"Robbie ain't worried about that kind of hurt, Miss. He don't like no one touching him," one of the other men spoke up.

"Shut up!" Robbie shouted. "You don't know nothing about me."

"I know enough."

"Robbie, not everyone is unkind or mean-spirited," Angelica said to him. "Most people are kind at heart. Maybe they are afraid of you because you're angry and wary." He looked at her, his brow furrowed as he listened to what she said. "Don't alienate yourself from others. Trust people. Trust that just because you open yourself, even a little, that they will not treat you badly. Treat everyone the way you want to be treated, with kindness and empathy."

"Empathy?"

"Yes. If we listen to and watch others, we can understand their experiences. That's why I said I won't hurt you. I sense that others have hurt you, not so much physically as emotionally. They say things or do things that are judgmental or out of fear. That makes you feel bad. You are trying to start a new life, but some people react to your past. The names, the condescending remarks, the distrust—it all hurts. I understand, Robbie."

Robbie was silent for a while—too long—and the other prisoners began shuffling and gripping the bars. They had witnessed—and been the victims of—Robbie's anger. They expected an eruption, and the little girl would be his latest victim. They tried to warn the officer, but they were too late.

Robbie reached through the bars for Angelica. The officer sprinted forward. "Stop," Angelica ordered. "Everything is all right." Robbie reached for her hand and held it. She trusted him. Few people ever had.

The other men still wondered what would happen. After all, this was a new experience for all of them. Never were they more shocked than when Robbie leaned his head against the bars and cried. He cried for more than ten minutes, and then lifted his shirttail to wipe his eyes. Julien stepped to the cell and handed Robbie his handkerchief. When Robbie offered it back, Julien shook his head.

"Oh, I see. It's got my taint."

"Not at all. I can launder it, but I have several handkerchiefs. I figured since you do not have any, you could keep that one," Julien calmly explained.

Robbie looked at the linen handkerchief. "Thank you," he said and stuck his right hand between two bars. Julien shook his hand without hesitation. Everyone breathed, relieved.

Angelica talked with each of the other men. Before she and Julien left, Robbie asked if they would sing *Silent Night, Holy Night* for him and the other prisoners. Angelica looked up at her father, and Julien nodded. "Only if you all sing it with us," Angelica requested. They agreed. Angelica began, and then everyone, including the officer, joined.

When they finished, Angelica asked, "Would you mind if I pray for you before I leave?"

"No one minds," Robbie replied.

Angelica and Julien bowed their heads. "Dear God, Please protect Robbie, Dan, Quintin, Merrill, Dave, Steve, Bram, John, Richard, and Mark with your grace and your love. Let them know that you are with them even when no one else is. Help them to always remember that they are valuable. They have much to offer the world. All they have to do is turn over their sadness, anger, and fear to you. Help them learn to love themselves so that others can love them. Help them, God, as only you can. Most of all, show them what is most important this Christmas and every day—love. In your holy name, I ask this of you. Amen."

The men repeated the Amen and thanked her and Julien for visiting.

That evening after dinner, they sat in the living room with Aurélie, Ophelia, and Rogier. The fire warmed their bodies, and the feelings of the day warmed their souls. They relaxed and listened to Christmas music until it was time to leave for the midnight church service.

When they returned home, Angelica grabbed her parents' hands and looked at them. The Christmas tree lights reflected in her eyes and befitted the happiness shown in them. "This has been the most miraculous Christmas Eve. Thank you for today, I will remember it always. Now I know more than ever that I want to help people for the rest of my life, no matter how long my life is." She kissed them and declared, "I love you so very much, Daddy and Mom."

$$\text{\SS\SS\SS}$$

The next morning when Aurélie left her bedroom, she noticed Angelica seated at her desk writing. She smiled and stood watching her for several minutes before she lightly tapped on the open door. "You are up early, ma petite," Aurélie greeted her and kissed her cheek

"Merry Christmas, Mom." Angelica returned the kiss and explained, "I wanted to write about yesterday in my journal before today creates a whole bunch of its own special memories I'll want to record."

"All right, darling. I am going to start breakfast. I will call you when it is done."

Angelica finished her journal entry several minutes later, and stood at the window admiring the winter landscape. She turned, intending to go downstairs, when Julien emerged from his room. Angelica audibly gasped. In his black trousers and forest green sweater, he resembled a dashing film star, akin to those she had seen in movie magazines in the past few months.

"What is wrong, Chouchou?"

"Nothing is wrong. Everything is perfect. My life is perfect. You are perfect."

"No one is perfect, Angelica."

"You are," Angelica whispered as she hugged him. "I am so happy that you are my father. I can never tell you how much I love you, Daddy."

"You do not have to, Chouchou. I feel it," Julien choked and kissed the top of her head.

Aurélie announced breakfast, so they walked to the breakfast table hand in hand. Julien kissed his wife and then said the prayer before they ate. Afterward, they placed the plates, cups, and utensils in the dishwasher and then went to the music room.

Julien put a Christmas album on the stereo and let it play in the background as they sat together on the sofa.

"It is so quiet and peaceful for a Friday morning," Aurélie noted.

"It takes Christmas Day to stop the hustle and business of everyday life. Most people never slow down and just enjoy life. I have been guilty of that, I admit it," Julien commented.

"I don't think you are," Angelica objected.

"Merci, Chouchou. I try not to be rushing all the time. Not anymore. I was more like that before my father got sick. But that changed me. Taking care of my father and sharing his death with him made me see just how precious every moment of life is. I hope it has made me a better human being. I like to think it has," Julien confessed.

"You were never anything but a wonderfully caring and attentive and thoughtful human being, mon amour. You were never one of those people who rush, rush, rush. But your father's illness and death did make you even more aware of the importance of every moment," Aurélie explained. "You do an incredible amount of work between the hotel, the foundation, and the art. But you prioritize things. I always knew that I came first. Now we both come first," she added and pulled Angelica close to her.

"You most certainly do, mes belles filles," Julien affirmed and leaned over to kiss each of them—Aurélie on her lips, Angelica on the cheek.

"Hello! We made it!" Rogier announced from the foyer as he and Ophelia hung up their coats.

Angelica ran to hug her grandmother and suggested they go to the living room where the fire was blazing. Soon, Aurélie and Julien carried in hot chocolate, which quickly warmed them all.

Ophelia excused herself and went to the foyer to retrieve three large gift bags. From one, she removed three wrapped gifts and handed one each to her son, daughter-in-law, and Rogier. She placed the other two bags—filled with gifts—before Angelica.

"What is all of this?" Angelica asked.

"Why, your Christmas presents from your grandmother, dearie, of course," Ophelia gleefully answered.

"All of this? This is too much," Angelica marveled.

"Nonsense. I am a grandmother. It is my duty to indulge you. Now, open them," Ophelia commanded. Rogier could not help but chortle, nearly spitting out his hot chocolate. He relished the family's bliss.

Angelica opened the gifts one by one to reveal three pairs of shoes and one dozen dresses. "You will be a university student in a few weeks. You can never have too many outfits," Ophelia justified when Angelica once more told her that the gifts were too much for her.

"Thank you, Grandmother. They are each lovely," Angelica wept as she hugged Ophelia. "I love you, Grandmother."

Ophelia held Angelica close against her and sniffed, "I waited sixty-seven years to hear that. Oh, dear girl, I love you."

"Let us pass out the rest of the gifts, cher," Aurélie suggested to Julien. Several minutes later, each person had a small pile of gifts. "Mother, you open yours first."

Ophelia happened to open Rogier's gift first, which was an original Renoir painting. From Julien and Aurélie, she received a mother's bracelet with her family's birthstones: Gerald's topaz, Julien's pearl, Aurélie's garnet, and Angelica's amethyst. She instantly clasped it around her wrist. She smiled when she picked up Angelica's gift and opened it. However, she burst into tears at her first sight of the gift.

"Don't you get upset, Angelica," Ophelia wept. "This is beautiful, the most beautiful drawing I have ever seen." Ophelia dried her eyes and then added, "This is one of the most priceless gifts I have ever received. You have captured my Gerald perfectly, dear." Ophelia pulled her granddaughter close to her and told the others to open their presents from Angelica. They, too, would be priceless.

Rogier, Aurélie, and Julien obliged, and each had a reaction similar to Ophelia's. "My father," Rogier gasped. "How could you know? He died in 1943."

"I'm so sorry, Rogier. Daddy has some pictures of him in the photograph albums. I debated whether to do it. I didn't want it to upset you."

"No. No, sweetheart. This is just like him. Thank you."

"Chouchou, this is incredible. So beautiful, just beautiful, just like ma belle femme. I will treasure this all of the days of my life," Julien gushed. He knelt before Angelica and put his hands on her cheeks. "Je t'aime, ma Chouchou. With all of my heart, forever and always.'

Aurélie smiled, kissed her husband, and wept, "And I will treasure this drawing of you, mon mari. Our daughter is as talented an artist as you. This is such a beautiful gift, ma fille. I am so happy." Aurélie kissed Angelica's cheek.

"I am, too, Mom. This is the best Christmas of my life, and not because of the presents. Because I have all of you with whom to share Christmas. Christmas is all about love to me, and I have never felt love, real love, before. Renée and I went to the midnight service, and on Christmas we read the Bible. She taught me about the Bible and God and Jesus, and I'm grateful she did. Renée was kind, but very different from all of you."

"Yes, I can see that," Aurélie stated. "There is nothing wrong in celebrating Christmas or in telling your daughter that you love her."

"No, there is not," Julien agreed. "Gift giving began on the day Jesus was born, and commemorates that. So now your Mom and I have gifts for you, Chouchou." Julien placed three presents on the table near Angelica. She looked at them in amazement, and her parents told her to open them.

Angelica opened a rather large box to reveal a typewriter. "For me?"

"Of course. You begin university in February, and you will need a typewriter for all of your essays and assignments," Julien explained.

"It's wonderful. Thank you." Angelica then unwrapped a leather satchel, which Aurélie told her was for her text books and notebooks. "It looks like yours, Daddy. I don't know what to say except thank you."

"After university, you will use it in your work with the foundation. I look forward to that," Julien smiled.

"So do I," Angelica whispered through her tears.

Aurélie smiled and handed her daughter a small gift. Angelica gasped and looked at her parents when she saw what it contained. "This is too beautiful and expensive for me."

"No, Chouchou, it is not. It is just right for you. Let me fasten it," Julien offered and removed the diamond heart pendant from its velvet box. He clasped it and then kissed the top of her head. "This was made for you, a symbol of our love for you."

"We do love you so, notre fille Angelica," Aurélie added.

"I am so blessed that you do." Angelica fingered the diamond heart and her birth mother's heart locket. "I have two very special heart pendants, too, Mom, just like you: one from you and one from my birth parents. I will wear both forever." Even after I die, Angelica thought. I want to be buried wearing them. "I love the four of you more than my words could ever say. This has been the most blessed year of my life. Meeting you, loving you, and becoming part of your family. This is more than I ever dared to hope for. My life is a dream."

"A dream come true, Chouchou," Julien whispered.

§§§§§

The following Tuesday, December 29, Julien went to Angelia's bedroom to make sure she was awake. She was accompanying him to the hospital for their weekly visits. Her door was open, and he noticed that she lay across her bed, attired in a blue dress. "Angelica?" She didn't respond or move.

Julien walked to her bed and gently touched her shoulder. "Angelica?"

She moaned and opened her eyes slightly. "Daddy," she gasped, "I'm sorry."

Julien placed his hand on her cheek. She was burning with fever. He ran to the top of the stairs and screamed for his wife. Aurélie rushed up the stairs. "Stay with Angelica while I telephone Dr. Sutfield." Aurélie quickly realized how serious the situation—Angelica's fever was obviously very high. She cradled her daughter's head on her lap until Julien returned.

"Dr. Sutfield wants us to bring her to the hospital. He will meet us there."

Aurélie ran ahead to start the car, while Julien wrapped Angelica in a blanket and picked her up. Finally, they entered the hospital, where Dr. Sutfield led them to an examination room. He took her temperature—41.11$^{\circ\text{C}}$ (106$^{\circ\text{F}}$).

"I am admitting her immediately. We need to determine the cause of the fever so that we can treat it. I also need to start her on fluids to prevent dehydration. We will perform some tests and begin treatment. A nurse will let you know when you can come into her room."

Julien and Aurélie watched helplessly as their precious daughter was wheeled away. "Oh, Julien, how, why could this happen? She was fine last might, smiling, talking about her classes." She cried and leaned against Julien.

"I am scared, Aurélie. Very scared." His words only made her cry more.

They refused to move, to leave their vigil outside her hospital room. They stood there, praying and holding one another. Two hours later, the door opened and a nurse beckoned them in. Angelica was still and unconscious, with an IV in her right arm and an oxygen mask over her mouth and nose.

Dr. Sutfield explained, "Angelica has a viral infection, which has caused her fever. We have saline solution pumping into her body to ward off dehydration. I am constantly monitoring her heart. A heart monitor is attached to her. Viral infections are resistant to antibiotics. The best course of treatment is rest and fluids. We will keep her comfortable and under observation until the fever breaks. Her immune system should fight the infection on its own. We have a waiting game until then."

Julien went to the hospital bed, kissed her forehead, and said through his tears, "I love you, Chouchou." She was so very hot, and Julien was terrified.

Aurélie was, too, and she stood beside him in solidarity. She lifted Angelica's hand and kissed it. She looked at Julien and began crying. Julien put his arms around her, held her close, and cried as well.

Julien and Aurélie stayed beside her throughout the day and night, just as they had in March. Early the next morning, while Aurélie slept curled in a chair, Angelica moved her left hand, feeling for something. Julien curled his hand around hers. "Daddy," she murmured.

Julien leaned close to her as Dr. Sutfield stood. "I am here, Chouchou. I am here." She curled her fingers weakly around his. "I love you, bébé."

Dr. Sutfield listened to her heart and checked her vital signs on the monitor. Her temperature was still $40^{\circ C}$ $(104^{\circ F})$, far too high. "We will make you well, Angelica. Your father and mother are here. You go to sleep. That is the best thing you can do for yourself and everyone else."

Julien stroked her head, soothing her to sleep. He looked fearfully at Dr. Sutfield, who softly reassured Julien. "Her fever will break. She needs rest so that her immune system can work and fight the infection. She is lucid and aware. I know this is frightening, but there is no need to be overly alarmed."

Julien nodded, fought back his tears, and thanked the doctor. Neither he nor Aurélie left the hospital, although Aurélie did telephone Ophelia and let her know the situation. By midmorning, Rogier and Ophelia arrived, both keeping vigil with Julien and Aurélie.

Thomas found out, and he came to the hospital and checked on Angelica. Dr. Sutfield refused to let him enter her hospital room, much to Thomas' frustration. "Thomas, you cannot risk getting ill. Angelica's fever will break soon, and she will be well. The best thing you can do is to keep yourself healthy and to pray."

Thomas understood. "Give her a message from me. Tell her I was here and that I love her." Dr. Sutfield promised to do so.

It was not until Friday—the first day of 1965—that Angelica opened her eyes. She saw Julien first. "Daddy. I'm so sorry." Her voice was weak and was muffled under the oxygen mask.

"No, Chouchou, do not apologize. Never. We love you," Julien said and kissed her forehead. Aurélie, Ophelia, and Rogier added their sentiments before Dr. Sutfield spoke.

"Hello there, Angelica," he smiled and removed the oxygen mask. "I'm going to ask these fine people to go get coffee and sandwiches while I examine you." They all kissed her and left, relieved and exhausted. However, they remained in the hallway, anxious to learn her condition. With her heart problems, they worried that the fever had caused more damage.

Over one hour later, Dr. Sutfield came into the hallway, while Nurse Ramsey remained with Angelica. "How is she?" Julien asked. "The truth."

"Her temperature is classified as low-grade at this point—37.78$^{\circ C}$ (100$^{\circ F}$). She is understandably weak. She has not eaten solid food since Monday evening. Her body has expended energy in fighting the viral infection. She needs rest, yes, but she also needs to eat and to begin working her muscles again.

"Her heart is also weaker. This may be temporary due to the infection. Time will tell us this. I will keep her here at least until Monday to monitor her and to make sure she regains her physical strength. I am also keeping her on the saline solution until she is fully recovered and the temperature back to normal. She is sitting up. She asked for you. Go on in. I will be back soon. I need to check on my other patients."

They thanked him, and Julien opened Angelica's door to see the bed inclined and Angelica propped up against pillows. "Bonjour, Chouchou. We have returned to visit with you." He entered, and the others followed. They each gently hugged and kissed her, feeling how hot her body still was. Aurélie held Julien's arm tightly, her only defense to overcome her tears. He understood and patted her hand.

"I'm sorry I ruined your New Year's."

"No, darling, you did not. This is a miraculous New Year's Day to see you sitting here," Aurélie said through her tears.

"I have put you through so much since the day we met. You wanted a child so desperately. You have suffered too much loss and pain. I have just added to your pain. I never intended to, and I'm so sorry," Angelica began crying. Aurélie looked at Julien, heartbreak and desperation on her face.

Julien sat on the edge of Angelica's bed facing her. The tears that filled his eyes broke her heart. His words filled her heart with joy. "Angelica, you are my daughter, and Aurélie's, and we love you. We love you. When Aurélie and I married, we took vows to love and to honor, in sickness and health, all the days of our lives. That day we also made a vow between us and God that we would do the same for our children. You are our child. Our love for you is so very deep and strong that nothing we do for you is a sacrifice. Nothing. Your life is the most important, and we will do anything, everything for you. Oh, Chouchou, the pain we feel when you are hurt or sick is born of our love for you."

Angelica hugged him. Aurélie wrapped her arms around Julien and Angelica. Ophelia was crying as she stood near them, and Rogier put his arm around her. Rogier had known Julien since they became best friends at university. The Lacoeurs had always been a loving, supportive family. However, the love between these four members of the Lacoeur family seemed stronger than any love Rogier had ever witnessed or felt. Their love was alive, tangible—he could literally feel it in the atmosphere. That love, he knew, would carry them through whatever fate dealt them. He offered a silent prayer that they would now have many years of peace and joy. They deserved mothing less.

Saturday morning, Dr. Sutfield performed an electrocardiogram on

Angelica.   Her   irregular   heartbeat persisted, although it was now rapid. She also had shortness of breath, even while resting, but at times she experienced rapid breathing.   As he had told Julien and Aurélie, these symptoms may be related to the viral infection, fever, and their combined stress on her body. Dr. Sutfield noted all of the information in Angelica's chart. He also ordered a battery of blood tests, so a phlebotomist drew seven vials of her blood.   Thankfully, those tests didn't indicate any issues of concern.

Dr. Sutfield started Angelica on a regimen of Furosemide, which would help to treat and prevent fluid build-up in and around her heart. He would monitor its effects on her over the next forty-eight hours. He explained all of that to the Lacoeurs and Rogier.

"I understand how frightening this is, especially after last March.   Please know that I am doing all I can safely do for Angelica. I know I said she would likely be released on Monday, but I will not release her if her condition is not stable enough. I am closely monitoring her. If the Furosemide works with no ill effects, she will take it every day for the rest of her life."

"How will this affect her life? Her activities, her plans, her dreams? She is supposed to begin university on February 8. She is so looking forward to that," Aurélie sobbed.

"The restrictions she has been under will remain in place, of course. As long as the myocarditis persists, she will grow tired more easily. It is of utmost importance that she not exhaust herself."

"We will make sure she does not. You said *if this persists*. Does that mean it may be alleviated?" Julien asked.

"Yes. This is likely caused by the turmoil of the fever and the infection. When she fully recovers, this may resolve itself. Time. We will know in time. I will examine her every week for the next few months. I will be aware of any changes as soon as I can be. I will do all in my power that I can do. You do as you have done. Love her, protect her, and enjoy her."

MOUVEMENT

QUATRE

Ophelia arrived during breakfast, as usual, on January 11. She poured herself a cup of coffee and joined her family at the breakfast table. The four of them chatted until Aurélie left for work. No one hinted at anything out of the ordinary when she kissed them and said she would be home around 5:30.

As soon as they heard her car pull out, Julien told Angelica, "I will return at 3:00 so that we can pick up your gift for Mom. We also have to get flowers and a few other things."

"Thank you, Daddy. I want today to be perfect for Mom."

"It will be, Chouchou. Her first birthday with you will become one of her treasured memories."

After Julien left, Ophelia and Angelica cleared the table. Angelica gathered the ingredients and began making a cake for that afternoon. Ophelia smiled as she sat sipping coffee and watching her granddaughter. Angelica had been released from the hospital one week before, and as Dr. Sutfield had said, she did become tired after any exertion. Despite that, she seemed to be doing all right. No one let her do too much, so she thus far had not intensified her heart condition.

"Join me, dear," Ophelia requested while the cake baked. Angelica poured herself a glass of orange juice and sat across from Ophelia.

Angelica stared out of the window for several moments before she spoke. When she did, her questions stunned Ophelia. "Have you ever wondered why our lives play out as they do? Why do the things that happen to us happen? What are we supposed to learn from everything that happens to us? Are we in control of our lives, or is destiny in control? If we aren't, then why are our lives planned as they are? What is the purpose?"

Ophelia placed her hand over Angelica's and sat silent for a few minutes, pondering the girl's deeply philosophical questions—questions similar to those her young son had asked her years earlier. "I do not have the answers to your questions, dear. I am not sure if anyone can answer them with complete authority. Except your father. Julien has surely contemplated these questions for many years. He asked me very similar questions when he was twelve years old."

Angelica's eyes sparkled. "He did?"

"Yes. Julien has long been interested in such matters. I tend to accept what happens as part of God's plan, although it is difficult to reconcile a tragedy. I do not know why terrible, tragic things happen. Murder. Illness, like the people Julien helps. I cannot understand it. I do believe there is a purpose to everyone's life. I also believe only God knows the truth."

"I believe that, too, but I also don't think it's wrong to ask such questions. If we are supposed to learn from our experiences, then we must analyze and think about those experiences."

"I am sure you are right. This is just too metaphysical for my brain." Ophelia patted Angelica's hand.

Angelica smiled, realizing that her questions were not to everyone's preference; indeed, they made some people uncomfortable. "I will talk with Daddy. Right now, I need to take the cake out of the oven and let it cool," she said when the oven timer sounded. Once the cake was on the rack, Angelica made the icing.

"What else needs to be done?" Angelica asked.

"Not a thing. Why not take a nap before the excitement of this afternoon?"

Angelica heeded her grandmother's suggestion. She went to her room and slept for nearly two hours. Not long after she came downstairs, Julien arrived home. He kissed his mother and then his daughter.

"I was able to leave earlier than I planned. We need to stop at the market, too, Chouchou, so I can get food for tonight's dinner."

"You're cooking tonight?" Angelica asked with a smile.

"Oui. Mom's favorite, poulet sauté. Chicken cacciatore," he translated when he noticed her furrowed brow. "We should leave now so there is plenty of time."

Julien and Angelica went to an art shop, where she picked up her birthday gift for her mother. Julien had no clue what exactly it was—it could be a painting, a drawing, or a photograph—but he enjoyed her happiness. She smiled and radiated when the shop owner showed it to her before wrapping it in brown paper. Julien, too, smiled as he paid. He thrilled seeing her so truly happy. He knew that whatever the gift, Aurélie would treasure it because it was given with all of Angelica's love for her.

They next walked to a nearby florist, where they bought a bouquet of Aurélie's favorite flowers. Others in the shop stared at them, as usually happened, some even approaching Julien for his autograph. Angelica beamed. "People love you, Daddy. I can't blame them.

You are gorgeous, inside and outside." He blushed; his humility made her admire him even more, which she told him as they walked to their car.

"You are a sweetheart. I am who I am, how God made me. I cannot take credit for the way I look, and my appearance should not be that important."

"I know, but people can't help but notice. Your kindness and generosity and mind are far more important. Most people know that. Your physical beauty only adds to the appeal."

"I know people do not mean to, or know this does, upset me. They mean nothing by it. I am flattered that people appreciate what I do." Julien unlocked the car door and placed the flowers and the gift carefully on the seat. "Let us buy the food for tonight."

Thirty-five minutes later, Julien and Angelica were on the way home. "Daddy, may I ask you some questions?" He said she could, of course, so she told him about her conversation with Ophelia that morning.

"First of all, I do not believe there is any harm in asking such questions. We are created for a reason. Each of us has a purpose. I do believe our lives are predestined by God. However, we can alter that destiny through the choices we make. God gave us free will. We have freedom to live according to our will rather than by God's will. Human beings are not robots, programmed to do anything against our will. We do not even have to believe in God." He breathed deeply before he continued. "We also cannot control other people and their actions. Those actions can alter God's plan. Murder, for example."

Julien stared straight ahead. Angelica looked out of her window. "My father," she very softly whispered. Julien heard her sadness.

"Yes. And nearly you."

"That's what made me think of all this. I mean, God did not let me die. Why? What am I supposed to do? What is my purpose?"

Julien pulled his car onto the shoulder of the road. He turned to face Angelica. "Oh, my dearest darling. You will touch the world. Your music will be heard by people. They will respond and be touched, as Mom and I have. You have a gift from God. He would expect you to use that gift, as you do, but I have already seen how people do respond to your music.

"You also touch people through your work with the foundation. You have compassion, empathy, sympathy, and this amazing ability to connect with people. Your very first visit was with Mr. Fortner, and you immediately connected with him. You care about people, and they know it. It shows. The prisoners on Christmas Eve felt it and responded to it. You are already remarkable at this work. You are the perfect person to take over for me. You are inherently natural at this.

"You are also a gifted artist. Your drawings are emotive, beautiful, and technically exemplary. I have not yet told you of one of my dreams. I look forward to the day that your art works are exhibited alongside mine. I will be so honored and happy when that day comes.

"You, Chouchou, are meant to touch and to affect the world."

Angelica's eyes filled with tears. "Just as you do?"

Julien hugged her, kissed her forehead, and said, "You are my daughter."

"I am."

"And Aurélie's. We have a party to prepare. Let us go home."

Angelica wrapped her gift to Aurélie at the breakfast table while Julien prepared the vegetables and chicken. She watched him, impressed by his skill with the knife. She studied his every move as he cooked the chicken in a skillet, then the vegetables, and added spices—he moved gracefully, elegantly, like a dancer. When he placed the skillet in the oven, he turned and noticed Angelica watching him. He had a flashback, instantly reminded of the day they had met. She had looked at him in the café. Her eyes. That day they had been filled with sadness and love. Now they reflected joyfulness and love.

Father and daughter stared into one another's souls for a long while. Neither spoke words. Words were unnecessary. Both of them had felt a soul connection on that first day, a connection that had strengthened and deepened over the past ten months.

Ophelia entered the kitchen, but stopped, stunned. She could see and feel the love that flowed between Julien and Angelica. She knew how very much Angelica meant to her son and daughter-in-law. They loved her. She was their child in every sense. Angelica was so like Julien that she could be his biological daughter. If anything happened to Angelica, Julien's heartbreak would be unprecedented. Ophelia offered a silent prayer for Angelica's health and long life.

The oven timer roused Julien, and he very slowly returned his attention to the present. He smiled at his mother before he removed the skillet from the oven and returned it to the stovetop for final cooking. Angelica said she would get the music room ready for the party. She hugged Julien before she picked up the cake plate and left.

"I love her, Mother."

"Oh, I know, Julien. I know. I see it and I feel it," Ophelia said.

"I am terrified," he whispered. Ophelia lifted her hand to her throat. "I never knew a man could be this terrified."

"Oh, Julien," Ophelia sobbed.

"She survived what should have killed her. Now this infection. . . . . I cannot lose her, Mother. I cannot," Julien muttered through clenched teeth while his fist pounded the counter. "I waited my entire life for her, and I found her just ten months ago. She cannot die."

What could Ophelia say? Would anything she said matter? She fully understood how Julien felt. Any parent would. All she could do was hold him, try to comfort him.

Neither of them saw or heard Angelica walk away from the kitchen entrance. She went to the piano and played her pain away before Aurélie came home. She could not do what she longed to—cry. She vowed to never again do anything that hurt Julien. His pain affected her far more harshly than any physical pain.

Julien was drawn to the music room. Her music was so sad and. . .angry. Angry? Angelica had not gotten angry once in the past ten months. Why now, today, a happy day? What had happened? Angelica looked at him, stopped playing, and ran to him. She grabbed Julien in a tight hug and said, "I love you, Daddy, more than you can ever know."

Ophelia cleared her throat and alerted them that Aurélie had just pulled up. Julien assured Angelica, "I do know, Chouchou. I know." He kissed the top of her head. "I best get dinner ready to serve."

Aurélie came into the kitchen just after Julien had taken the last dish to the dining room. "I should start dinner," she commented to herself, not realizing that Angelica had come in.

"You don't need to. Daddy already made dinner."

"Oh, well, we are in for a treat, my dear. I am just going to wash my hands in the powder room, and I will be right in to the dining room."

Angelica informed Julien and Ophelia, who acted as normal as possible when Aurélie entered the dining room. She kissed her mother-in-law's cheek and then gave her husband a passionate kiss.

"What a nice treat to come home to," she smiled at Julien. "My favorite. Thank you, mon cher."

The four of them thoroughly enjoyed dinner, talking, laughing, and sharing their memories of their most special birthdays—except for Angelica, who had never had a birthday celebration.

"I have already told you about my tenth birthday, when I met Aurélie. Last year was the other very special birthday, the first with Angelica. That piece you composed for me, Chouchou, is the most wonderful gift anyone has ever given me," Julien shared and reached across the table to hold Angelica's hand.

Aurélie smiled and shared hers. "My first birthday after we were married was magical, just Julien and me here at home. He cooked my favorite dinner, just as he has done today, and then we went upstairs, to the sunroom. We danced under the moonlight for hours. It was so romantic." Angelica smiled when her parents kissed. "Your turn, Mother."

"That is easy. Last year. My beloved family all together, including my granddaughter." Ophelia put her arm around Angelica. "The surprise party you gave me stays in my heart."

"Thank you all. You have shown me what a family really is, how a family shares love and everything that happens. I read about such families in novels, but I never knew one until I met you. You, my family, are one of the greatest gifts I have been granted," Angelica choked and clasped Julien's and Aurélie's hands.

Aurélie moved to Angelica and pulled her into an embrace. "You, my daughter, are the greatest gift I will ever receive. God brought you to us, and I am eternally grateful."

"So am I," Julien whispered as tears threatened to possess him.

"We all are," Ophelia stated.

Angelica stood and took Aurélie's hand. She led Aurélie to the music room, and Julien and Ophelia followed. Aurélie instantly noticed the flowers and the cake and hugged Angelica. "This is lovely, ma petite. That cake is too pretty to eat. Those flowers. Did you do all of that?" Angelica told her mother that Julien and she had—she the cake, he the flowers. "You and Julien could open a restaurant. He could be the master chef and you the pastry chef."

Angelica giggled. "I couldn't be a very good pastry chef, but Daddy is an excellent chef."

"Shall I serve this exquisite cake?" Julien asked, diverting the subject.

Julien handed his three ladies cake plates, cut a slice for himself, and soon they sat continuing their conversation. Two hours later, Aurélie smiled and said, "Thank you. This has been a fabulous birthday."

"It is not over yet," Julien told her. "You have to open your presents." He wanted her to open Angelica's last, so he gave his gift to her.

Aurélie opened the box and immediately pulled Julien close to her. "This is the most beautiful bracelet, mon amour."

"A beautiful bracelet for my beautiful wife," Julien smiled and clasped the bracelet on her wrist. "Je t'aime." He kissed his wife.

Angelica's eyes filled with tears as she watched them. Their love was epic. She had seen it from the first minute in the café. She had never known that kind of deep, abiding love, even in books. She thanked God every night for allowing her to witness their love daily.

Julien motioned for his mother to give Aurélie her gift next. "Your ring!" Aurélie exclaimed. "Your beautiful ring."

"It was my mother's and her mother's before. I was the third owner. I want you to have it. Someday, our Angelica will be the ring's fifth owner, and it will be passed to a daughter in every generation of our family."

"That is a lovely heritage, Mother. Thank you for entrusting it to me," Aurélie said, kissed Ophelia's cheek, and slipped the ring on her right ring finger.

Angelica leaned over and looked at the ring. "It's very pretty. Family heritage means so much. I never knew how much until our trip to Lucerne. Having some of my birth parents' things is more than I ever dared imagine."

"Yes. That trip inspired me to give this ring today. Why wait until I am dead to give people the family heirlooms I want them to have? It looks lovely on your long, slender finger, my dear," Ophelia told her daughter-in-law.

"It does," Angelica agreed. "Are those rubies?"

"Yes, dear, rubies and white sapphires," Ophelia answered. "Now, what about your gift to your mother?"

Angelica picked up the rectangular package, which she had wrapped in rose-covered paper, and handed it to Aurélie. She carefully, slowly removed the paper, wanting to savor her first sight. She gasped. Then cried. She held the frame to her chest for several minutes, and then passed it to Julien.

He stared at it, mesmerized. His emotions overrode his logic for a few moments. Soon, though, his art training took over and he found his brain analyzing Angelica's pastel. The composition, the symmetry, the lines, the light and shadow, the perspective—all possessed the mark of an experienced, expert artist. The pastel was exceptionally well done, and he could detect the influence of Monet, Renoir, and Degas.

The subjects of the pastel were another matter altogether. He could never remain impartial. He and Aurélie were depicted in their wedding attire, alone in an opulent fairy-tale ballroom, waltzing. She had, of course, seen their wedding pictures; she knew what the gown and tuxedo looked like. However, she had not copied or mimicked one of the pictures. She had created a captivating work akin to a fairy-tale illustration from the 18th or 19th centuries, very romantic and soft.

Julien and Aurélie evoked a Hollywood film couple, passionate and completely absorbed in one another. Julien held Aurélie close, and her skirts swished, suggesting that theirs was not a staid waltz. Their waltz was as vibrant as their love, which seemed to emanate from them like a halo.

"This is truer than any photograph of Aurélie and me. This captures how we feel. This is absolutely magnificent, Chouchou. It is perfect."

Aurélie sat leaning against Julien, her head on his shoulder as she looked at the painting. "It is," she whispered.

"I had hoped you would like it. I don't think it's all you said, Daddy. You are too kind. But thank you. I have known you for nearly eleven months. This is how I see you, so beautiful and in love."

Julien had been right. Aurélie was sobbing again, too overcome to speak. He put his arms around his wife and looked at his daughter. "I am so in love with you, my little girl. You are a most remarkable girl. Your love for us fills my heart—our hearts—with the highest joy. Thank you for that, and for making Aurélie's birthday so very special."

That night, Aurélie entered Angelica's bedroom just as the teenager stood from her prayer. "I know you do not need me to tuck you in bed, but indulge me. I want to."

"I'd like that, Mom."

Aurélie helped Angelica in bed, pulled the covers up, and kissed her cheek. "Every time you call me Mom, I am so very happy. It is such an emotional experience, because I had desired for so long to be a mother. Now I am. You are so much like Julien that I now have a hard time remembering that you are not our birth daughter. You were meant to be ours, Angelica. Fate aligned our lives and brought us together. Je t'aime, ma fille." Aurélie kissed Angelica's forehead, turned off the light, and wished her "Sweetest dreams" before crossing the hall to the bedroom she shared with Julien.

When Julien emerged from the bathroom, he saw Aurélie standing at the window, seemingly lost in thought. He stood behind her, put his hands on her shoulders, and asked, "What is wrong, mon amour? Your birthday party was magical."

"Yes, it was, Julien. Nothing is really wrong. I have been thinking a lot about what I truly want, and now I know with certainty. I have worked since before we married, and I do like my job. Now things are different. We have Angelica. I want to quit my job and be a full-time mother. I want to take her to and pick her up from the university, take her to doctor appointments, meet her for lunch, take her shopping. I want to be here for her. That is what I dreamed of doing."

"I know, ma chère. Do it."

"Oh, Julien, I knew you would understand. I will submit my resignation tomorrow, and my two weeks will end before she begins classes. Oh, mon cher, I am the happiest I have ever been."

§§§§§

Julien took Angelica to her doctor appointments that Thursday and the following Thursday. At both, Dr. Sutfield performed an EKG and an ultrasound of Angelica's heart. Her heartbeat was still rapid, and her breathing was as well. She had completely recovered from the infection and the fever. As Dr. Sutfield explained to a visibly distraught Julien, that indicated that her heart had been permanently damaged.

By the time of Angelica's February 28 appointment, Aurélie was free to take Angelica. Her condition had not changed. Aurélie thanked God that Angelica's condition had not worsened. Every week, she and Julien feared that Dr. Sutfield would tell them it had.

"Your classes begin Monday. Let us do some shopping and then have lunch."

"Really? That sounds wonderful."

Aurélie pulled into the parking garage of a huge department store. She and Angelica went to the stationery department. "I just realized that you need school supplies. Notebooks, paper, folders. A notebook and folder for each class, a binder, and anything else you need." Angelica stood looking at the shelves of notebooks, tablets, binders, pens, pencils, erasers, and sundry other items that most students bought at the start of every academic year. "Go on, dear," Aurélie gently encouraged.

"I never imaged there was so much for school. I'm sorry. I must sound like someone from a deserted island. There is so much I don't know and have never seen."

"Not at all, darling. You were very sheltered, and for good reason. Now go ahead and get whatever you want."

Angelica picked out notebooks and folders for each class, a binder in which to keep papers, pens, pencils, erasers, and a pencil case. Aurélie assured her it was not too much. "You are taking six classes, after all. If there is anything else your professors say that you need, we will get it then. Let us pay for this and have lunch in the store restaurant."

The waiter had just approached their table when Angelica saw Thomas enter the restaurant. "Thomas is here." Aurélie told her to invite him to their table, so Angelica motioned for him to join then, and he happily greeted them and sat. They ordered and then enjoyed the unexpected company for nearly ninety minutes.

"Are you excited to begin university classes Monday?" Thomas asked Angelica.

"I am. I have never been to any school, you know, so I have no idea what to expect, not really."

"School is very social. You're in classes with several other students, and some of them become friends. Others become study partners. School is a great place to learn from many people, not just the teachers. You'll enjoy it, Angelica."

"I think so, too. It's just that social experiences are fairly new to me. Even when I was a waitress, I rarely talked with customers, I mean really talked. The first time I did was the day Mom and Daddy came in. But going to the hospitals with Daddy has helped me learn to be more comfortable in meeting and talking to people."

"You're natural at it. Mr. Fortner told me how you just walked in his room by yourself and got to know him. And me. You had no problem becoming my friend. I'm glad you did. I know we haven't known each other very long, but you are the best friend I have ever had."

"Really? Thank you, Thomas. I'm glad we met, too. How is your school term going?"

"Fine. I finish next year. I got behind being in the hospital so much, but I don't mind. I'm alive. That's what matters most. Everything else will work itself out. I'm only here today because the teachers have meetings all day. Do you have special plans for this weekend?"

"Other than church on Sunday, no."

"There is a new movie playing, and I thought we could go. If it's all right with Julien and Mrs. Lacoeur. Ma'am?" Thomas asked Aurélie.

She smiled and replied, "It is fine with me, and I am certain with Julien, too. What time is the film?" Thomas told her it started at 1:00 that Saturday afternoon. "Then come to the house a couple of hours before that and have lunch with us."

"I'd like that very much. Thank you. I better go now. I have homework I have to finish. I will see you Saturday, Angelica."

After he left, Angelica looked into her water glass. "I have never been to a theatre. I never even saw a film until I lived with you and Daddy. I never had a family until I met you, Daddy, and Grandmother. I never had a friend until the day I met Thomas. I never attended school. Monday will be my first day. My life is fuller and more glorious since that day we met. I could never have dreamed of such a wonderful life."

§§§§§

On Saturday, Thomas arrived at the Lacoeur's home shortly before 11:00. Julien opened the door and warmly welcomed Thomas. "Come in out of the cold. Let me take your coat," Julien offered, hung it in the foyer closet, and gestured Thomas to follow him. "Aurélie is fixing lunch now. You join Angelica in the music room while I help Aurélie. I bought some new record albums you two can listen to if you want."

"Thank you," Thomas said and went into the music room, where Angelica was flipping through a stack of albums. "Hello, Angelica."

"Thomas. Hello! I'm so glad you came," she greeted him and flashed him a smile.

"How are you feeling? I mean, the movie is three hours long. We can see something else if you're not up for that."

"I'm fine, Thomas. I do get tired more often when I'm active, so Dr. Sutfield, Daddy, and Mom make sure I rest and take naps. A movie won't cause any problems, though. What about you?"

"It's been almost three months since my transplant. The antirejection drugs cause this puffiness and high cholesterol, but the doctors are treating them. I take high cholesterol medication. I have to limit my salt, and that helps with both. Dr. Corland will probably start me on diuretics to help with the edema at my next appointment. We were both dealt these challenges. They're scary and tough, but we will overcome them. Both of us. Won't we?"

"We'll do everything we can."

Julien had stood outside the music room, intending to call them to lunch, when he overheard their conversation. He bowed his head and silently prayed that both Angelica and Thomas regain their health and live long, productive, happy lives. He swallowed his tears and entered the music room. "Lunch is ready in the dining room." He put his arms around the teenagers and walked to the dining room with them.

Julien said grace, and then opened the conversation by asking Thomas which film they were seeing.

"*The Sound of Music.* It just opened this week. It's based on Maria von Trapp's memoir. I read the book a few years ago, so I'm excited to see the film."

"I read it, too. Renée bought it for me. I'm so happy you asked me to go see it with you. Thank you."

"I was going to even if I hadn't seen you and Mrs. Lacoeur in the restaurant Thursday. I planned to call you that afternoon or Friday afternoon. I wanted you to go with me."

Julien smiled and squeezed Aurélie's hand. He and Aurélie became best friends nearly thirty-seven years earlier. He saw a similar friendship developing between Angelica and Thomas. Whether that would lead to marriage was far too soon to predict or know, but he would not be surprised—or disappointed—if it did.

Aurélie squeezed his hand in return. She had come to know Thomas; he was polite, smart, and not only shared a love of music with Angelica but loved Angelica. Aurélie had seen it since the day she met Thomas. Furthermore, even though Angelica was fourteen and had been sheltered, she was wise beyond her years and emotionally mature. Aurélie knew that Angelica considered Thomas her closest and most trusted friend. Aurélie trusted both Thomas and Angelica.

Before they left, Thomas told Julien and Aurélie to which theatre they were going. "If it's all right, I thought we could go for ice cream after the movie. That will give us a chance to talk about it."

"That is fine, Thomas. Have fun and enjoy the film," Julien wished them. He and Aurélie watched Thomas help

Angelica into the car and then drive away. He closed the door, turned to Aurélie, and said, "Our little girl is beginning to grow up. This is her first date, n'est-ce-pas?"

"Date? At fourteen?"

"But of course. We had our first date at twelve."

Aurélie laughed. "The fall carnival. Fair enough, mon mari. I suppose this is technically Angelica's first date. She is so young, Julien, and so inexperienced. But she is so wise and intelligent, far more than her age should allow. Our fourteen-year-old daughter begins university in two days. Is it wrong to feel as nervous as I do?"

"No, ma chère. I think all parents feel that. I feel it, too, I admit. She is young, but she is very smart. She will not do anything risky or unwise. Neither will Thomas. I have known him long enough to trust him with Angelica." Julien and Aurélie walked to the sunroom on the third floor and snuggled on the sofa there. "Besides, I have a strong feeling that in a few years, Thomas will be our son-in-law."

Four hours later, the sound of the front door opening and closing roused Aurélie from her nap. On her way to her bedroom, Angelica looked for her parents. After hanging her coat, she went to the third floor and peered into the sunroom. Julien turned his head, smiled at her, and said, "Join us, Chouchou."

Angelica sat beside Julien, leaving Aurélie resting against him, her head on his shoulder.

"How was your da. . .the movie?" Aurélie asked. Julien heard her slip and squeezed her shoulder.

"The movie was very good, even if it took some liberties with Maria von Trapp's memoir. Julie Andrews is so talented and beautiful. She portrayed Maria. The music is exquisite. It's pretty much all Thomas and I talked about at the ice cream parlour. I have never seen a film on such a large screen. As wonderful as *The Sound of Music* is, I think going to the movie theatre for the first time is what I'll remember most," Angelica gushed.

"I am so happy for you, my little princess. We will have to go to more films, the three of us. Of course, as you make more friends at the university, you can do things like this with them, too," Julien smiled.

"Do you really think so? That would be nice," Angelica said, put her arms around him, and leaned against him. He and Aurélie smiled and watched their daughter as she napped.

§§§§§

Monday morning, Angelica came down to breakfast, and soon Ophelia arrived to join them. "I cannot miss my granddaughter's first day at university. My fourteen-year-old granddaughter. I have been telling all of my friends. Yesterday, at lunch with my church friends, I shocked them by saying that. Most of them have grandchildren who have gone or are going to university, but none of them have a fourteen-year-old grandchild in university. I know pride is a sin, but I can't help but be proud of this young lady," Ophelia admitted and hugged Angelica.

"We are all proud of her, Mother," Julien smiled. "Even the Admissions counselor made mention of Angelica's young age. She has overcome quite a lot to get to this point."

Angelica blushed and stared down at her oatmeal. "Julien, I swear she is your daughter!" Aurélie exclaimed. "That is exactly how you look whenever anyone mentions your beautiful looks." She gasped. "There. That look," she said as Julien himself blushed and looked down at his hands.

"So it is," Ophelia marveled.

"Must you make both of us uncomfortable?" Julien asked his wife and mother.

"Why on earth should the truth make you uncomfortable? You are forty-six years old. People have been praising your beauty since you were born. You should be used to it by now."

"Mother, please," Julien pleaded, picked up his bowl, placed it in the sink, and stood with his head bowed.

"It's impossible to see yourself as others do," Angelica said. "And vain."

Julien went to Angelica, bent, and kissed the top of her head. "Merci, Chouchou."

"I am sorry for the times I made you feel this way. I had no idea until now."

"Neither did I, mon cher. I am sorry, too," Aurélie apologized, stood, and kissed her husband. "I never meant any harm, but if this is how it makes you feel, I will never do it again. Je promets."

"I promise, too," Ophelia stated. "I honestly had no idea. Your uncle Henri enjoyed such attention."

Julien snorted. "He would. Henri was a veritable playboy. He squandered his inheritance from grandfather on travel, parties, clothes, cars, and women. He never worked one day in his life. His looks and his money were his tickets to anything he wanted."

"Isn't that harsh, Julien? He was your father's brother," Ophelia reprimanded.

"It is true, and you know it."

"Yes, it is," Aurélie agreed. "He flirted with every woman, expecting each one to fawn over him. He was handsome and charming, yes, but he knew it. Very well."

"You are the exact opposite, Daddy. That's one reason people admire you so. There is no ego in you," Angelica said and looked up at him with those brown eyes that mirrored his.

"Merci." Julien kissed her cheek, his mother's cheek, and his wife's mouth. "I must go to the office now. I have some meetings today. I should be home around 5:00."

After Julien left, Aurélie asked Angelica, "What time is your first class?"

"8:00."

"We will leave in half an hour."

Angelica went upstairs to her room to get her satchel, coat, and purse. She checked her wallet to make sure she had the lunch and telephone money that Julien had given her. Before she went downstairs, she picked up her father's portrait. "Father, I begin university today. Art history is my major. I admit I'm nervous. I have never attended school before, and I don't know exactly what to expect. But I am also excited, because I have thought of this possibility for so long. I want to learn all I can. I want to make you proud. I am very happy and loved, Father; I hope you know that. The beautiful part is, you can be with me all the time, especially when Daddy can't be. You are with me, in my heart. I love you." She replaced the frame on her dresser and went downstairs.

Moments later, Aurélie drove Angelica to the École Normale Supérieure. "Do you have enough money? Do you know where to go?"

"Yes, Mom. Daddy gave me more than enough money for lunch and anything I might need at the bookstore. He also gave me coins for the telephone. I know where everything is. I was given a tour the day I got my identification card. I'll be fine."

"I know, darling. It is just that this is your very first day of school. Most mothers get anxious and emotional on their children's first day of school. I know you are not six years old, but it is still the same for me. Maybe more, because I dreamed about this many times. A little child who looks like Julien, with a book satchel, going to school. And here you are." Aurélie stroked Angelica's hair.

"Oh, Mom. This is an emotional day for me, too. I'll tell you and Daddy all about today this evening. I love you." She kissed Aurélie's cheek and walked toward the classroom building, followed by the security officer.

Aurélie watched Angelica until she was out of view, tears blurring her vision. She had to stay in the parking lot until she stopped crying, and then she went home, where she attempted to work off her emotions by cleaning the entire kitchen.

Ophelia understood. Angelica was her only child, one who had been hospitalized with serious conditions twice in the first nine months she and Julien had known her. Angelica had nearly died once and was now in precarious health. She was also a young girl in a sea of much older classmates. Aurélie was proud, excited, anxious, and scared.

After two hours and thirty minutes, Aurélie collapsed on a chair in tears. "Oh, Mother, I am all mixed up. I am happy for Angelica, that she is living one of her dreams. But I am terrified. She has no one to protect her. The security officer follows her everywhere. He is always there but discreet. You know all of that. But he cannot go everywhere on the university campus. He cannot go into the classrooms, studios, theatres. I am so scared that those people from FREE will have a way to get near her. I have not told Julien my fear. I do not want to upset him and cause him to worry. What can I do?"

"Aurélie, dear, Angelica will be safe. There has been no word from or sighting of anyone connected to FREE in months."

"I know. That scares me, too. They are too quiet, too inactive. Why? I thought I would be all right today, but she is in a public place without one of us beside her for the first time."

"What time does her last class end?"

"3:00."

"That is just over three hours from now."

"That is an eternity when I feel like this."

"Then we need to take your mind off of this. It is lunch time. Let us make lunch together. Sandwiches and soup?

Do not tell me you are not hungry. Come, Aurélie."

Ophelia looked at Angelica's course schedule taped to the refrigerator door. "Angelica is sitting in her Art Theory class right now, no doubt absorbing the professor's lecture, taking notes, and enjoying every second."

"You are right, Mother. I know I probably overreacted, but I cannot help but worry."

"It gets easier with each passing day. Take my word. I worried about Julien on his first day of school."

"You did?"

"Yes. All of my friends worried about their children, too. Worry is part of motherhood."

"I am sure it is. Most children do not have assassins hunting them, though." Aurélie was on the verge of tears again.

"Her schedule says she will eat lunch in thirty minutes. Her art history class is in DHTA 301. Why not go meet up with her when she leaves class and have lunch with her? Go on."

"Thank you, Mother. I will."

Aurélie waited in the hallway outside of room 301 until the class was dismissed. She was relieved to see the security officer standing next to the door. She smiled at him and explained, "I thought I would have lunch with Angelica." He smiled in return.

The classroom door finally opened, and students began leaving. Angelica emerged, to Aurélie's delight, talking with a classmate. The other girl hurried away, saying she had another class. Angelica then saw Aurélie and went to her. "Is something wrong, Mom?"

"No, darling. I thought I would have lunch with you, unless you have plans to eat with someone else."

"No, I don't. I have a class at 1:30, so we have plenty of time. I was planning to go to the campus cafeteria."

"I ate there a few times when Julien was a student here," Aurélie winked.

"Has the campus changed since then?"

"It has, but not too much. Of course, I never knew the buildings very well, but nothing looks drastically different. He and I used to talk about where our children would go to university: my alma mater or his, or somewhere else altogether. We would have never forced one or the other. This university does make the most sense for you, though, given your age. You do not drive, and you cannot live on your own, and this university is the closest to our home."

"I know. Daddy told me about it when we talked about universities. The Art History department is excellent. I am so happy to be here. Thank you and Daddy for allowing me to attend."

"Do not thank us for anything we do. We want to, because you are the most important person in the world to us and we love you."

"I love you and Daddy," Angelica said as they entered the cafeteria. They found a table, where Angelica left her satchel while they bought their lunches. They carried their trays back to the table, and Angelica laughed joyfully. Her first school lunch.

"I feel as if I have traveled back in time. How very many times I did this when I was a student. That all seems so long ago, another lifetime. Now I understand how my mother felt each time I reached a milestone. She had lived through those experiences herself, and my experiences gave her pause for reflection and memories. You will understand this, too, when you are a mother, Angelica. Oh, how I look forward to being a grandmother."

"You are the best mother. You will be an amazing grandmother."

"Listen to us. You are fourteen, not twenty-four. You have many years yet before we will think of you being a mother."

"We can dream about it, though."

"That we can, ma petite. We will always have our dreams," Aurélie said wistfully.

When Angelica went to her 1:30 class, Aurélie went to the art gallery and remembered Julien's first exhibit in that gallery. He had been nineteen. So many memories flooded her mind as she slowly moved from painting to painting. She became so absorbed in her memories that she completely lost sense of time and place.

"Mom. Mom?"

"What?" Aurélie was startled back into the present and looked at her daughter. "Angelica. Is your class over already?"

"Yes. It is ten after three. Are you all right?"

"Yes, darling. I was lost in thought. I did not expect this campus to be loaded with so many memories. All of them happy."

Aurélie drove them home, followed as always by the security officer. Ophelia greeted Angelica and asked about her first day. Angelica told her everything and ended by saying, "It was grand."

"I knew it would be, my dear. My girls, I must be going. I have some shopping to do before my Ladies Club meeting this afternoon. She kissed them and left, wanting to give Aurélie more time and space to deal with the emotions of the day.

"Thanks for lunch, Mom. I want to do my homework before Daddy gets home." Angelica spent the next couple of hours in her room reading and completing assignments. She reviewed her work before she put the typewritten sheets in their respective folders and packed her satchel with the books and folders needed for the next day.

Julien had arrived home, kissed Aurélie, and sprinted upstairs in time to watch Angelica prepare her books for the following morning. She saw him when she stood to place her satchel on the table next to her door.

"Daddy!" she bubbled and leapt into his embrace.

"My, what a greeting." Julien hugged her close. "How was your first day at university?"

"Just wonderful, Daddy. My professors are so smart, full of information, and I can tell they want to teach us."

"How can you tell that from just one day?"

"Each of them assigned homework that is due on Wednesday. They got us reading, thinking, doing, and learning right away. I have one of your former professors, Monsieur Delacort."

"He is still teaching? He had been at the university twenty years when I was in his class. He is highly intelligent. You will learn a lot from him, Chouchou. Take as many of his classes as you can."

"I will," Angelica said and stifled a yawn.

"You rest for a while before dinner. This has been an exciting and busy day for you, my little scholar."

§§§§§

Angelica had her weekly appointment with Dr. Sutfield after her Thursday classes. He noted that her heartbeat was more irregular than before. Her tachycardia was more rapid. She now also had heart palpitations. He knew that her university term had begun on Monday. She had been more active than usual, what with all of the walking and studying. He decided to wait one week and see if her condition returned to normal. Until then, he would not say anything to Angelica or the Lacoeurs.

Angelica's first week of classes went smoothly and successfully. She truly enjoyed learning, and she did find school engaging. She particularly relished sharing ideas with her classmates, just as Thomas had said. Her work had received perfect scores, indicating her knowledge of art.

Sunday, Saint Valentine's Day, would be a very important day to Julien and Aurélie. For several days, they planned Angelica's surprise birthday party. It was her first birthday with them, the first birthday she would celebrate, the first year she knew her actual birthdate—and a miracle. She had nearly died one year earlier. They would celebrate her life.

"This is her first birthday party. It has to be perfect, beautiful, and happy. It must reflect Angelica and everything she means to us. I want her first birthday party to remain a beautiful memory for her," Julien explained to Aurélie, Ophelia, and Rogier as they discussed the final preparations Friday morning.

"We all want that," Aurélie added.

"We invited Thomas, of course," Julien said. "There are some people she has come to know who work with with the foundation. I invited them. They adore her. Should we invite Dr. Sutfield? He has done so much for her."

"We can ask him. It would be a way to let him know how much we do appreciate him. I will call him today," Aurélie told them. "There is a girl in her Art Theory class she talks with often. They have gone to lunch together twice this week. I will invite her. Angelica exchanged telephone numbers with her. I will call her today, too. Of course, she may already have plans, but it would be nice if one of her university friends can come."

"I have invited a few of my friends' grandchildren who are close to Angelica's age. It will be a nice chance for her to meet other teenagers," Ophelia informed them.

"That will be nice, Mother," Aurélie smiled.

"The hotel chef has the food menu and the cake design. His staff will have everything except the cake in the ballroom before we arrive. The musicians will also be there. All of the guests should be in the ballroom before we go up with Angelica. When she enters, the band will play a fanfare. We want the party to be a true surprise," Julien said and clasped Aurélie's hand. "I can take our gifts for her to the hotel today and have them brought to the ballroom Sunday morning."

"The florist is setting up the flowers tomorrow afternoon. The banner and the balloons should already be there. I have to pick Angelica up at 3:00. Can one of you make sure everything has been done?" Aurélie asked Julien and Ophelia.

"I will, darling. I am spending the day at the hotel. I want to make sure everything is on schedule. I plan to go again tomorrow afternoon to double check. I know this is just a birthday party, but it is a very important party." Julien closed his eyes and took a deep breath. "Angelica deserves this party. I called her my princess since last March, before we knew she was born a princess. I want to do all I can to make up for the life she was forced into. I want to make her feel like the princess she is. I want her to feel love every second of her life. She deserves nothing less."

§§§§§

Sunday morning, Julien, Aurélie, and Angelica enjoyed the church sermon over the various kinds of love humans feel. When Pastor Bornio discussed the love of parents for their children, Aurélie held Julien's hand. He smiled at her. Pastor Bornio next discussed a child's love for her or his parents. Angelica smiled at Julien and put her hand on his arm.

His sermon complete, Pastor Bornio announced, "A member of our congregation has composed a hymn which expresses a daughter's love for her parents. I have asked her to play it today." Pastor Bornio nodded once, and Angelica stood and walked to the piano.

Julien and Aurélie stared at Angelica. Their hearts overflowed with love and gratitude. Their beautiful daughter loved them with every molecule of her being. They knew that. They heard it in the hymn she played, the hymn she had composed about that love.

The entire congregation heard that love, and it filled them with joy and appreciation. The regular parishioners knew the Lacoeurs' story, and had rejoiced with them when the adoption had been finalized two months prior. As they listened to Angelica's hymn, they thanked God for bringing Angelica, Julien, and Aurélie together.

§§§§

Julien, Aurélie, and Angelica entered the Hotel du Raphael and instantly garnered attention. Julien was asked to sign a few autographs, which was normal whenever he was in public. No matter how common it was, though, the notice Julien drew elated Angelica. As she watched her father sign autographs and chat with guests, a young voice suddenly declared, "Happy birthday, Princess Angelica."

Angelica turned her head in surprise and saw a young girl offering her a bouquet of flowers. "Thank you. What is your name?"

"Veronica."

"Thank you, Veronica. These are so lovely," Angelica gestured toward the flowers.

Several other guests wished Angelica a happy birthday, which shocked her. In the elevator, she asked her parents, "How does anyone know today is my birthday?"

"It was published in many newspapers during our trip to Lucerne, darling," Aurélie replied.

"Oh. It feels strange having strangers know such things about me."

"Yes, I know, Chouchou," Julien groaned.

"Mon pauvre chéris," Aurélie sympathized.

The elevator door opened, and Julien directed Angelica toward the ballroom. He motioned for Angelica to precede him and Aurélie. Angelica stooped at the closed door, and Julien said, "Go on, Chouchou." Angelica opened the doors, took her first step inside, and was astonished into immobility.

Those gathered in the ballroom applauded, and the band played a fanfare. Angelica looked at her friends and grandmother, who stood smiling at her. When the band finished, she turned to face her parents and hugged them. Through her tears, she murmured, "I don't know what to say. I never expected this. I can't believe you did all of this for me."

"Oh, darling, this is not enough to match how much Daddy and I love you," Aurélie hugged her daughter.

"No, it is not, Chouchou. We will do anything and everything for you. You are the love of our lives, the answer to our prayers, our joy and sunshine. This is your day," Julien smiled and kissed the top of her head.

Ophelia ran to Angelica and hugged her. "My precious granddaughter, this is not nearly as grand as it should be. Your first birthday with us is the most important day of the year."

Rogier, Thomas, and everyone else in attendance greeted Angelica. Thomas kissed her cheek, a gesture noticed by everyone. Her classmate, Gena, playfully nudged Angelica's arm and asked—in a discreet whisper—"Is he your boyfriend?"

"No. Thomas is my best friend."

Gena started to say how much Thomas loved Angelica, but had second thoughts when she saw the innocence in Angelica's eyes. "May I ask how old you are today?"

"Fifteen."

"Really? I had no idea you're a wunderkind. Happy birthday, kiddo," Gena smiled, hugged her new friend, and knew that Angelica would recognize Thomas' love for her—and her love for him—in due course.

Angelica was talking with the grandchildren of Ophelia's friends when she felt a hand on her shoulder. "Dr. Sutfield!"

"I apologize for arriving late, but I had to wait for your birthday present."

"You didn't have to get me anything."

"I wanted to get my favorite patient a very special birthday present. It's in the hallway. Let me go get it, and I will be right back."

Julien came to Angelica, and she asked him, "Do you know what Dr. Sutfield brought?"

"No, Chouchou. Your mother told him he did not have to bring you anything. You will find out any second now."

"Nicky!"

The little boy walked to Angelica and hugged her. She put her arms around him and cried. "Oh, Nicky, I am so very happy you are here."

"I am, too. I have to go back to the hospital when the party is over, but this is fun."

"Thank you, darling, for coming. You are the best present of all."

Nicky giggled. "Dr. Sutfield said I would be a surprise for you. I've been excited since he told me about it Friday. Is Thomas here?"

"You bet I am, buddy," Thomas answered from behind Nicky. He knelt down next to Nicky and hugged him. "I miss seeing you every day. I'm back in school, but I try to come every week."

"I like it when you, Angelica, and Julien visit me. Where is Julien?"

"Right here, Nicky." Julien bent and put his hands on the boy's shoulders. "Thank you for doing this for Angelica. I can see how happy she is."

"I am, Nicky," Angelica beamed.

"There is a lot to eat, Nicky. Would you like me to show you the buffet?" Nicky nodded, and as he and Julien walked away, Angelica and Thomas heard Julien whisper, "We will have a huge cake later, with lots of icing and ice cream."

Angelica smiled up at Thomas. "What a truly wonderful surprise. I need to thank Dr. Sutfield. Excuse me."

Angelica walked to her cardiologist. "Dr. Sutfield, thank you so much for arranging this. Nicky is such a sweet boy, and I know how exciting it is for him to have an adventure away from the hospital."

"I knew both Nicky and you would enjoy this. I am pleased Nicky's doctor and I were able to arrange this. Go, enjoy your friends and party. You see enough of me."

"Thank you for everything," Angelica smiled and gave him a kiss on his cheek. Dr. Sutfield watched her join her father and Nicky, and he felt his heart ache. Nicky was dying of leukemia. Angelica's heart was getting weaker, and if it did not improve by her Thursday appointment, he feared for her.

A young couple began dancing to the band's music, and were soon joined by others. Thomas stood near Angelica, Nicky, and Julien, smiling. Angelica noticed him tapping his foot, shaking his knee, and slapping his thigh. "Go on. Join them, Thomas."

"Huh? Oh, no, I can't leave you out of your own party."

"It's okay. Go on. Have fun. Gena isn't dancing. Ask her." Thomas hesitated. "Go on. You shouldn't be left out, either."

"You're sure?"

"Of course. I'll be happy if everyone has a good time."

Thomas patted her shoulder and went to Gena. Angelica smiled as she watched them. She suddenly noticed how

Nicky shuffled his feet and realized he was tired. He needed to sit. "Daddy, why don't you dance with Mom? The two of you deserve fun, too." Julien nodded, smiled, and crossed the room to his wife. Angelica got Nicky a cup of punch and a sandwich. "Come on, Nicky. Let's sit for a while." She helped Nicky settle comfortably and then looked at the dance floor.

Julien and Aurélie looked happy, elegant, beautiful, and in love. Angelica inhaled, and her hands went to her throat. "Julien is having fun. I'm glad," Nicky said.

"So am I," Angelica whispered. She watched them until the dance was over. Aurélie leaned her head back and laughed joyously. Julien leaned into her and kissed her throat.

Nicky gently tapped Angelica's arm and asked if he could have another sandwich. When she went to the buffet, she didn't see Julien speak with the band.

When she placed the plate before Nicky, Julien took her hand and walked her onto the dance floor. The band played a ballad, and Julien led his daughter in a slow dance. She stared into his eyes.

Her first dance, with the man she most loved. Cinderella's dance with the prince at the ball had not been as magical and meaningful.

Julien smiled down at his daughter, knowing it was her first dance. When the music ended, she stood on her toes and wrapped her arms around his neck. He put his arms around her, lifted her, and kissed her cheek. "Je vous aime tellement, Chouchou," Julien choked as everyone applauded.

"Je t'aime, Daddy. You make me feel like a fairy-tale princess."

"You are. You are my princess."

Aurélie and Ophelia were crying. They, too, knew that Julien had gifted Angelica her first dance. The love and light in her eyes as she had looked at him spoke volumes. Such a simple thing as a slow dance, which many girls took for granted, meant more than riches and jewels to Angelica. That dance meant so much because her beloved Daddy had shared it with her.

Julien put his arm around Angelica and led her to Thomas. "The next dance is yours," he bowed.

Thomas smiled and walked with Angelica to the center of the dance floor. The band played another slow song, and Thomas and Angelica shared their first dance. Everyone watched them. Gena smiled; she had been right. Thomas did love Angelica. Her father knew that, too. Nicky smiled and ran to Dr. Sutfield. "Look at Thomas and Angelica! They're dancing!"

"Yes, I know, Nicky. I am very glad that Angelica's fifteenth birthday is so very happy for her."

"So am I."

Aurélie went to her husband and leaned against him. "This is so magical, mon cher. You wanted her birthday to be a fairy-tale come true, and it is. You are the best father ever. Je t'aime." She kissed him and put her arms around him.

Everyone applauded when the dance ended, and Thomas escorted Angelica to her parents. Many people got food and sat at tables eating. "Let us eat now," Aurélie suggested. She knew that Angelica had not eaten since breakfast; neither had she and Julien.

Julien and Thomas helped Aurélie and Angelica onto their seats and got plates of food and cups of punch for them. When all four were seated, they joined hands and Aurélie said grace. Ophelia and Rogier joined them, and the six of them talked and laughed. Dr. Sutfield smiled as he watched them from his table with Nicky—who was eating his fourth sandwich.

After everyone finished eating, waiters cleared the dishes in preparation for the next surprise. A trumpeter played a fanfare, and a door opened. The chef pushed a table into the ballroom. Everyone gasped.

Atop the table rose a six foot confection, a birthday cake unlike any other. Pale green icing dripped with sugar flowers, predominantly her namesake, the delicate angelica flower.   Rosebuds, violets, and lilies-of-the-valley mingled with the angelica and cascaded down the towering layers in a rainbow of delicate colors. "Wow!" exclaimed Nicky, and everyone agreed.

"For me?   This is for me?" Angelica asked through her astonishment.

Julien turned her to face him. "For you, Chouchou. Only you."

"I have never seen a more beautiful cake."

"For our most beautiful daughter," Aurélie smiled and kissed Angelica. "Why not cut the first piece?"

Angelica smiled and walked to the cake. The chef handed her the cake knife, and she asked him for two plates. She carried them to her parents and kissed their cheeks. "I love you both more than words can say. Thank you for everything."

Ophelia began sobbing. Rogier dabbed the tears in his eyes. Thomas bowed his head. By now, he knew Angelica's story, and he knew what she, Julien, and Aurélie meant to one another. He also knew how close she had come to dying nearly one year earlier and that she was alive for a purpose. He looked at her and found himself hoping that he was part of her destiny.

The chef began cutting pieces of cake for everyone. He gave the third piece to Nicky, who charmed everyone by giving it to Angelica. She kissed his cheek. "You are such a gentleman, Nicky. I'm so glad I know you. I love you."

"I love you, Angelica. Will you marry me when I grow up?"

"I will be honored, Nicky."

"Don't forget your promise." Nicky turned and looked at Thomas. "I'm sorry, Thomas, but I asked Angelica first." Thomas hung his head to hide his tears. "Don't be sad. You can be her friend still. You can even be our best man, can't he, Angelica?"

"Of course he can," Angelica replied, her arm around Nicky's shoulders.

Thomas forced his tears away and went to Nicky, knelt beside him, and hugged him. "Of course I will, buddy."

"I forgot one question," Nicky suddenly said, sounding panicked, and stood in front of Julien. "Julien, can I marry your daughter Angelica?"

"Of course you may, Nicky," Julien managed to say despite the tears that threatened him. He clasped Nicky's small hand between both of his.

"I don't have an engagement ring for Angelica!"

"Come here," Thomas told him and pulled him close. Thomas took a small box from his pocket, quickly removed a ribbon, and handed it to Nicky.

Nicky opened the box, looked inside, and exclaimed, "Wow! She'll like this." He stood before Angelica and knelt on one knee. "Here is your engagement ring, Angelica darling."

Angelica—and everyone else— had seen Thomas pull the ring from his pocket. His act of kindness touched Angelica, and when she opened the box, she knew he had sacrificed a gift to someone very special just to make Nicky happy. "Put it on my finger, Nicky?"

"Okay," he smiled, pulled the ring from the velvet box, slid it on her left ring finger, and kissed her cheek. Angelica kissed his cheek and hugged him. "Now it's official. If you'll excuse me, Angelica, I'd like to have a piece of cake now."

"Of course, darling."

Thomas left the ballroom, and Dr. Sutfield followed. Thomas was sitting at the top of the stairs, crying. Dr. Sutfield sat beside him. "That was a very kind and noble thing to do. I know how painful it was, too."

"He doesn't know."

"No. His parents decided not to tell him. They want him to be as happy and carefree as he can be. Nicky knows he is very sick, but he doesn't know it is terminal, no. That's why today is so important. I know how fond Angelica is of Nicky, and I knew how much he would enjoy today. This will be one of the most special memories he has. I have a pretty good idea what that ring was meant to be, and what you did was very generous."

"Angelica," Thomas said before his voce croaked from unshed tears. "Angelica is the strong one. She never let her feelings show. Her heart is breaking, I know that. She made him feel special and loved. She gave me the strength to do what I did. How could I not? She's so selfless. How could I be selfish and claim I love her? Besides, she's got the ring, she just got it from Nicky."

"You are a greater man than most, and you made Nicky feel like a man."

Thomas shrugged his shoulders. "Yeah, well, he'll never grow up and ask a girl to marry him. That's why Angelica accepted his proposal. She wants to work with Julien's foundation. She will be amazing. I know that first hand, but what she just did for Nicky, never giving in to her pain. She's so incredible. I love her more than ever after this."

"I know, Thomas. It shows. Take a little time to yourself, and then come back to the party." Dr. Sutfield returned to the ballroom, where Julien met him near the entrance.

"How is Thomas?"

"Upset about Nicky." Dr. Sutfield explained everything.

"That is what I feared. That ring was his birthday gift to Angelica?" Dr. Sutfield nodded. "It is a friendship ring. He talked to me about that a while back. She thinks it was meant for someone else, that he sacrificed a gift to someone for Nicky." Julien suddenly grabbed Dr. Sutfield's arm. "Where is Thomas?"

"Just outside on the landing."

"I have an idea." Julien quickly found Thomas and told the surprised boy to follow him. Moments later, Julien unlocked his office door on the first floor and ushered Thomas inside. Julien quickly unlocked the safe and removed a locked box. He unlocked it and placed it on his desk. "Choose a ring."

"What?"

"To replace the one you let Nicky give to Angelica. Go one."

After some persuading, Thomas perused the rings in the jewel box, finally selecting a delicate diamond filigree ring. Thomas looked at it before he put it safely in his jacket pocket. "Thank you."

"What you did was so kind and selfless. I am just glad these were in the hotel safe and available. Let us return to the party. It will be time for gifts soon."

The two rejoined the party as if nothing had happened. Aurélie and Julien got everyone's attention. "It is now time for Angelica to open her birthday presents," Aurélie announced. "Come, darling."

They had requested that invited guests not bring gifts, and most of them didn't. Gena, however, bought Angelica a book about the Impressionists, Angelica's favorite artists. Julien motioned for Thomas, who had retrieved the ring box and ribbon and placed the ring from Julien inside. Thomas kissed Angelica's cheek and told her, "I am so grateful we met, Angelica. You are the dearest friend I've ever known." He slipped the small box in her hand.

Angelica looked at Thomas, confused. He had given that same box to Nicky. As she stared into his eyes, she suddenly understood. The ring he had allowed Nicky to give her had been his birthday gift for her. How, then, had he gotten a replacement so quickly? Her thoughts, though, were interrupted by Nicky's anxious, "Open it!"

Sure enough, another ring sparkled at her. Thomas gently lifted the ring and slipped it on her right ring finger. "A token and symbol of our friendship," Thomas smiled. Ophelia instantly recognized the ring as a family heirloom, and she patted her son's back.

"Thank you, Thomas. It's lovely. I will wear it always and think of you every time I see it." She kissed his cheek.

"Now Angelica has rings from both of us, Thomas," Nicky pointed out, much to everyone's amusement.

"Yes, I do, Nicky," Angelica smiled. She leaned close to Thomas and whispered, "Thank you." He knew what she meant, that she had figured out Nicky's ring was supposed to be her gift from him. He squeezed her elbow in acknowledgement.

Rogier cleared his throat and suggested, "How about my gift next?"

Aurélie handed it to Angelica, who gasped in delight at the Degas painting of a ballerina. He knew Degas was a favorite of Angelica's. "Rogier, thank you. You know how much I appreciate this and what it means to me." She stood on her toes and kissed his cheek. He hugged her close and whispered in her ear.

"You are so very special, Angelica. I have come to love you very much."

"You're very special, too, Rogier. Thank you for everything."

Angelica opened Ophelia's present next, which was a Fabergé music box of a castle with a king and a queen on the balcony. "This reminded me of Henri and Stephanie, dearest. I wanted to give this to you."

"Thank you, Grandmother. This is gorgeous. It does remind me of Father and Mother." She handed the music box to Aurélie and hugged Ophelia, who held Angelica close to her for several minutes.

Aurélie hugged her daughter next, and sobbed, "You mean the universe to me, ma belle fille. You are the answer to my prayers and dreams. More than that, you are a remarkable young woman, and I am privileged to know you. I love you."

"I love you, Mom, more than you know."

Aurélie wiped her eyes and handed Angelica an oblong box wrapped in silver paper and ribbons. Angelica tore off the paper, opened the box, and saw a delicate, intricate figurine of cherubs and bluebirds amongst wildflowers. The card nestled in the box informed Angelica that the piece was an 18th-century Volkstedt Dresden.

"I wanted to get you something pretty and impractical. No one needs something like this, but such things bring joy and beauty into our lives. Like the Degas painting," Aurélie explained.

"Thank you. It is very pretty. The cherubs are adorable. They do make me smile," Angelica responded. She sat the box carefully on the table, and felt Julien's hands on her shoulders, turning her to face him.

"What can I say, Chouchou? How can I say what I truly feel for you? To say I love you can never tell you exactly how I feel and what you mean to me. You have become part of me, my soul, and I can never live without you."

Tears filled Angelica's eyes as she looked up at him, her love for him, as always, so evident. "Nor I you. From that first day when you entered the café, I felt connected to you. I can never explain it, not even to myself, but it was real then. It has only grown stronger. I do love you, but it's so much more than that." Angelica put her arms around him and snuggled against him. "I can't find the words anywhere that mean how I feel.

That's why I use music to express my feelings."

"Je sais, Chouchou, je sais." Julien held her at arm's length and looked down at her. "I wanted to do something very special for you, for your first birthday party and your first birthday with us. I have told you how I feel a connection with your father Henri. He is part of you, part of our lives." Julien picked up a large rectangular box. "This is for you, Chouchou, from my heart to yours."

No one knew what the box contained. Aurélie only knew that Julien had begun work on the gift several months earlier, sneaking items from the house in his briefcase. He had kept the completed gift in the safe at his hotel office. She had never asked him about it, knowing he wanted to surprise Angelica.

While Julien held the heavy box, Angelica lifted the lid and then the tissue paper that cocooned the contents. A large leather-bound book nestled inside, a gold title embossed on the cover. *Letters of Henri Thurmaldi.* Angelica looked from the book to Julien, her face betraying her bewilderment.

"Chouchou, I had your father's letters bound in chronological order, a few from his childhood. Some were in the boxes Monsieur and Madame Warne gave you in Switzerland. Others, Rogier helped me to track down. President Kobelt had some, which he sent to me when I explained why I wanted them. He even wrote a letter to you, which is in the box, too."

"My father's letters? This book is thick. The boxes that the Warnes gave me had thirteen letters. I went through all of the papers and organized them into folders. You found that many letters?" She looked at the book again, and then at Julien. "I am sure not everyone just sent you the letters. You went to a lot of trouble to get them. And a lot of money. For me." Her eyes filled with tears once more.

"Mais bien sûr pour vous. Je vous aime le coeur et l'âme."

Angelica bowed her head and cried. Julien placed the book on the table and held her close to him. He let her cry. When she stopped and wiped her eyes with the back of her hand, he gave her his handkerchief.

"May I look at the book now?"

"Oui," Julien softly answered.

Angelica lifted the heavy volume from the box and gingerly placed it on the table. Her father's letters were encased in clear protective archival sleeves that served as the leaves in the book. Facing each letter was an illuminated manuscript of the letter, with illustrations from Henri's life along the borders. The end pages were specially designed with Henri's coat of arms.

Angelica read the first letter, a thank you for a birthday card when Henri was ten years old. It was addressed to Mrs. Rebecca Fikes in Horsham, England. Even as a child, Henri was well liked, Angelica thought, and he was also appreciative and considerate. A stranger cared enough to wish him a happy birthday, and he cared enough to acknowledge her thoughtfulness. Angelica voiced her thoughts, and Aurélie put her arm around Angelica's shoulders.

"You inherited Henri's kindness and compassion, ma petite," Aurélie said. "This book is such a beautiful heirloom and preservation of your father's letters. This is so incredible and generous. You are incredible. I love you, Julien." She kissed her husband.

Angelica clutched the book close to her and smiled as she watched them. "Ever since the day we met, when you came into the café and Mom had that huge bouquet of roses you gave her, I adored your love. Your love story is my favorite. Your love is eternal and real. I fell in love with both of you that day, and I am so blessed to have you."

Aurélie began crying. She and Julien embraced Angelica, their emotions heightened, while most guests stood with their heads bowed. Rogier put his arm around Ophelia. Nicky reached for Thomas' hand, and Dr. Sutfield put a hand on Thomas' shoulder. Few of them had witnessed such an emotionally-charged scene before.

While they remained in the embrace, Angelica softly asked Julien and Aurélie, "May I invite hotel guests to the rest of the party? There is a lot of food and cake left."

Aurélie beamed. "I think that is a wonderful idea, and I know just where you got it."

Julien laughed and kissed his wife. "Of course, Chouchou. Do you want me to come with you?"

"Of course, Daddy," Angelica smiled.

Soon father and daughter were in the lobby, where they invited each person they encountered. Angelica stopped a woman who had just picked up her messages at the desk. "Ma'am, I am Angelica Lacoeur, and my parents and I are having a party in the ballroom. Would you care to join us?"

"Lacoeur? You are related to the hotel owner?"

"Yes, Ma'am. Julien Lacoeur is my father."

The woman looked around the lobby and spotted Julien talking to a family. "There he is, yes," she said to no one in particular and went over to him. "Excuse me, Monsieur Lacoeur. I am sure you do not remember me. My husband and I stayed at this hotel on our twenty-fifth anniversary in 1927. We had just returned from a stroll and entered the lobby, which was full of people, even a newspaper photographer. You were playing that piano," she pointed. "You were a boy, no more than ten, I would say. You played beautifully. I have always remembered that, because my husband and I so enjoyed piano music. He put his arm around my waist as we stood here listening to your music. Harold died eleven years ago, but I still come here twice a year, on our anniversary and on Saint Valentine's Day. Would you play for an old lady on this sentimental day? Let me relive the memories."

Julien blushed and was on the verge of protesting when he saw the sadness in the woman's eyes. Julien nodded, sat at the piano and played Mozart's *Piano Concerto No. 14, E-flat Major, 3rd Movement*, which lasted more than six minutes. Angelica watched him in admiration, her hands clasped before her and her brown eyes gleaming.

The woman looked at Angelica and remarked, "You have your father's eyes."

"I know," Angelica whispered.

When Julien finished, everyone crowding the lobby applauded. Julien waved them quiet and smiled at Angelica. "My daughter Angelica is an exceptional pianist and composer. She composes the music she plays. Come, Chouchou." Angelica shook her head, but several people pleaded with her. Finally, she relented and played one of her shorter compositions.

When she finished, she ignored the applause and asked Julien to duet with her, which thrilled the guests. Many of them took pictures of the attractive father and daughter—including a newspaper photographer who went unnoticed by Julien and Angelica.

When the duet ended, they stood, and Julien got everyone's attention. "Today happens to be Angelica's fifteenth birthday. We held her private party in the ballroom, but we came down here to ask you all to join us. There is plenty of food and cake, so please come up and enjoy some refreshments on this beautiful day."

People began chattering excitedly, and within minutes, the four elevators were filled to capacity and headed to the ballroom. Dozens of people mingled, eating sandwiches or cake, dancing, and meeting one another. Nicky charmed everyone, especially when he held Angelica's hand and announced,

"Angelica is my fiancée. We will get married in a few years, when I'm older."

Angelica put her arms around him, kissed both of his cheeks, and said, "I love you, Nicky. You are such an incredible boy."

Dr. Sutfield came to Nicky's side at that moment and told Angelica, Nicky, and Julien that it was time for Nicky to return to the hospital. "Okay, Dr. Sutfield. I have to get healthy so I can grow up and marry you, Angelica. When will you visit me?"

"Thursday afternoon, after my appointment with Dr. Sutfield." Angelica stood and hugged her doctor. "Thank you, Dr. Sutfield."

"My pleasure, dear. I will see you on Thursday."

Nicky waved to everyone as he and Dr. Sutfield left. Other guests began leaving, each one wishing Angelica a happy birthday and thanking Julien and Aurélie. Once the family, Rogier, and Thomas were alone, they gathered around Angelica.

Ophelia wrapped her arms around Angelica. "My dear girl, I love you so. In a few short months, you have made my life so happy and complete."

Rogier next hugged her and held her close for several moments. "You are more remarkable than I thought. What you did today was the most generous and loving act I have ever seen. You deserve everything wonderful and beautiful that this world can give you. Happy birthday, Angelica." He kissed her cheek and quickly left before anyone could say anything and make him cry.

Ophelia quickly kissed her family, said her good-byes, and followed. "Rogier is my ride home. I will see you all tomorrow, my loves."

They all giggled. Thomas cleared his throat and looked into Angelica's eyes. "Happy birthday, Angelica. You do deserve only the best this life has to offer. I want to know you all of our lives. I love you, my friend." Thomas held her arms and bent to kiss her cheek.

"Thank you, Thomas. You are the best friend I will ever have. I love you, too." Angelica stood on her toes and kissed his cheek. "Thank you for everything," she softly said in his ear. Thomas smiled through the tears in his eyes, squeezed her arms, and left before the tears overtook him.

"It is nearly dinner time. We need to do something very special tonight. We will stay here tonight and have dinner in the hotel restaurant. Let us take the birthday presents to the suite," Julien suggested.

"All right," Aurélie smiled. "Oh, one thing," she remembered and went to the chef, who was beginning to pack and clean up. "I would like the top layer of Angelica's cake, please. It is her first birthday cake and is very special."

"Certainly. I will box it and bring it to your suite, Madame Lacoeur."

She thanked him and picked up some of the presents. Julien, Angelica, and Aurélie went to the family's suite on the twenty-fifth floor, which Angelica had never seen before. She looked around the living room for a few minutes.

"Chouchou, let me show you your room," Julien said and led Angelica to one of two bedrooms in the suite. The décor was classic, with antique French Provencal furniture and blue walls.

"This was your room."

"Oui.   Mother, Father, and I stayed here a few weeks every year, and often came here for weekend getaways. We need to redecorate this room for you."

"No, please don't.   It's perfect. It's yours. I want it just like it is."

"All right, ma fille." Julien kissed her forehead.   "You do not have an evening dress here. Mom and I keep a few things here, but you need something. Here," Julien said, pulled 3000F from his wallet and gave it to her. "Mom will take you to the boutique to get a dress."

"No.   I don't need such an expensive dress.   You and Mom go without me. It is Valentine's Day, and you can have a romantic dinner."

"Nonsense." Julien took her hand and led her to Aurélie in the bedroom next door.   "Aurélie, ma chère, take Chouchou to the boutique and buy her an evening dress. While you are gone, I will confirm our reservations."

"Confirm our reservations?   I thought all of this was a last-minute thought," Angelica told Aurélie while they walked to the elevator.

"Oh, darling, no.   This has all been carefully planned. Come on."

Inside the boutique, Angelica seemed drawn to a pink silk dress, so Aurélie had the clerk wrap it for them. In the elevator back to the twenty-fifth floor, Angelica once again voiced her bewilderment. "Daddy actually planned all of this, the dinner, the dress, the overnight stay? Why?"

"Angelica, sweetheart, because he loves you, and today is your birthday."

"But this is too much."

"No, it is not.   Nothing is too much for you. Julien and I want to do and give everything we can for you. You will have many more birthdays, but today will only happen once. This is your first birthday with us. This is a very special day, ma petite fille. Very special," Aurélie hugged Angelica as they entered their suite.

Inside, the ladies showered and Julien dressed; he had showered while they were shopping. Soon, Angelica stepped out of her bedroom and browsed the suite while she waited for her parents. Julien saw her looking at a portrait of his father. He stood behind her.

"I wish I could have known Grandfather."

"He would have adored you, Chouchou," Julien whispered, his voice filled with emotion. "He looked forward to becoming a grandfather. He would have spoiled you."

"I don't need to be spoiled. I don't need lots of things. I need you," Angelica assured him and turned to hug him.

"I know, Chouchou. I know. But there is no harm in having things. I am able to indulge and treat you, so I will. I enjoy it. I do it because I love you and I want to. Indulge me, my darling girl, and let me.

"All right. It's not that I'm ungrateful, it's just that I'm not used to this."

"You should be. You would be if Henri were here. You would have tiaras, gowns, jewels, and all that a princess needs. Why should I not give you pretty things? You are my princess. I called you that when you were in the hospital, before we knew the truth of your birth. You will always be my princess."

"I love you," Angelica choked against him.

Aurélie smiled as she came upon them. "I love both of you," she softly said.

"And I love both of my gorgeous girls. Let us go to dinner," Julien smiled and linked his arms with theirs.

Moments later, the family entered the restaurant and caught the attention of diners. "Is that Julien Lacoeur? Oh my gosh, he's beautiful!" a young American woman not-so-softly whispered. Angelica smiled, but she understood how much Julien disliked such comments. She felt him cringe, and she gently squeezed his arm. Thankfully, they were led to their table and were no longer the central focus.

Angelica looked around the room and out of the window. "This is lovely, especially at this time of day. To see Paris in evening and from this height is so special."

"The view is more amazing at night. The city is lit, and from here you can see for miles. In fact, I wanted you to see Paris at night from the top of the hotel," Julien revealed.

A waiter approached, took their drink orders, and soon brought their drinks: coffee for Aurélie and carbonated water for Julien and Angelica. He then took their food orders, and while they waited, Julien and Aurélie told Angelica about their first dinner together in the hotel restaurant.

"It was July 19, 1928, one month to the day that we met. It was a Thursday. A few days before, I had asked Father and Mother if I could ask Aurélie to dinner in the restaurant. Just the two of us. They approved, so I asked Aurélie. Remember, her family was staying at the hotel, so I went to their suite to meet her and to escort her to the restaurant. Father told me later that he had alerted the restaurant staff and to have our meals charged to him. I had saved money, so I was prepared, but that was typical of father.

"I had made the reservations, and this was the table I requested. We spent over three hours here, through dinner and dessert, and talked about what we envisioned for our lives."

"We were ten years old, but I felt so grown up. I wore one of my prettiest dresses and patent leather shoes, and it was such a magical evening. We had permission to stay until ten that night to see the city all lit up. I even brought my camera and took some pictures. They are in one of the albums at home."

"We walked around the perimeter of the dining room, seeing the different views of Paris. I had seen Paris at night many times, coming to the restaurant with Father and Mother. But Paris was extra special that night. Seeing it with my best friend made it special. Seeing it with my darling daughter will make it special tonight," Julien softly said.

At dusk, the many city lights came on, illuminating the city. Even the Eiffel Tower, which they could see in the distance, shone brightly. Angelica gasped in delight. After they finished dinner, they went from window to window enjoying the views.

"This has been amazing. I want to write about it in my journal. Oh, thank you, Daddy and Mom."

§§§§§

When they returned to their suite, Aurélie suggested that they get into their pajamas and enjoy hot cocoa while they savored the night sky from the large window.

"We didn't pack anything," Angelica reminded her mom.

"I know," Aurélie simply smiled and followed Julien into their room.

Angelica soon knew why. On her bed laid a new nightgown and robe, matching slippers beside them. She smiled, realizing that her parents had planned every detail of the day. She removed the evening dress, placed it in the closet, and put on the gown, robe, and slippers.

When she entered the living room, the doorbell rang, and Julien quickly opened the door. A waiter pushed a cart inside which held a pot of cocoa, cups, and saucers, as well as the box containing the top layer of the birthday cake. Aurélie gushed when she saw the pink and green ribbons tied around the box and a card inscribed with the event, date, and contents. "I love you, ma femme. You are beautifully sentimental."

"How can I not be sentimental about our daughter's first birthday party? I want to document every moment and milestone of Angelica's life," Aurélie sobbed, put her arms around Angelica, and walked to the sofa with her.

Julien pushed the tea cart near the coffee table, poured the cocoa, and sat on Angelica's other side. She kissed both of them. "Thank you for today. I will remember it every day of my life. Everything was special and so beautiful. I've only read of such parties in novels. I've never seen one. You went to an awful lot of time and effort to do this. Thank you."

"No, darling. Planning your party was no effort at all. We both enjoyed every moment. I dreamed so very long of planning a party for our child, and today it came to fruition. I truly enjoyed every moment," Aurélie assured Angelica.

"I did, too, Chouchou. Today filled my heart with happiness. Look! A shooting star! How special on your birthday," Julien kissed her. "Today has been beautiful but long, and someone has class in the morning. Let us say goodnight and get some sleep. Come, I will tuck you in." Aurélie and Julien made sure Angelica was comfortable in bed, kissed her, and turned off the light.

Soon Aurélie and Julien were in bed, as well, and felt happy and content. The party had gone as planned and had created glorious memories for Angelica. Aurélie was quickly asleep, while Julien lay staring at the ceiling. Suddenly he heard what sounded like sobbing and became alarmed. Angelica. Something was wrong.

Julien quickly got out of bed and went to Angelica's bedroom. She was crying. Julien entered and sat on the edge of the bed. "What is wrong? Are you sick? In pain?" he asked anxiously. Angelica shook her head. "Something is wrong, Chouchou. Tell me please. Can I do anything?"

"Oh, Daddy, you have done so much. You do things for people every day."

"What can I do for you?"

"Nothing. I don't need anything."

"You are hurting. Let me in. Let me help. I want to, darling. Please. You do not need to go through this alone."

"I don't want to burden you. You deal with so much every day."

"You can never burden me. Believe me. You will worry me more if you do not tell me," Julien softly said and smoothed her hair.

"Nicky," Angelica cried.

Julien bowed his head for a moment. The doctors and Nicky's parents had told him more than one week earlier that Nicky was nearing death. He had talked with Pastor Bornio and with Aurélie in dealing with his feelings. He had anticipated Angelica's emotions when she learned. He had planned to tell her, but Nicky's appearance at her party had brought his situation to light.

"Angelica, my darling," Julien cooed and lifted her into an embrace. "I know. I understand. Nicky has become very special to us. This is never easy, darling, no matter how often it happens. Can I tell you how very proud I am of you? You were awe-inspiring. You made Nicky happy and made him feel special. No one else knew the pain you felt. What you and Thomas did for Nicky is so very loving and selfless. You hid your pain for Nicky's sake. That was hard, I know that, but now is the time to let it all out. Cry, get mad, whatever you need to do."

"I'm not mad. I just can't understand. I never will understand. I guess I don't have to, though. Oh, Daddy, Nicky just broke my heart. He's still Nicky, but he's different. He's lost weight, and his color is more ashen. And I saw Dr. Sutfield give him injections through the IV. Nicky doesn't know, does he?"

Julien shook his head. "No, Chouchou, he does not. He knows that he is very, very sick. The doctors did tell him that today was a one-time deal. He will never leave the hospital again. He will die within a few weeks. That is why today was so special. He got to do something normal for the first and only time since he was admitted to the hospital more than one year ago. You in particular made him so happy, my little girl, and my heart is so full of love for you. I also ache for you, because I know what today did to you.

You will carry today in your soul forever." Angelica nodded through her tears. "You earned your angel wings today, Chouchou. Je t'aime. I love you."

§§§§§

Aurélie picked up Angelica after classes on Thursday and drove her to her weekly appointment with Dr. Sutfield. As usual, he performed an EKG and took her blood pressure. The tachycardia and heart palpitations had not improved, her pulse was low, and her blood pressure was also low.

Angelica noticed his expression. "Tell me, Dr. Sutfield. Please."

He sat on a stool across from her. "You know I have been monitoring your heart since the fever." She nodded. He explained the results of her February 11 and current tests and his concerns. "Angelica, at this point all of the evidence tells me that your heart is permanently damaged. My dear, you have congestive heart failure. Your heart cannot pump blood as strongly as it should, and this causes increased pressure in your heart that results in blood moving through your body more slowly than it should. Your body is not getting the oxygen it needs."

"I am going to die soon. How long do I have?"

"Not soon, dear. A few years, I would venture. Your heart is damaged and weak, Angelica. The shooting and the fever were too much for your heart."

"Don't tell Mom and Daddy. Please."

"Angelica, I have to."

"Not yet. Please wait. Please."

Dr. Sutfield took a deep breath. "Three weeks. Your one-year appointment is March 11. If there is no improvement, I need to tell them then. I have to tell them, Angelica."

"Thank you. The saddest part of this is that I won't be able to work with Daddy's foundation. I thought that was my life's purpose."

§§§§§

That evening, Angelica went to the den, where Julien had gone to work on a painting. "Do you mind if I stay, Daddy?"

"Of course not, Chouchou. This will not be very interesting, though."

"Yes, it will. I have never seen you work on a painting. I want to."

Julien smiled as he worked. Just having her there made his soul happy. She also inspired him, and he quickly resolved the indecision he had battled with the painting and finished the majority of it by 10:00.

"Merci, Chouchou. You are my charm.   I am almost done with this painting now. I shall call it *Angel's Haven.*"

Angelica came closer and stared at the painting, a misty, mystical landscape covered in dew and just the hint of sunlight, with moss, wildflowers, and the most ethereal wings peeking from behind a tree. "This is perfect, like Eden," she sighed.

"Maybe it is. I did not want to do just a landscape, I knew that, but I did not know how to make it what I wanted. I did know once you were here, so thank you. You are the unseen angel in the scene, my angel." Julien turned to her, stroked her hair, and said, "I want to paint you, Chouchou. You will be my next project. May I?"

"If it means spending a lot of time with you, yes. I want to spend as much time as possible with you. I want to create a lifetime of memories with you."

Julien smiled. "So do I."

§§§§§

One week later, Aurélie once again took Angelica to her appointment with Dr. Sutfield. He told her that nothing had changed and reminded her that he needed to tell her parents on March 11. "I know, Dr. Sutfield, but I don't want the news to change anything. I'm scared it will."

He put his hand on her cheek. "This kind of news always changes things for families, darling. Of course it does. But they must know. You know that."

Angelica nodded, then got dressed and joined Aurélie. Julien arrived before they left, which brought a smile to Angelica. "I have been visiting patients today. I have one more visit to make. Would you like to go with me, Chouchou?"

"Yes, Daddy. Nicky? Please say it's Nicky."

"Yes, it is." He turned to Aurélie and kissed her. "Do you mind, dearest?"

"Not at all. I will have dinner ready by 5:30. I love you both."

"How is Nicky?"

"Weaker, darling. He does not leave the bed. He is still the same sweet boy, but there will be a time soon that he will begin to shut down. His body will begin the end of life process, Angelica. He will start to sleep most of the time. The doctors say one week, no more than two weeks. I want you to be aware, Angelica. If you no longer want to come, you do not have to. I will understand."

"I want to come. I have to visit Nicky, Daddy. I could never forsake him because his illness is painful to see. I can't do that to him. I won't do that to him. I want to visit him as often as I can."

"All right, darling. Come on."

Julien and Angelica entered Nicky's room, and he smiled. Angelica went to his bed, bent, and kissed him.

"Hi, Nicky, dear." She showed him her left hand. "I've worn your ring every day since you gave it to me."

"Will you wear it forever, Angelica?"

"I promise."

"Will you tell me a story?"

Angelica told Nicky a story of a brave little boy who went on a long journey to a beautiful new land all by himself. He reclined, completely enraptured, thoroughly enjoying the story and her company. He began yawning, so Angelica finished the story.

"That was so cool, Angelica," Nicky yawned. "I wish I could go on a journey like that."

"I will visit again on Saturday. I have a lot more stories to tell you." She kissed his cheek. "I love you, Nicky."

"I love you, Angelica. Love you, too, Julien."

Julien bent and kissed Nicky. "I love you, Nicky. Sleep now."

In the hallway, Angelica held Julien's hand. "I can't imagine how hard this is for Nicky's parents."

"I know. There is no pain comparable to the pain of a parent whose child dies. None. Aurélie and I know that." He smiled down at her. "Now we have you, Chouchou, and we will never feel that pain again."

Angelica saw Dr. Sutfield nearby, and she gave him a sad look. She didn't want to hurt her parents, but how could she prevent that? Julien said that the pain of grief equaled one's love. He and Aurélie did love her, she knew that, so she knew that her death would cause them pain. She prayed it wouldn't cause them much pain.

"I love you, Daddy. I don't ever want to cause you pain," Angelica said and put her arms around him.

§§§§§

"Do you have plans for this weekend, Chouchou?" Julien asked during dinner on Thursday, March 4.

"No, nothing special. I was going to read my homework."

"Pack a weekend bag. We are leaving on a weekend vacation after your classes tomorrow. Mom and I will pick you up and we will start on our way."

"Just the three of us? No one else?"

"The security officer will follow us, of course." Julien knew she felt safer now, but he refused to take any chances.

"I understand. It's worth it to protect you, Mom, Grandmother, and Rogier, or anyone else with me. I don't want anyone else to get hurt because of me."

Aurélie always felt uneasy when the topic of FREE came up, so she changed the subject. "Where are we going?"

"Southern France, to the Côte d'Azur. We are taking the train, actually. I have everything arranged, the hotel and even reservations at a restaurant for Saturday evening. I want us to have time alone, have fun, and just get away."

Angelica finished eating and asked if she could go pack. Aurélie and Julien smiled as they watched her leave. "This is so wonderfully kind, Julien. We do need this. Angelica deserves this after everything she has been through. I can pack while she is at classes tomorrow. Maybe I should help her pack. Let me get the dishes in the dishwasher first."

Aurélie began picking up the plates when the doorbell rang. Julien opened the door to Inspector Beaumont, whose late evening visit concerned him. "Come in. Is anything wrong? It has been a while since you have updated us."

"Nothing is wrong, actually. I do have an update for you, though. Are Madame Lacoeur and Angelica available to join us?"

Julien escorted Inspector Beaumont to the living room, and then told Aurélie to bring Angelica to the living room. She was extremely curious, so ran upstairs to get Angelica. A few minutes later, the two of them entered the living room.

"Inspector Beaumont. What happened?" Angelica asked.

"I have good news. INTERPOL and French police closed in on FREE members, including the remaining leaders.

All of them were killed. They also tracked down the remaining members and arrested them. They are in a high-security prison. FREE no longer exists. There is no longer any threat to Angelica."

Aurélie fell onto the chair behind her. "This is true? They are gone?"

"Yes, Madame Lacoeur, they are."

"It's over. Finally. I have lived with the nightmare of my father's murder all of my life. I never wish for anyone's death, but I'm grateful that these people can't hurt anyone else again. Thank you."

Julien put his arm around Angelica and smiled. "Yes, thank you, Inspector Beaumont."

Julien escorted Inspector Beaumont to the front porch, where the security officer was on watch. "Officer Binder, thank you for guarding and protecting Angelica all of these months. I can never thank you for that. Inspector Beaumont just informed us that FREE has been destroyed. There is no longer a threat to Angelica."

Inspector Beaumont confirmed Julien's comments. Julien removed 6000F from his wallet and gave them to the officer. "Thank you for all you have done." Officer Binder thanked Julien and wished him and his family well.

Julien returned to Aurélie and Angelica. "We are going on our vacation alone, truly alone. You go finish packing, Chouchou, and then get a good night's sleep. Tomorrow will be an exciting day for us."

"We are free now," Angelica said and smiled. "This weekend will be truly awesome. It will be the first time there hasn't been someone else present when we go somewhere."

§§§§§

Angelica rushed from the classroom Friday afternoon, eager for the weekend getaway with her parents. Julien's car was waiting, and she got in the backseat with a beaming smile. Soon they were boarded on the train, in a private compartment, for the six hour trip to the Côte d'Azur.

Angelica sat across from Julien, and he stared at her as she looked at the passing landscape. He pulled a piece of paper and his pen from his jacket pocket, and he made an ink sketch of her. Aurélie watched him with a contented smile. "That is so lovely, mon cher, just lovely. I want to have it framed."

Julien giggled. "If you desire. It is just a quick sketch."

"What did you sketch, Daddy? May I see?"

"You, darling," Aurélie replied and handed Angelica the paper.

"This is me? I never see myself this way."

"I do," Julien whispered, leaned forward, and clasped her hand between both of his. "I always have."

§§§§§

That evening, they had dinner in their hotel suite and then sat on the balcony watching the stars dance on the sea. Angelica fell asleep in Julien's arms, so he carried her to her bed. He removed her shoes and pulled the covers over her.

He stood watching her sleep for a long while. "Dear God, Please do not take her from us yet. Not yet. We waited so long for her, and we want her here with us. She is so young and is just starting to really live. She wants so much to help people, and she is so gifted at that. She has already made differences in people's lives, and I know how much more she will do. Her music. Her art. She has so much to offer. Please do not take her yet. If this prayer makes me selfish, so be it. We love her. We need her. You know that. Amen."

Julien's silent prayer was the most earnest he had ever prayed. Ironically, with the threat of FREE eradicated, Julien feared more for Angelica's future than he had since she had been shot nearly one year earlier.

"Daddy?"

Her soft whisper revived him, and he smiled down at her. "Yes, Chouchou. You fell asleep, so I carried you to bed. I was watching you sleep, my angel." He bent and kissed her forehead. "Sleep well. my precious daughter. Je t'aime."

"Je t'aime, Daddy."

§§§§§

Julien, Aurélie, and Angelica spent Saturday morning strolling along the coast, enjoying the cool breeze and the sunshine. After more than two hours, Angelica sat upon some rocks. Her shoulder-length hair and long white skirt blew in the breeze. Her eyes shone in the sunlight.

Julien stood staring at her, his hands in his pockets and his eyes full of love. Aurélie took pictures of both of them. She would have the film developed that afternoon. She smiled. The love and connection between Julien and Angelica began the instant they met, natural and strong. Aurélie found their bond a beautiful blessing that she treasured. She was so fortunate to witness it.

After lunch, Angelica napped on the balcony for a while. That was the perfect time for Aurélie to slip away. She found a kiosk where her film was developed in one hour, and then a gift shop where she bought two picture frames. When she returned to the suite, she placed the picture of Angelica on Julien's pillow and the photograph of Julien on Angelica's pillow.

That evening, after an afternoon of sightseeing, the three family members dressed for dinner. Julien had made reservations at one of Southern France's best restaurants, and they enjoyed not only the food and atmosphere but the drive along the coast. In the car on the drive back to the hotel, Angelica leaned against Julien and fell asleep.

"Les pauvres bébé, she is tired," Aurélie murmured.

"Oui," Julien softly replied. He masked his fear. Angelica became tired more frequently now. He knew enough to understand that her lethargy was likely due to her weakened heart. That terrified him.

His own heart trembling, he gently woke her when they arrived at the hotel. She smiled at him and apologized for falling asleep. "All of the sea air must make me sleepy," she attempted to pass it off. Aurélie accepted her explanation. Julien did not.

Back in their suite, they dressed for bed, and then both Angelica and Julien found the snapshots from Aurélie. Angelica hugged the picture to her and stood it on the bedside table. She stared at it until she fell asleep.

Julien began crying and held the picture of Angelica to his heart. "I love her so. I never knew I could love someone this much."

"Oh, Julien, I know. She knows. She adores you, worships you, mon cher. I always knew the amazing and loving father you would be, and you are. I love you both."

§§§§§

Sunday morning, the Lacoeur family held their own worship service. Each of them read scriptures and led prayers. They ended by singing their favorite hymns, which filled their souls with peace. "I feel wonderful, Mom and Daddy," Angelica enthused. "What are we doing today?"

"We have to leave no later than two so we can be home by nightfall. You need a night's sleep for classes tomorrow," Aurélie reminded her.

"I can sleep on the train. My books are already in the car, and I completed my homework already. Can't we stay all day?"

Julien and Aurélie smiled at one another. "I think we can manage that," Julien said and tickled Angelica. Her laughter made his heart soar with joy. What a glorious sound. "What do we want to do?"

"I don't care; I really don't. I just want to be with you both," Angelica answered.

"How about taking a ride up into the mountains?" Julien suggested. "We can easily get to Saint-Paul-de-Vence. They have monuments, history, art museums, and art galleries. Aurélie and I were there years ago, and we enjoyed everything about the commune. I know you will enjoy it, too, Chouchou. Would you like to go?"

"Oh, yes."

Within the hour, they were in one of the oldest medieval towns on the Côte d'Azur. "This is magical! I dreamed of a place like this when I was very young. The village where I lived with Renée was sort of similar to this, removed from the major towns and cities. It was smaller, though, and not as densely populated. I used to imagine a place like this where artists of all types gathered to create beauty."

"That place is here, Chouchou. Many artists live here, painters, writers, actors, musicians," Julien explained.

"Really? I wish I could live here at least some of the time, a few months a year."

"Maybe you will, darling," Aurélie smiled.

"Maybe," Angelica whispered and walked to one of the ancient buildings.

Julien stood behind her, put his hands on her shoulders, and softly said, "I pray that you do."

Angelica smiled up at him. "It would be nice, but God probably has other plans for me. I can't always do what I want, can I?" She grabbed his hand. "Come on. Let's not waste one minute of our day here."

Julien smiled. Her enthusiasm and excitement pushed his melancholy aside and proved contagious. "All right. Let us explore."

They went down a narrow road. An artist had his easel set up and was painting. Angelica was mesmerized and stopped to watch him. He never looked away from his canvas; Angelica didn't want to interrupt him, so she walked on. She smiled up at Julien. They came upon several artists at work. "This is incredible. It's like an open-air art studio. I wish I could do this."

"Then we will stay here tonight and tomorrow." He noticed the confusion on her face. "Missing one day of classes will not cause any problems. You do not have tests tomorrow, and you will learn so much from being here. Tomorrow, you can draw."

"Really? Oh, Daddy, thank you!" She hugged him.

"We will come here again. This summer, we will plan a one-month visit."

"You will do that for me?"

"Absolutely. It is for me, too, you know, because I will be with you and get to see you work. I love you."

"I love you. I never loved anyone this much, Daddy," Angelica softly said and held him tight. She leaned against him, and Julien bowed his head onto hers. They stood silent and still for several minutes, while Aurélie watched with tears and love.

When they finally began walking, one of the artists approached them and handed Angelica a drawing. She stared at it, overwhelmed. He had drawn Julien and her as they had stood embracing. He had captured that moment between them. Julien looked down at the drawing, and then at the artist.

"Merci. Merci beaucuop. This is. . . . . I cannot find the words. Merci," Julien wept.

"I had to. The feelings, the love, that surround you. I had to capture that. I did not mean to pry."

"Not at all. This is priceless." Julien pulled out his wallet.

"No. No money. This moment was too real and too intense. Honest. From the heart. You gave me the gift of seeing it. I repay the gift with this. My gift to you and your daughter."

"We will treasure this," Angelica stated. She kissed the artist's cheek, and he kissed her hand.

Aurélie put her arm around Angelica as they walked away. Their lives were indeed perfect, everything they had prayed they would be—and more. She silently thanked God for their blessings and asked him to watch over them. They were so incredibly happy and in love. She wanted their lives to forever remain that way.

§§§§

After a late lunch at a small café, Aurélie suggested where they should next go. "There are some art galleries here you need to see, Angelica. The best one is inside the ramparts. We need to go there first."

"We do not need to, ma chère," Julien countered.

"Yes, we do. I want to," Angelica said with a pout.

"All right. It is on the other side of the commune."

As they walked, Angelica requested, "Tell me about this gallery. What makes it so special?"

"This was one of the first galleries to open here in Saint-Paul, and it is considered one of the most prestigious art galleries. It is called the Galerie Frédéric Gallong. Many fine artists have their work on display in this gallery," Julien explained.

"They most certainly do," Aurélie said with a beaming smile. Julien smiled and shook his head.

"It is right ahead," Julien said and led Angelica to the entrance.

Several people browsed the gallery, and a few more entered just before the Lacoeurs. When they entered, Angelica looked around, taking it all in at once. "There is so much to see."

"We have time, darling. Look at everything," Aurélie told her.

Angelica did just that, looking carefully at each piece. Paintings, engravings, sculptures, lithographs, and rare posters filled the walls, tables, and display cases. Julien enjoyed looking at each piece. As he mentioned to Angelica, "There are many new works since Aurélie and I were here. The gallery has acquired quite a lot of excellent work."

"When did you come, Daddy?"

"1958. We had intended to return before now, but, well, the foundation took over most of my attention."

"Julien Lacoeur!" a woman shrieked. "I cannot believe you are here! I am a huge fan of your work. I bought one of your paintings a few years ago. *The Light of the Darkness.* That is my favorite painting of all time."

"Merci. That is very kind of you."

"May I have your autograph? I would love to frame it with a picture of you and display it with the painting. I cannot tell you how excited I am. I never thought I would meet you."

"I am flattered," Julien replied and signed the museum brochure she held.

The woman's excited exclamations drew attention, and soon several people lined up to get Julien's autograph. He signed each one in gratitude, knowing that any support his work received benefitted the foundation. Angelica watched with spellbound love, always delighted by her Daddy's popularity. He was so good at so many things, and people responded to him by the thousands.

"You are just as or more respected and admired as the other artists represented in this gallery. And I, for one, think you are the best artist ever."

"Ah, merci, Chouchou, but hardly."

Aurélie motioned for Angelica not to protest, and encouraged her to continue her gallery tour. After several minutes, Angelica turned a corner, trailed by her parents, and studied the works there.

Halfway down the wall, she gasped and pointed to a painting. "This is one of yours!" she practically screamed and looked at Julien. She looked at the painting, leaning closer to read the signature. "It is. I knew it. It's your style. Oh, Daddy, this is breathtaking, and to see one of your paintings in a gallery means everything to me."

Aurélie beamed and put her arm around Julien. "Read the card, darling."

"I hadn't even noticed it yet."

Julien Lacoeur

Rebirth

Oil on stretched canvas

1957

"This is why you were here in 1958. You didn't tell me."

"That is mostly my fault, Angelica. When I mentioned the gallery at lunch, I knew you would be surprised to see Julien's painting here. I did not tell you, because I wanted you to be surprised. And Julien never tells anyone about his exhibitions. He should, but he does not," Aurélie explained.

Julien stood next to Angelica and put his arm around her shoulders. "The gallery's director contacted me in 1958 and said they wanted one of my paintings. They left it to me to choose the painting, so this is the one I brought."

"Can you tell me who or what inspired it?"

Julien inhaled deeply. "Sharing death with people. My father was the first person I was with when he died. Then, with the foundation, there have been many others. The end of life is painful for us, because we do not want to be parted from those whom we love. At the same time, the transition from this life to the next life is an incredibly spiritual experience. The body dies. I have seen that. Often it is painful for the person who is dying, physically painful. But it is indescribable to feel the soul leave the body and to know that it will continue living eternally. There are times when the person is lucid and feels this, too, and realizes that this life is temporary. The life that never ends begins when this life ends."

Aurélie and Angelica remained silent for several minutes. "You are so wise, brave, and selfless, Daddy. I know each death hurts you deeply, but you put your own pain aside for other people. This painting, though, does show the beauty of death, the gift we receive when our bodies die.

"The human body is like a flower, just as you show. A flower dies in the winter and is reborn in the spring. When

I die, I will leave this earth forever and be reborn in Heaven. I will always live."

Julien pulled Angelica closer to him as he fought his tears.

§§§§§

After they left the gallery, they found boutiques where they purchased clothes for the next day and pajamas for that night. They then went into a shop for toiletries. Finally, Julien led them to the Hotel Le Saint-Paul, where Julien got them the last two suites.

They settled in, refreshed, and relaxed before dinner. When Julien went to get Angelica, his shoulders drooped when he saw her curled in the chair asleep. He gently woke her, and she smiled up at him. "It is time for dinner, Chouchou." She stood, smoothed her dress and hair, and accompanied him and Aurélie to the hotel restaurant.

"Today has been one of the best days of my life. Thank you for this, Daddy and Mom."

"You do not need to thank us, darling, but your gratitude touches me. Julien and I want to do everything for you that we possibly can. You bring us so much joy, Angelica."

"Yes, you do, my angel," Julien smiled.

Aurélie ran her hand through Angelica's hair, smiled, and said, "I so look forward to watching you become a woman, to seeing all of the wonderful, beautiful things you do and create. Your future is so full of light, wonder, and goodness. I am honored to be part of it."

"I love you, Mom," was all Angelica said in response. She hugged Aurélie. Neither Angelica nor Aurélie saw Julien wipe tears from his eyes. Neither of them knew he offered another silent prayer for Angelica.

§§§§§

After an early breakfast on Monday, Julien, Aurélie, and Angelica set off for their last day in the commune. Julien asked directions to a store where they could buy art supplies, and he bought Angelica a sketch pad, pencils, pastels, and a bag in which to carry everything.

They walked slowly, and whenever Angelica found something she wanted to capture, they stopped. Julien watched her, relishing her joy. She drew multiple scenes before she asked to stop near some ancient buildings.

A sidewalk café across from where Angelica sat caught Aurélie's attention. She and Julien found a table in the front where they could watch her. They ordered coffee and pastries, and, as always, cherished each other completely. Angelica had begun sketching the buildings, but stopped when she saw someone take her parents' picture. She looked at them, so in love and best friends.

She smiled, turned to a clean page in her sketch book, and did a pastel drawing of her beautiful parents. Julien and Aurélie talked, laughed, fed one another bites of pastry, and kissed. As she watched them, Angelica could not stop herself from crying.

She loved them. Last summer, she had written in her journal how she would take care of them when they grew older. She looked forward to that, to repaying all they did for her. She would do all she could for them.

She would never be able to do anything for them. She would be dead in a few short years, and she would leave them. She didn't want to leave them, and that alone caused her pain.

Julien looked over at her, noticed she was crying, and ran to her. "Chouchou, what is wrong?"

Angelica wiped her eyes and looked at him. "I am just overcome by everything." That was true, even though she didn't reveal exactly what overwhelmed her.

"You are such a sensitive soul. Come, join us for a while. You can do more drawing after a break." Julien packed her supplies in the bag and helped her to their table.

Julien ordered her some carbonated water, and Aurélie gave her some pastries. "Darling, you cannot see and do everything today. We will return, especially in the summer when we can stay for a few weeks. I do not want you to exhaust yourself."

"I won't, I promise. I'm all right. I got emotional, that's all."

"That may be, Chouchou, but Mom is right. You cannot let yourself become sick or exhausted. We will eat dinner in the hotel restaurant at 5:00, and then go to the train station. You need to sleep well and be ready for your Tuesday classes."

One hour later, they set off again, and Angelica stopped twice to draw. They entered the busiest spot in the village, with many shops and restaurants, as well as street musicians and artists. "Please, may we stop here? That fountain is stunning."

"Ah, yes, that has been here for centuries. La Place de la Grande Fontaine is what this square is called. This is where people got their water and washed their clothes three centuries ago. Saint-Paul has so much history. You want to draw the fountain?" Angelica nodded. "All right. Find your angle, and we will wait."

Angelica chose a view from under the arches behind the fountain, standing at an angle to see the fountain framed by an arch. That view allowed her a perspective most artists didn't explore. Nearly one hour later, she completed her pastel drawing and packed her supplies in the tote bag. She rejoined her parents and sat between them on a low wall.

"Are you finished?" Aurélie asked.

"Yes."

"May I see?" Julien asked. Angelica pulled out her sketch pad, opened it to the drawing of the fountain, and handed it to Julien. He studied the drawing for a few moments. "This is very good. The shading, perspective, lines, colors, shapes—very well done, Angelica. Very well done." He returned the sketch book.

"Thank you. I will never be as good as you, but I enjoy drawing."

"No. Never compare yourself to anyone. You are unique. Your talent is amazing and unlike anyone's. You do not need to be like or imitate anyone. Capiche?"

"Yes. Thank you, Daddy. You make everything better," she said and hugged him.

"It is late in the afternoon. How about a slow walk back to the hotel? We will have a little time to relax before dinner."

"All right. I'm just grateful to have this experience," Angelica smiled at Julien and Aurélie.

"So are we, darling," Aurélie said.

The three of them did enjoy their walk. Julien and Angelica stopped to admire an ancient monument, and Aurélie asked them to pose in front of it. She took their picture and smiled. "We have many pictures to add to our family album. I look forward to someday showing them to my grandchildren." Angelica didn't say anything, but she hugged Aurélie tight. Julien gently squeezed Aurélie's shoulder.

Soon, they were on their way again. They arrived at the hotel at 4:14 and relaxed in Julien's and Aurélie's suite. Julien stretched out on the overstuffed chair and ottoman, and he pulled Angelica onto his lap. She lay her head against his shoulder and fell asleep. He kissed the top of her head and held her protectively.

"Julien, dear, it is 5:00. You best wake her so we can eat and get to the train. We still have to get our luggage from the other hotel and catch the train back to Paris."

Julien nodded and nudged Angelica awake. "We will be on the train back to Paris in a couple of hours, Chouchou, and you can sleep all night. Come on."

As promised, they managed to board the 7:00 train to Paris. Once their luggage was secured on the overhead racks, Julien and Aurélie made sure the beds were ready. They changed into their pajamas and tucked Angelica in bed, then climbed into their bed and held each other.

Neither Aurélie nor Julien slept, though for different reasons. Aurélie had thoroughly enjoyed their first real vacation as a family. She possessed so many precious memories from the four days. Julien did, as well, although he remained constantly aware of Angelica's frailty. Her condition had worsened; he knew that— he had seen it numerous times. Her next appointment with Dr. Sutfield was in three days, on Thursday, March 11.

March 11, 1965—one year to the day that their three lives changed irrevocably.

§§§§

Thursday morning, Julien awoke at 4:30. He noticed a wrapped gift on his bedside table and sat up. He picked it up, saw a card tucked under the ribbon, and *"Mom and Daddy"* written on a gift tag. Angelica's handwriting. He leaned down, kissed Aurélie's neck and whispered, "Wake up, ma chère," in her ear.

Aurélie moaned, stretched, and turned over. "Did I miss the alarm?"

"No. I found something for us."

"You found something?" Aurélie asked, confused, as she sat up.

"Here," he smiled and handed her the gift.

"Oh," she gasped. "It is from Angelica." She slid the card out and gave him the gift. "You open one, and I will open one."

The card was handmade, more beautiful and special than any manufactured card. Aurélie's eyes filled with tears as she read Angelica's handwritten message inside the card:

Dearest Mom and Daddy,

Happy 26th Anniversary!

I love you with every fiber of my being. Your love is eternal and beautiful. Your love is inspirational. Your love touches my soul. It has since you entered the café and my life one year ago today.

What a glorious year we have shared.

XOXO

Your Loving Daughter,

Angelica

"Oh, Julien, you have to read this. How glorious."

Julien had opened the gift, which took his breath—literally. He stared at it, not breathing. Aurélie gently nudged him, and he looked at her. "This is incredible. Look." He showed her a framed pastel drawing of them.

"Oh! What? When? When did she do this?"

"Monday in Saint-Paul, when we were sitting at the café while she drew."

"But she drew the buildings. That's what she wanted to draw. She was watching us? This is magnificent."

"Yes," Julien softly said. "She was crying that day, and when I went to her and asked why, she said she was overcome. I thought she meant by the ancient history of Saint-Paul. I had no idea she had just drawn this."

Aurélie smiled and leaned her head on Julien's shoulder. "Her love for us is the most precious gift we have ever received. Even with the scary times of the shooting and the fever, this has been such a dream of a year. One year ago, we prayed for God to bring our child to us, and he did. Angelica is such an amazing young lady. She is a loving, thoughtful, compassionate daughter. She will do many great things in the years to come."

Julien kissed Aurélie. "Yes," he whispered.

§§§§§

That afternoon, Aurélie picked up Angelica at the university and drove to the hospital for the appointment with Dr. Sutfield. When they exited the elevator,

Julien met them. Aurélie kissed him, and then Angelica did likewise.

"How is Nicky?"

"He is sleeping, Chouchou. He has been asleep most of the past two days."

"Soon?"

"Yes, my angel. We will visit with him on Saturday. You can talk to him and read to him. Even if he is unconscious, he will hear you."

Angelica nodded. "I will. I want to stay with him as much as I can."

Julien nodded, put his arm around her, and escorted his wife and daughter into Dr. Sutfield's office. Dr. Sutfield greeted them and explained, "I am going to examine Angelica and perform some tests. Everything will take ninety minutes. Why don't you go for coffee?"

"Thank you. We will wait here," Julien stated.

Neither Julien nor Aurélie spoke during the long wait. Aurélie stared down at her hands, which lay clutched in her lap. Julien learned forward, his arms resting on his knees, his hands clenched, all the while staring at the floor. He was transported back to the evening one year earlier as they awaited news about Angelica.

During that time, Dr. Sutfield listened to Angelica's heart, checked her blood pressure, did an EKG, and had several vials of blood drawn. He ordered a rush on the blood test results. The results were delivered within thirty minutes. He finally talked with Angelica.

He began by asking her questions, and she had to confess that she became tired more often. "Then you know that your condition has not improved, Angelica. The blood tests confirm what I knew. Your heart failure is not caused by another condition, such as leukemia, other organ failure, anemia, diabetes, or hypertension, which means we cannot cure it by treating an underlying cause. I wish I could tell you otherwise, my dear."

"I know. It's all right. My life has been good, especially this past year. Whatever time I have left will be spent with Daddy, Mom, Grandmother, Thomas, and my other friends. I couldn't ask for more."

Dr. Sutfield put his hand on her cheek. "I wish I could give you more. You should have more, many more, years of life."

"It's not up to us. It can't be changed, so I just have to accept it. The worst part of all is the pain it will cause Daddy and Mom."

"I know, dear, but I need to tell them today. I'll do that while you get dressed, and I'll buzz the nurse when we're ready for you."

Dr. Sutfield returned to his office, where Julien and Aurélie still sat. "Julien, Aurélie, I need to talk with you. I have asked Angelica to dress while we talk. I'll have her come in when we're through."

"Please tell us she is getting well," Aurélie pleaded.

"I need to tell you the truth. Angelica's tachycardia has not improved. Her heart palpitations are far more frequent. I have monitored her heart every week since the fever. Angelia's heart is permanently damaged."

"You can treat her, give her medications to halt this," Aurélie disputed.

"She has been taking the best cardiac medications that exist, Aurélie," Dr. Sutfield explained. "The damage is irreversible, and has led to congestive heart failure."

"What does that mean?" Aurélie asked, fear on her face and in her voice.

"It means she is going to die in a few short years. Our little girl is going to die," Julien quavered.

"No. No, it cannot mean that. Tell me she will not," Aurélie demanded, on the verge of hyperventilating.

"I can't tell you that, Aurélie. That would be a lie," Dr. Sutfield gently said.

"No! No, not Angelica!" Aurélie shrieked. "No! No! No!"

Angelica heard Aurélie, and she went into Dr. Sutfield's office. "You know. I'm so sorry. I never wanted to hurt you, Mom, Daddy. Never. That's the worst part of this. I hate that I cause you pain," Angelica sobbed.

Julien instantly stood, went to her, and held her close to him. "You do not hurt us, Chouchou. You never could. What has happened to you hurts, worse than any pain I have ever felt, I will not lie. I told you that our pain equals our love. Mom and I love you so incredibly much, so much. We will hurt and grieve for the rest of our lives."

"You can adopt another child."

"No," Aurélie wept. "We can never replace you, never. We will never love anyone the way we love you. Oh, Dear God, why? Why is this happening?" Aurélie cried so much, she gasped for air.

Angelica knelt and hugged her mother. "Dr. Sutfield explained how the fever weakened my heart? We may never know how I got sick, but I did. It's no one's fault. It just happened. Never blame yourselves or God. Please. It happened."

Aurélie held Angelica for a long while until she stopped crying. "You are so amazing and wise, darling. I need time to process this. You have been so happy that I thought you were getting better. This has been such a shock, a devastating nightmare."

"I know. But we have a few years together. We can enjoy them, can't we?"

Aurélie sobbed again. "Yes, darling, we can." She looked up at Julien and stretched out her arm. He held her hand and smiled through his own tears. "Well, we have plans for this evening. Shall we get ready?" Julien nodded, put his arm around Angelica, and helped Aurélie stand. They thanked Dr. Sutfield and went home to prepare for dinner and the theatre.

§§§§§

Julien had reserved a table at the restaurant he and Aurélie had eaten at on their engagement day. After they had ordered, Angelica smiled at them. "We met one year ago on your twenty-fifth anniversary. This past year has been a dream come true for me. I have been happier than I ever thought I could be. I love you both more than my words can tell you. I will remain happy every day that I have left. Believe that. I could never be anything but happy with you,

479

sharing your lives and your love. I feel your love. I hope you feel mine.

"I pray that you remain happy, even after I am gone. I know you will be sad, but I pray it passes. You deserve happiness. You deserve everything beautiful and glorious. The pain and the grief will subside. Someday I will be just a distant memory. Your lives will continue. They must continue."

Aurélie wept, unable to talk.

Julien held Angelica's hands. "You will never be just a memory. Your soul has fused to mine. You are part of me. You are part of my life force. I love you deeply and eternally, my angel."

POSTLUDE

"**W**elcome to the morning news on this sunny Tuesday, May 12, 2015. In our top stories today. . . . ."

Thomas cooked breakfast as he listened to the news that morning, and then he and Julien ate in silence. After they finished, Julien went upstairs and sat in Angelica's bedroom for a while. That was his daily ritual. Her bedroom had remained untouched.

Julien sat on Henri's rocking chair while he prayed, remembered, and talked to Angelica. He looked around the room, at the teddy bear on her bed, the doll he had bought her in 1964, the figurines and music boxes she had received as gifts, the framed university degree. Every item in her room held memories, memories that constantly flooded Julien's brain.

After Thomas cleaned the kitchen, he went upstairs to his bedroom. Julien then went downstairs, using his cane and taking the stairs one at a time. He went into the music room and stood staring at the portrait of Angelica he had painted in 1965. "I love you, Chouchou," he softly said. Then he sat on the piano bench and relived that last day—as he had done every day since.

Julien and Angelica arrived home at 5:00 from a day of hospital visits and a foundation meeting. They greeted Aurélie, who was beginning dinner in the kitchen. Julien kissed and hugged her, relishing the feel of her soft, warm skin.

Angelica kissed her mother's cheek. "Do you want me to help you, Mom?"

"No, darling, you have both had a long day. Go relax before dinner. You know I enjoy preparing meals and cooking. This is my relaxation. Scoot," she playfully commanded.

"Come, Chouchou, let us go to the music room."

"Play something," they both said at the same time. They giggled and sat on the piano bench.

"Play for me, Daddy."

Julien played one of his favorite Chopin selections. Angelica inhaled deeply, affected by the emotions Julien imparted as he played.

Just as he finished, Aurélie yelled that she had to go to the grocery for a couple of things. They both shouted back that they loved her.

"Now your turn," Julien said to his daughter.

Angelica played one of her compositions, one he had not heard before. The piece was sad, and Julien listened with his head bowed and his eyes closed. When it ended, he slowly opened his eyes and suggested, "You and Thomas need to record that one. Why not play it at your concert on Saturday?"

Angelica smiled. "We plan to. We've rehearsed it a few times, and his violin adds just the perfect tones this needs. I swear, his violin sounds like crying in this one. It's breathtaking."

"I look forward to hearing it. I am so very proud of you, Angelica. Of Thomas, too. I knew your music would touch people, affect people, and it does. I am so grateful to both of you for donating the proceeds of your concerts and recordings to the foundation. You are too much."

"I learned from you, Daddy. I am just doing what you have done for years. You and my birth father are two of the most giving and caring people. I am honored to belong to both of you. I love you both so very much."

"We both love you, Henri and I." Julien put his forehead against hers, kissed her nose, and smiled. "Play with me, a duet."

Angelica nodded. "What shall we play?"

"Do you know this one? It is quite challenging."

"Oh. I'll try to follow. You might have to play it more than once."

Julien began playing. Angelica laughed. She jumped in and joined him, and when they finished, they both laughed uproariously. Angelica felt her heart flutter and felt light-headed. She didn't let it show, and as their laughter stopped, they hugged. She held onto him and smiled. "You really got me. 'Chopsticks'. Can't we play something beautiful?"

"Of course. How about Strauss' Blue Danube Waltz'."

"Perfect."

For the next ten minutes, they played the waltz, which had never sounded more beautiful. When it ended, Julien looked at her and smiled. "Now I have a request, Chouchou. Please play 'Heartsong Sonata' for me."

Angelica smiled and kissed his cheek. "Anytime you want. It is yours, Daddy."

Angelica began playing the piece she had composed for him in June 1964. He watched her as he listened. She had never played the piece with more emotion. He smiled, completely besotted.

Angelica suddenly stopped playing. Julien looked at her in concern and noticed that she struggled to breathe. "Chouchou?"

"Daddy," she panted. "Hold me."

Julien put his arms around her and leaned her against him. "Let me call Dr. Sutfield. He can get here soon."

"No, please. Let me die in your arms."

"Angelica?"

"I'm dying, Daddy."

"No," Julien choked.

"The past six years have been more than I could have dreamed," she gasped. "I have no regrets. I love you, Daddy."

"I love you, my precious angel. I love you."

Angelica smiled up at him. Then her eyes closed.

§§§§§

Julien sat on the piano bench remembering that day in vivid detail. Angelica had been caring, concerned, and engaged as they had visited patients in the hospital that morning and early afternoon. She read to some, drew pictures with others, played card games, or held their hands. She was naturally attuned to each patient's needs. She was intuitive and compassionate, and she had consistently astounded him.

After the patient visits, they had gone to the foundation offices for a board meeting. Angelica had been typically alert and attentive, not only listening to ideas and questions but sharing her own. She had proposed building housing near the hospitals, for families of patients so that they could remain close to their sick family members. The board said they would research the proposal and get quotes from land owners and architects.

Then Julien and Angelica had come home and played the piano. They had laughed over *Chopsticks*. Angelica's laugh had always filled him with joy.

He had asked her to play the piece she had composed for him. So beautiful. So tranquil.

Without any warning, she had died in his arms. His precious daughter's soul slipped away from her body as he held her. As painful as that was and remained, Julien was grateful that he had shared her last moments.

She had been happy. Their last words were proclamations of love for one another. More important than that, though, she felt his love as she died. She left this world feeling Julien's love for her. For that, he thanked God.

§§§§§

Meanwhile, upstairs in his bedroom, Thomas looked at the mementoes of his life with Angelica. The record albums they had recorded of her compositions—one per year. They had planned to record a fifth in the summer of 1970. His gold records hung on his wall; Angelica had kept hers in a stack on her bookshelf. He smiled, remembering when he had visited and asked her where they were. She brushed them off, saying they made her feel vain.

He picked up a picture frame from his desk. The drawing she had done of him in the hospital in December 1964. He treasured it.

A picture of them from their first concert stood atop his bookshelf. The concert had been a benefit for the Donner du Coeur Foundation in the spring of 1966.

A scrapbook contained news clippings about Angelica: her work with the foundation, her art exhibits, and her recordings and performances with Thomas. He flipped through it, reliving key moments from his life with her, the only woman he had ever loved.

Angelica had turned twenty on Saint Valentine's Day 1970. Thomas had planned to propose on her twenty-first birthday. He never got to.

Thomas began working with Julien's foundation after his university graduation in 1974. He had planned to work alongside Angelica. Instead, he honored her in his work with *Angel's Haven*, the family housing that had been built and named for her. He always remembered how selfless and compassionate she had been with the patients, and he strove to be like her.

Thomas missed her each day. The ache deep within him remained as strong as when Rogier had called him forty-five years earlier. Most nights, he cried himself to sleep. During the days, he hid his pain from the world. He had not gotten over Angelica's death. It had become part of his life, something constantly there.

He knew it remained with Julien, too. Thomas had moved into Julien's house after Aurélie's death in 1991. He wanted to. Julien had devoted his life to helping people. He had saved Thomas' life. The least he could do was to help and to take care of Julien now that he was without any family. Thomas loved his friend.

§§§§

At 11:00, Thomas quietly entered the music room. "Julien, are you ready for our visit?"

"Yes, Thomas," Julien replied and stood. Thomas assisted him into the car's passenger seat and drove to a florist shop. As usual, Julien's standing orders were ready: one bouquet of red roses and one bouquet of angelica flowers. Thomas gave them to Julien to hold, and then he drove to the church.

Thomas parked in the back, near the cemetery, and helped Julien from the car. He held Julien's arm as they walked to the graves. Fresh flowers covered Angelica's tombstone; people still remembered and loved her, just as did Julien and Thomas.

They stopped at Aurélie's first. Julien bowed his head for a moment and then said, "Je t'aime, ma chère." Thomas removed the previous day's roses from the vase. He then helped Julien kneel and place the red roses in the vase on her tombstone. "Je t'aime." He kissed his fingers and touched the tombstone.

"Aurélie never recovered from her grief for Angelia. The last twenty-one years of her life were filled with sadness and despair. She broke my heart. My consolation is that for the past twenty-four years she has been with Angelica."

"I know, Julien," Thomas softly said.

"I miss her, too," Julien whispered and stepped to Angelica's grave.

"I do, too," Thomas wept.

Julien patted Thomas' hand. "I know you do. We both love her. She knows that. She does. She did when she was here, Thomas." Julien bowed his head; so did Thomas. Both men silently prayed.

"Oh, Chouchou, ma petite fille, how I love you. How I wish you could feel what my heart says. I miss you. I wish you were here. You are not a memory, Chouchou. You remain part of my soul. The memories live inside of me. They are always present. They allow me to see you and to hear you. I treasure them. I treasure you. The six years you were with us were the happiest of my life. Thank you for that. Je t'aime, Chouchou. I love you."

Thomas wiped his tears and knelt with Julien. Thomas removed the previous day's flowers. Julien placed the fresh angelica flowers in the vase. He traced his finger over the letters of her name as tears fell from his eyes.

Thomas cried, too, as he read her tombstone.

Angelica Anna Maria Thurmaldi Lacoeur

February 14, 1950

May 12, 1970

Our gift from God.

--Psalm 127:3

Sheilah R. Craft is an English professor, writer, blogger, poet, artist, ardent genealogist, and book lover. Born and raised in the Midwestern United States, Sheilah was born surrounded by a close family—including several educators—books, and animals. She began reading and writing very early, and has published novels, short stories, articles, and poems. She was literally born a writer. Her series of novels centered on the lives of one family dynasty and spanning more than two centuries began in the fall of 2012 with the first volume, *Heart-Glow*. Sheilah has written and published one novel per year since then.

Published by STARLIGHT Books:

•HEART-GLOW: A NOVEL

•FIRST LOVE NEVER DIES: HEART-GLOW VOLUME II

•HEART ETERNAL: HEART-GLOW VOLUME III

•LIFE ETERNAL: HEART-GLOW VOLUME IV

•MARY MAGDALENE: A MYSTERY PLAY

•HEARTSONG SONATA

Published by Little Butterfly:

•THE QUEST FOR PERFECTION: SHELLEY AND THE POET-HERO

•A DAY WITH TEDDY BEAR